PENGUIN BOOKS

The Guests

'A gripping story of betrayal and secrets set against the beautiful backdrop of the Maldives, this heart-pounding thriller kept me on the edge of my seat until the last page'
Jo Jakeman, *What His Wife Knew*

'A cracking thriller!'
Emma Curtis, *One Little Mistake*

'Nikki Smith has written the perfect beach read . . . the twists had me gripped and I devoured it in a matter of days'
Emily Freud, *What She Left Behind*

'Lies, betrayal, greed and murder – this is the destination thriller of the year. Bursting with flawed characters who all have something to hide, *The Guests* is a perfect summer read that will keep you gripped to the final page'
Eleni Kyriacou, *The Unspeakable Acts of Zina Pavlou*

'Thoughtful, twisty and suspenseful, this is the perfect holiday read*
*. . . except if you're going to the Maldives'
Caroline Hulse, *Reasonable People*

'Think this one may well be Nikki's best book yet (which is saying something!!). A fiercely compelling human drama of secrets and deception, sprinkled with well-timed shocks and pitch-perfect twists'
Barnaby Walter, *Scuttle*

'Nikki expertly examines human nature at its worst'
Emma Christie, *Find Her First*

The Guests

NIKKI SMITH

PENGUIN BOOKS

To Saffi – so loved and much missed

PENGUIN BOOKS

UK | USA | Canada | Ireland | Australia
India | New Zealand | South Africa

Penguin Books is part of the Penguin Random House group of companies
whose addresses can be found at global.penguinrandomhouse.com.

Penguin
Random House
UK

First published 2024
001

Copyright © Nikki Smith, 2024

The moral right of the author has been asserted

Set in 12.5/14.75pt Garamond MT
Typeset by Falcon Oast Graphic Art Ltd
Printed and bound in Great Britain by Clays Ltd, Elcograf S.p.A.

The authorized representative in the EEA is Penguin Random House Ireland, Morrison Chambers,
32 Nassau Street, Dublin D02 YH68

A CIP catalogue record for this book is available from the British Library

ISBN: 978–0–241–99736–9
www.greenpenguin.co.uk

'The only paradise is paradise lost.'

— Marcel Proust

Prologue

Three months later – March 2024

Jamie Ellis lies on his stomach and reaches down to dig out the final part of his sandcastle moat when he comes across it. Something hard that his fingernails scrape against as he leans over the deep hole. He'd read in his nature book how most beaches in the world are made of quartz; it's only in a few places like the Maldives where they are formed from the remains of coral. The white powder trickles through his hands like the icing sugar he and his mum used last week to decorate the cupcakes for his seventh birthday. He'd had to mix it up in his bucket with seawater to get it to stick together to make the turrets on his castle.

The sun reflects off the expanse of smooth turquoise water at the edge of the sand, making him squint. He pulls on the brim of his sunhat that his mum insisted he wore at all times, despite slathering his entire body in sun cream. He peers into the dark hole again and stretches out his arm to reach the bottom, running his fingers over the rigid lump. He traces around the shape to find the edges, forming cups with his hands to dig out the damp sand, dumping it in small piles next to the turrets. The lump becomes looser, less embedded, until Jamie feels it move beneath his fingers. If he stretches a bit further, he'll be able to get it out.

He wipes away the line of sweat which trickles down his forehead on to his nose. His mum was right. This is the hottest place he's ever been. Way hotter than when they go to the beach at Branksome. Even this close to the shiny green bushes and palm trees there's hardly any shade. Every time he shifts his position, he feels the sand burn his skin. He can see his mum looking over in his direction, stretched out on the sun-lounger she'd asked their butler to drag over to this part of the beach, away from everyone else. He waves at her, then reaches into the hole again, welcoming the coolness of the dark space, grasps hold of the object and pulls until it gives way with a sudden jolt.

He grins, a bubble of excitement bursting in his chest. A piece of buried treasure to show her. Maybe his dad will come and have a look too – it's been nice to spend more time with him. He always used to be away working until recently. Jamie can see him snorkelling out on the reef, a pink shape bobbing on the surface of the ocean.

He clasps the lumpy object in one hand as he runs across the deserted beach towards his mother, the fabric of his green swimming trunks swishing as he moves, the soles of his feet on fire.

She is lying propped up on her lounger, her oversized sunglasses watching him like the giant black eyes of an insect. Jamie keeps both hands behind his back.

'Guess what I found?' he asks.

She turns her head towards him, her glasses slipping slightly down her nose.

'What, sweetheart?'

'Treasure. Do you want to see?'

She nods. He brings one hand around from behind him as she holds hers outstretched to receive his gift.

She is still screaming by the time his father reaches them, his flippers discarded at the edge of the shallow water. A livid red mark outlines where his snorkel mask has been and his eyes widen in horror when he spots the human skull, pieces of hair still attached, lying discarded on the cream cushion of the sun-lounger.

1. 4 days 3 hours left

Cara can see at least a dozen seaplanes bobbing in the water as she walks across the wooden boards of the jetty behind Zach. The quickest mode of transport for guests to get from Malé to one of the resort islands, a hundred and thirty tiny green jewels floating in an aquamarine paradise. She makes a bet with herself that theirs is the one which seems to be tilting to one side, its faded paintwork looking as if it's seen better days. Before she had Alexa, she wouldn't have thought twice about getting on a plane – she had loved her job as cabin crew – but now her stomach clenches more tightly any time they start down a runway. No matter what Zach tells her about the odds of crashing being far worse in a car, she can't get the image out of her head of the three of them hurtling towards the ground, watching it come up to meet them with a terrifying inevitability. Her therapist would say the issue isn't flying at all; the issue is about not having control. She's got a point: so many things in her life feel as if they are slipping through her fingers right now.

Zach turns around to check she's still following. The wheels of her cabin bag, which he's dragging behind him, bump over the small gaps in the bleached boards, making a series of noises that seem to say *don't get on don't get on*. She flashes him a quick smile and gathers up her recently balayaged caramel hair into a ponytail, lifts it away from the back of her neck to wipe off a line of sweat. *Hundreds of people do this journey every day. There is nothing to worry about.*

Her husband waits for her to catch up, slides one arm across her shoulders. She catches the musky scent of his new responsibly sourced aftershave, a recent purchase from a company that claims to put sustainability front and centre. She can't bring herself to tell him she actually prefers his old one. He smells like a stranger, not the man she's shared her life with for the last nineteen years.

'You OK?' he asks.

She nods.

'You used to do this kind of thing all the time. We'll be there before you know it.'

He strokes her cheek and tucks a loose strand of hair behind her ear.

'Think of that white-sand beach and crystal-clear water.' He plants a kiss on the side of her head, before adding, 'And our own plunge pool – even brought my Speedos. I know you can't wait to see me in those.'

He winks, and Cara smiles despite herself as she looks ahead of her at the seaplane. One propeller attached to each wing, like one of those battery fans the woman in the seat next to her had pulled out of her bag on the flight over from Heathrow. That had been in an A380, an aircraft so huge she'd almost forgotten they were in the air, even at thirty-five thousand feet. Seaplanes have a worse safety record than commercial airliners, but Zach had refused to endure the hour-long boat ride with his seasickness, and there isn't an alternative method of transport to get to the Asana Fushi resort.

Cara glances behind her to where her daughter is busy taking selfies at the side of the jetty, the clear blue water stretching out in the background. Lips pouted for some, others with her tongue out, two fingers held up in a peace sign, her long brown hair still effortlessly chic despite the ten-hour flight. Her blue-gel nails match the colour of the Plant Faced T-shirt Zach bought her last week. *God, they need this holiday. Especially Alexa.* Cara wants to tell her to put her phone down and hurry up, but suspects she'll get an eyeroll in response if she says anything.

Was she like that at sixteen? Constantly pushing the boundaries? Alexa's life is so different to how hers was at that age that she can't begin to make a comparison. Cara's every move wasn't recorded on social media, for a start, *thank God.* Her holidays had consisted of a trip to a caravan park in Wales for a long weekend, and that was only on the rare occasion her mother had worked extra shifts to scrape together enough cash to afford it.

Alexa doesn't know how lucky she is. But then Cara sees the livid red line that runs down her daughter's leg, like someone has drawn on it with a felt-tip pen, and a wave of nausea rises up at the guilt that overwhelms her. It still hasn't healed properly. Alexa isn't lucky – she could be scarred for life. She needs this break too.

To try and forget what happened.

Cara reaches the end of the wooden walkway and hands over her cabin bag to the Asana Fushi resort representative who had met them in the main terminal. He'd been holding up a sign with their names on, had greeted them with a smile and whisked away their suitcases before handing out cool, damp towels fragranced with lemon balm. Cara had buried her face in hers, inhaling the aroma and wiping away the hot stickiness that had settled on her skin.

Another couple climbs up the small set of steps into the plane ahead of them. Cara tenses. The man had been sitting a couple of rows in front of them on the flight over. American. Brash. Chewing gum and wearing a baseball cap with the letters 'USA' emblazoned across the front in stars and stripes. He'd pressed his call button constantly for much of the flight, demanding everything from extra pillows to more ice in his drink until his numerous gin and tonics had finally knocked him out. She'd exchanged sympathetic glances with the various cabin crew who had been summoned to his seat; wanted to tell them she knew exactly how they felt.

Alexa finally catches up with them, still holding her iPhone, the thin gold hoop in her nostril catching the sun. Zach had been furious when he'd first seen it, but he seems to have got used to it now. Alexa knows how to twist him round her little finger.

'Are you sure you haven't still got your data on?' Cara says. She knows the words sound accusatory as soon as she's said them but can never seem to find the right ones with Alexa.

'I'm not stupid.'

Alexa's retort makes something inside her shrink. Zach squeezes her hand, a silent plea not to start this holiday with an argument. 'She knows to wait until we've got wi-fi.'

She was already texting when we landed, Cara wants to reply, but swallows the words instead. Alexa stomps up the steps, and Cara follows, looking for two empty seats.

'Don't you want to go by the window?' Zach asks. 'Get the best view?'

Cara shakes her head and waits for Zach to sit down before sliding in beside him. She fastens her seatbelt, pulling it through the buckle and tight against her stomach. She reaches underneath her seat, her breath catching in her throat when she can't find what she's looking for. It's got to be here. She scrabbles around until her fingers encounter the familiar roll of plastic, and her body feels lighter, although she's unsure what use a whistle, a light and an inflatable jacket would be miles from land in the middle of the ocean.

The propellers start up and she grasps Zach's hand. He smiles at her, then glances at his Apple watch before staring out of the window as the plane glides across the surface of the water and rises into the air, leaving the Indian Ocean spread out like an enormous blue carpet beneath them. Cara looks out of the tiny window as Malé turns into a grey blur and other islands come into view, small dark green shapes fringed with yellow and white, encircled by turquoise water.

She turns away, focuses on the American woman's head poking out above the top of the seat in front of her, black roots peeking through her bleached blonde lights. Everyone in the plane can hear her loud drawl over the whine of the engines as she demands another bottle of water. *Can't she wait?* They've only been in the air a few minutes, for heaven's sake. Cara concentrates on her breathing, tells herself it's only a twenty-five-minute flight, that nothing is going to happen, that it will all be fine. Just like she had four weeks ago.

But it hadn't been then, had it?

2. 4 days 2 hours left

Alexa turns up the volume on her AirPods; even Drake is difficult to hear over the noise of the propellers. She looks across the aisle at her mother, who is staring straight ahead, gripping the armrest so hard her knuckles have turned white. Alexa knows how much she hates confined spaces. Another thing about her she only discovered recently.

Alexa's stomach lurches as the seaplane drops abruptly. The American woman lets out a sharp squeal. Alexa looks again at her mother, who has shut her eyes. The small plane judders, then bounces twice. She experiences the sensation that she's falling, her stomach sinking like it does on a roller coaster for those few seconds at the top of a loop. Her father reaches for the paper bag in the seat pocket in front of him. For someone who goes abroad on business as much as he does, he's a dreadful traveller. Alexa can't believe he'd made it through the flight from Heathrow without chucking his guts up.

She turns her music down as the co-pilot apologizes for the turbulence and asks everyone to check their seatbelts are securely fastened. Her mother fumbles unsuccessfully to pull hers tighter than it already is. The cockpit has no door and Alexa sees the pilot reach up above his head to flick switches and adjust dials.

Is he panicking?

Pilots are trained not to panic. Even in an emergency.

Alexa glances at the clock on her iPhone and takes a deep breath. Only ten minutes to go. She has no idea how many kilometres that is, but it's too far to swim.

There's another jolt and Alexa's stomach swoops before coming back to rest in its original position. Her mother turns her head towards her and opens her eyes. Alexa gives her a brief smile. It's hard to believe now, but her mother has been trained for this. To deal with emergencies. She's seen photographs of her in her twenties, wearing her navy uniform, laughing with the other cabin crew. Happy. The kind of person Alexa could see herself being friends with. But they aren't friends. Not at the moment. Every interaction between them ends up being confrontational, even when she tries so hard for it not to be. She doesn't know who she's more frustrated with, her mother or herself.

The noise of the propellers increases, as if they are straining to keep the plane in the air. Alexa glances out of the window. The islands dotted amongst the dark blue are still small circles, thousands of feet below them.

Imagine falling from this height.

As this thought flashes into her head, she watches her mother undo her seatbelt and try to stand up. Her dad puts his hand on her arm, but Cara shakes him off and grabs hold of the headrest in front of her, trapping the American woman's hair beneath her fingers. The woman lets out another shriek and tries to turn around, but Cara doesn't seem to notice. Alexa leans forward, stretches out her arm to block her.

'Sit down, Mum.'

For a few seconds, Alexa isn't sure whether her mother has heard. Then Cara turns and looks at her, eyes blinking frantically. Alexa feels the pressure of her mother's body against her arm decrease as she hesitates.

'It's just a bit of turbulence,' Alexa continues. 'It's fine. Honestly. Sit back in your seat.'

Cara meets her gaze, her eyes finally focusing on her daughter.

'It's going to be OK?' she asks.

Alexa reaches out and squeezes her mother's arm.

''Course it is.' She hesitates. 'Just like I told you before.'

She feels her mother's hands tremble as she helps her back into her seat. Zach leans across and fastens her mother's seatbelt. He mouths a silent *thank you* at Alexa, who turns up the volume on her Airpods and runs her finger over the mark on her leg, wincing as she touches the puckered skin.

3. 4 days 2 hours left

Zach lifts his hand to shade his eyes from the brightness as he steps out of the seaplane, bending down so he doesn't hit his head, scuffing his Ethletic trainers. The heat hits him like a wave; he breathes in the warmth as he stares out across the ocean. Miles and miles of blue that stretch all the way to the horizon with nothing to impede the view apart from the odd patch of green in the distance. He'd seen the resort photos online but hadn't expected it to be quite like this. The epitome of luxury. No wonder people rave about this place.

He turns around to help Cara down the steps. Her large sunglasses hide most of her face, but her skin has a grey tinge that wasn't there before the flight. She had booked this holiday to celebrate his fiftieth birthday, but she needs it more than he does. Her therapist had said the break would do them all good, a way to come to terms with what happened, but Zach is sure his wife's issues date back further than four weeks ago.

'Hi there.' The American grabs Zach's hand and pumps it up and down in time to the beat of the drummers who are standing in a group on the wooden jetty, the red, green and white stripes embroidered on the bottom of their skirts designed to reflect the colours of the country's flag.

'I'm Ryan Miller. And this is my wife, Cindy. It's Zach, isn't it? Zach Hamilton? I recognized you from the sustainability conference in London a few months ago. Your keynote speech – very impressive.' Zach catches a waft of halitosis beneath the stale mint as Ryan claps him on the shoulder. 'We should get together for a drink – throw a few ideas around – my business operates in the same space as yours, and Cindy and I spend a lot of time in the UK.'

Ryan's voice echoes above the drummers and Zach can only bring himself to nod in agreement as he mutters something non-committal then pulls his hand away, wishing Alexa would hurry up and get off the seaplane.

'Isn't this place just *amazing*?' Cindy trills, staring at Cara intently. 'Jeez, it can't be . . . there's no way . . . Cara? Cara Brown? Do you remember me? Cindy Johnson? We flew together with United? Oh my god, I can't believe it's you! I haven't seen you in, like, over fifteen years?'

Zach sees Cara stiffen, then smile. One of her polite smiles. The one she wears when his mother comes over.

'Wow,' his wife says. 'Such a small world. I'm amazed you recognized me after all this time. It's Cara Hamilton now. How are you? You're looking well.' Cindy opens her mouth to reply just as Alexa finally emerges from the plane, but Cara carries on talking. 'We'll catch up properly a bit later, yes? When we've settled in. So lovely to see you again.'

She reaches for Zach's hand as he follows one of the staff towards the reception area, trying to put as much distance as possible between them and the sound of Cindy's heels, which click irritatingly against the jetty.

The balau-wood building with open sides has a thatched roof, and a dozen gigantic fans hang from the ceiling, their gold blades spinning silently. Dark mahogany seats covered in velvet cushions are arranged around the sides of the room; koi carp swim lazily in circles amongst the water-lily leaves in a shallow pool in the centre of the floor. Zach looks at the tall vases brimming with tall stems of kaaminee phool that sit on the low tables beside each of the seats, the white blossom filling the room with a fragrant orange-like scent. The attention to detail is impressive.

A waiter holds out a tray of colourful drinks adorned with pieces of fresh fruit, and Zach takes one, grimacing at the sweetness but wanting something to wash away the furriness that coats the inside of his mouth. Pineapple juice is a bit passé; he needs to tell them to get in some of the ginger and turmeric shots he drinks every morning.

'Welcome to Asana Fushi.' A tall, stocky man of around his own age steps forward and reaches for Zach's hand. 'I'm Marc Geddes, the general manager.'

Zach notes his firm grip and receding hairline. Slick, but with a whiff of desperation. He's seen it in hotel managers the world over.

'We're delighted you've chosen to spend some time with us,' Marc continues, smoothing down his pale blue linen shirt. 'I'm sure you must be tired after your journey, so we'll get the administration out of the way as fast as we can and then I'll hand you over to your butler, who will check you in to your room. If you're happy with the idea, we ask you to exchange WhatsApp details so that you can contact him twenty-four seven with any requests. Nothing is too much trouble for us here. I'll see you at dinner later on, and if you have any questions in the meantime, please don't hesitate to ask. I'm always available.'

He flashes a smile.

'Is there a code for the wi-fi?' Alexa asks.

'You'll find all the details in your room.'

Zach watches his daughter fiddle with the helix piercing she'd had done last week despite Cara asking her to wait until they were back from this trip. At least it seems to have stopped her from picking at her cuticles; one compulsive habit replaced by another.

'Actually, could we get it now?' he asks.

Marc's smile widens until his skin is stretched tight, revealing his artificially white teeth. Zach runs his tongue over his set of perfect veneers and grins back.

'Sure,' Marc replies smoothly. 'Just give me a moment and I'll find it for you.'

He walks over to a desk in the open-plan reception and pulls a small card with the wi-fi details printed on it from a drawer. Alexa looks behind him to where a flatscreen television hangs on the wall, video footage of various activities at the resort playing on the screen. Hundreds of multicoloured fish swim around a group of divers, bubbles escaping from their respirators like tiny glass balls. A woman holds on to something underwater that looks a bit like part of a surfboard as it pulls her over the reef.

'Fancy having a go?' Marc asks. 'It's a Seabob. A cross between a jet-ski and a bodyboard. They can go down to forty metres. We've got a couple of them here.'

Zach's forehead creases.

'Maybe,' he says. 'We'll get settled in first.'

Marc hands Alexa the card, his smile still fixed on his face.

'I hope that does the trick,' he says. 'It's a bit patchier than in the UK, but after five years out here, I'm used to it.'

Zach hands him his glass, half full of viscous yellow liquid.

'I wanted to ask you about the water,' he says. 'Do we need to stick to bottled?'

Marc shakes his head. 'We've tried to ensure that Asana Fushi is as eco-friendly as possible,' he says.

'The resort's reputation is one of the reasons we chose to come here,' Zach replies. 'Environmental concerns should be on everyone's radar. I try to do my bit both personally and professionally.' He hesitates, waiting for Marc to ask a question, which fails to materialize, then adjusts his glasses as he adds, 'I run a business that funds ethical projects around the globe.'

'Really?' Marc puts his hand on Zach's shoulder. 'We should have a chat once you've settled in. We've recently installed a desalination plant here. It gives us all the water we need. It's safe to drink and there are recyclable glass bottles for you to use in your room. So much more environmentally friendly than plastic.'

Zach senses Cara begin to fidget beside him.

'Sorry, sweetheart, I know I said no business talk while we're away. I'll shut up now.' He squeezes her hand.

'Zach Hamilton?'

He turns around, takes a step backwards as he sees a familiar face staring at him.

'Skye Elliot,' he says. 'What the hell are you doing here?'

4. 4 days 2 hours left

Cara looks at the woman who is staring at her husband. Slim. At least fifteen years younger than her, probably more; it's difficult to be sure as she's so tanned. Piercing blue eyes and hair that's been bleached almost white by the sun.

'I'm Cara.' She holds out her hand. 'Zach's wife.'

The woman takes it, and Cara sees the various inkings that stretch down her arm. An octopus, its tentacles looping around in decorative swirls. A curling wave, the edges of breaking foam intricately detailed in black and grey. She can see Alexa staring too; tattoos are the one thing she and Zach have agreed their daughter is not allowed to even consider getting until she's at least eighteen.

'Hey, Cara, nice to meet you. How are you doing?'

Cara feels herself tense as the woman with the broad Australian accent looks her up and down, studying her Stella McCartney sweatpants and top, but before she can pronounce judgement they are disturbed by the sound of Cindy's heels clicking towards them.

'Oh my god, is that really you? *The* Skye Elliot? My daughter just *adores* you.'

Skye smiles.

'Thanks! That's nice to hear.'

'Would you mind if I get a selfie?'

Cindy puts one arm around Skye before she has a chance

to answer, and grins, her head tilted to one side as she holds up her phone.

'Doesn't that look great?' She points at the screen. 'Thanks so much. My Riley will be so psyched. Are you here for long?'

Skye opens her mouth to reply, but Ryan's booming tones cut her off; he's calling his wife over to the golf buggy that's about to leave for their villa.

'I need to go.' Cindy turns to Cara. 'We'll catch up later, yes?'

Cara nods.

'We used to fly together,' Cindy says to Skye. 'Cabin crew for United Airlines. Such good times. Fifteen years ago, and I still recognized her straight away.'

Cara smiles politely. She has a vague recollection of working a couple of flights with this woman, but Cindy makes it sound like they were best friends. As Cindy walks away, Skye raises her eyebrows and grins conspiratorially at Alexa.

'I thought it was you,' Alexa says. 'I've watched your videos on YouTube. The ten-questions-in-a-minute chat feature you did with my dad last year. You've had some amazing guests.' She hesitates. 'And I love your tattoos.'

Skye grins. 'Cool, aren't they?' She looks at Zach. 'I read that feature you wrote for the *Daily Economist* – "How to make a profit while saving the planet". You had some really interesting ideas.'

'Thanks.' Zach smiles. Cara notices he omits to mention that both she and ChatGPT had given him a helping hand coming up with a few of those concepts. 'It's really great to meet you in person,' he continues. 'Your social stats are through the roof – you must be delighted. Is it hard having to constantly come up with new ideas for content?'

'Nah. Not really.' Skye smiles sadly. 'That's the thing about environmental issues. There's always something to talk about when things are getting worse, not better. Another species disappears practically every day.'

'Are you staying here long?' Alexa echoes Cindy's question.

'A few days, maybe a week. Then I'm moving to another resort. Took me longer to get here than I expected. It's a tricky journey from Bali – that's where I'm based now. Great place for a digital nomad, but only marginally less accessible than Sydney.'

'You lived in Sydney?' Alexa asks.

Skye nods.

'Beautiful city,' Cara says, glancing at Zach. It's where they had their first date. She'd been on a lay-over and he'd travelled over for a business meeting. Zach winks at her but says nothing.

'Yeah. But Bali's great too,' Skye continues. 'I came here by sailboat. Finally arrived last night. Tore a leaf out of Greta's book. Couldn't justify flying – not exactly ethical on the carbon-neutral front.'

Cara notices a muscle in her husband's cheek twitch.

'A magazine asked me to do a feature on some of the resorts out here,' she continues. '"Can you experience luxury in paradise while saving the planet?" I'm here to find out if Asana can live up to its claims. They've certainly got the luxury bit figured out. Have you seen some of the overwater villas have slides out of the bedroom straight into the ocean? Fucking amazing.' She looks at

Alexa. 'Excuse my language. And you have to go to the underwater restaurant – it's incredible.'

Alexa grins.

'You guys know each other?' Marc asks as he comes over.

'Only online,' Zach says. 'Skye interviewed me over Zoom last year after I helped fund a sustainable-energy project she had an interest in. I don't think she'd mind me saying that we share certain values.'

'Hashtag environmentally conscious.' Skye smiles.

Cara remembers Zach doing an interview about the project, but he hadn't told her this was the person he was doing it with. A woman who both her daughter and husband are now staring at in adoration. And as she looks at the octopus wrapped around Skye's arm, she feels a hot layer of jealousy slide over her skin.

5. 4 days 1 hour left

Marc beckons to a man who is hovering at the side of the room.

'Devi is ready to take you to your villa,' he says.

They are ushered towards one of the electric golf buggies that are lined up outside reception. Zach climbs on to the leather seat, helps Alexa in beside him. Cara sits behind, their luggage already loaded on to the back.

Skye holds up her hand and Zach waves as they pull away. He crosses his legs and taps one foot against the metal floor, the taste of pineapple still acidic on his tongue.

The buggy travels silently along a sandy path surrounded on either side by dense green bushes and palm trees. Every thirty metres or so, smaller paths branch off to one side, leading down to one of the twenty beach villas set along one side of the island so they catch the view of the sunset each night. Located far enough apart to still be highly exclusive. Devi tells them the other side of the island has been left deliberately unoccupied to ensure the resort never feels crowded and guests can swim off a deserted beach without being overlooked.

Zach turns his head to see Cara gazing at the lanterns that have been strung up in the branches either side of the path. He had wanted to stay in a beach villa, but Cara had said it was his fiftieth and he deserved to have the best, so they went for an overwater villa at almost twice the cost. He hopes it will be worth it, that this will be a turning point. A literal line in the sand. As he'd said to his mother, who had made it very clear she thought this trip was an unnecessary expense, it will be a way to put everything behind them.

'Asana Fushi is basically a circle,' Devi says as the electric buggy whines. 'The resort is spread out over the entire island, and this path runs around the edge. It will take you about twenty minutes to walk the full loop. Or, if you want, you can stroll all the way around Asana on the beach. But unless you're going to walk in the water, wear something on your feet, as the sand gets very hot. Everywhere is signposted, but the main restaurant is next to reception, along with the infinity pool, diving centre, yoga pavilion and resort boutique. There are two places where we moor the boats, the main jetty that guests come in on, and another a short distance away on the deserted side of the island next to the desalination plant. It will take you about ten minutes to walk from your overwater villas to reception, but you can call me at any time and I'll collect you in the buggy if you'd prefer. The best snorkelling is on the sunset side of the lagoon, away from where all the villas are located' – he points over to their left – 'but the house reef stretches all the way around the island in front of the beach villas and there are also steps straight down into the sea from the deck of your overwater villa.'

Zach glances at his watch. Twelve o'clock here, so 8 a.m. at home. He thinks about what he'd usually be doing at this time on a Monday morning as he gets into the office and then stops himself. He needs to focus on making the most of this break. Concentrate on his wife and daughter. He owes them that.

The buggy judders as they come off the path and on to a long wooden jetty that has been built in a semicircle off the side of the island over the lagoon. The water is the clearest turquoise Zach has ever seen, with tropical coloured fish swimming around clumps of coral in the shallows. Ten overwater bungalows with dark wood-panelled walls and thatched roofs are positioned off the side of the jetty, facing out over the ocean.

Zach turns around to look at Cara, and she smiles, points at an eagle ray that is moving through the water, a grey diamond amid the blue. He has a good feeling about this place. A few sessions in the spa and the opportunity to spend some time together away from the business will do them the world of good. He wouldn't be without Alexa for anything, but sometimes he wishes he could turn the clock back for a few hours, for him and Cara to be like they were when it was just the two of them.

He glances across at his daughter, who has dragged her eyes away from her screen for a few seconds to admire the view. Miles of ocean as far as he can see, in every direction, civilization just a distant memory.

Her leg looks like it's healing nicely, but he needs to get Cara to remind her to cover it up when she's in the sun. Minimize any scarring. He swallows, remembering her screams. Thank God he'd been there.

It could have been so much worse.

6. 4 days left

Alexa looks at the white linen on the king-size four-poster bed in her bedroom, where the words *WELCOME TO ASANA FUSHI* have been spelt out with bright pink petals and palm leaves. She takes a photo before sweeping the foliage on to the floor, lies down and opens Snapchat to type a message to her best friend now the wi-fi has finally connected.

Just got here. 😉 *Seaplane journey.*

Sophie's Bitmoji and a think bubble appear, showing she is online and replying.

Nightmare. Is it hot?

Yeah, sweating atm, Alexa types. *Villa is amazing – lit like standing in the sea. Has an acc PLUNGE POOL on the deck!!* 😊

Wow v jell 😊

Alexa smiles and sends the photo of her room in which she'd captured the decoration on her bed along with the bowl of papaya, mango, coconut and lychees on the table and the view out over the ocean.

Sophie's response comes back immediately.

Ur so lucky!!

This place is epic. You'll never guess who's here.

???

SKYE ELLIOT!!!!

😲 *OMG.*

Ikr. She's so fucking cool. She hit 3.4 million on Insta last week. Want to get a selfie! She remembered my dad from last year and is staying for a few days. She's so lovely. Lives in Bali now and am defo gonna get a tattoo like hers.

There's a pause before Sophie replies.

Sounds incredible. Ttyl – am off to a party tonight.

Alexa's stomach tightens.

Spill the tea. Anywhere nice? She sends another photo of the outdoor shower and the marble bathtub that is big enough to swim in.

Holly's. Charlie's coming.

Charlie?

Didn't he tell you?

His dad went total psycho when he found his vapes last week, Alexa types, then wishes she hadn't. Now it's obvious he hasn't updated her on the fact he's now allowed out. She fiddles with the stud in her helix, twists it until it hurts, making her cartilage throb.

His dad? Are we talking ab the same man here? He doesn't give a fuck ab what Charlie does. Charlie said he's hardly ever at home. Btw do you like my nails?

Alexa looks at the photo Sophie has sent and types a thumbs-up, exactly the opposite of what she's actually feeling, then adds, *Cool. Wish u were here x*

There's a pause before Sophie responds.

Is everything alr now with ur mum & dad?

Alexa bites her lip. *Yeah*, she types. Then adds, *Kind of. Ok. Gtg.*

Sophie hasn't picked up on the hint.

Alexa hesitates. *Enjoy*, she types. *Let me know all the goss x*

She waits for a response, but nothing appears, checks

her other messages, but there's nothing new, so she sends Charlie a selfie of her in her new bikini blowing a kiss, adds a filter that smooths her skin, making her look less jetlagged than she feels, and positions a bunch of hearts that float across the screen. She adds a message underneath: *U in 2nite?*

Then she opens the door that leads into her bathroom, notes the rain shower on the decking outside, types Skye's name into YouTube on her phone and watches her latest vodcast. Taken on the sailboat on the way here. She zooms in so Skye's face fills the screen, stands in front of the mirror and looks at herself as she mimics what Skye is saying, tries to perfect an Australian accent, move her head so it's at the same slightly tilted angle when she's talking. Then she runs her fingers over her arm, wondering, if she had a tattoo, how long it would take to heal, and whether it would end up feeling different to the rest of her skin.

The video is still playing when she calls reception from the phone by her bed, and she mutes Skye's voice when someone answers.

'Hi, this is Alexa Hamilton. I've got something I need to give to Skye Elliot? We were chatting earlier, and I thought she said she was in villa five, but I think I might have misheard her.'

The woman on the other end of the line hesitates, and Alexa holds her breath.

'It's villa nine, not five, madam.'

'That's great. Thanks so much.'

Alexa unmutes the video and holds Skye's face above her as she lies back on her bed, racking her brain to think of a good reason to drop in for a visit.

7. 3 days 21 hours left

The man can't remember what he was thinking about as he steps out of his front door into the drizzle and pulls the hood of his jacket over his head. The weather forecast hadn't predicted rain, but he's brought an umbrella anyway — the app never seems to get it right. He hates the lead-up to Christmas. Too much going on. He flips his car key over and over in the palm of his hand, evidence, if any was needed, that he can never relax properly before a job. Marie had said to him once that she didn't think he'd ever stop moving until he was dead.

He wishes he didn't have to go. He would far rather stay at home, chill out with his wife on the sofa and then go and pick up his son from school later. But that's not an option. Not in his line of work. Vincent calls and he has to go in. Don't argue with the boss. That's been the deal for the last fifteen years.

His brand-new Mercedes EQS SUV is less than fifty metres ahead of him, parked at the side of the road, a motorbike behind it. A man is standing next to it. Perhaps he's waiting for someone. For him? He's learned to trust his instincts after this long in the job. Or maybe he's just being paranoid. They're probably here to deliver take-out; he can smell the familiar aroma of fish and chips. It makes him salivate; Marie told him he should have had something to eat before he left, but he couldn't face breakfast. Not this morning. Not when he knows what's around the corner.

He quickens his pace, thinks about what he's going to have to do. Remembers it's his wedding anniversary tomorrow. Ten years. He's going to have to find somewhere to get some flowers. Roses. Marie's favourite.

He presses the button on his key fob and the car lets out a couple of beeps as the amber lights flash. He puts his hand in his jacket pocket, checks he's got what he needs, lets his fingers stroke the cold metal.

The man standing by his car reaches down and picks up a helmet from the motorbike, puts it on before swinging his leg over the seat, then starts the engine and drives away. Something inside him relaxes. He reaches out to open his car door as his mobile rings, glances at the screen and rolls his eyes.

Bloody hell, Vincent. Really? There's nothing more annoying than a last-minute change of plan.

8. 3 days 18 hours left

There is a knock on the door of their villa just after 7 p.m. and Cara opens it to find Devi standing outside. He points at the buggy waiting on the jetty, a garland of fresh flowers draped over the back of the seats.

'Evening, Mrs Hamilton.'

His eyes are emerald green with gold flecks, his pupils expanding as he focuses on her, only blinking when she looks away first.

'I'm here to take you to dinner.'

'We're almost ready,' Cara says, smoothing down her dress. 'Just waiting for my daughter.' Her hand flutters to her neck, fiddles with the small bee on her gold chain. 'Teenagers. They take for ever.'

She sees him suppress a smile.

'I hope you've settled in OK?'

Cara nods. 'We can't stop looking at the view. It's incredible.'

'You know I'm on WhatsApp if you need anything.'

Cara notices he's standing very still with his hands clasped together but his fingers are still moving, the same pose her mother used to adopt when she was talking to the people whose houses she cleaned. She wonders how many guests he has to look after, whether he has a family, how old he is. Forty, maybe? Younger? She can see his arm muscles under his short-sleeved shirt, sinewy from so much physical labour.

'Thanks.' She smiles.

'I mean it,' he adds. 'Anything at all. Just drop me a message.'

She has an urge to tell him that she doesn't expect him to be at her beck and call. Her mother had done that for people her whole life, and look where it had got her. Constantly scrabbling around for loose change down the back of a sofa despite the arthritis in her fingers, then dead of a heart attack at sixty-five.

Devi reaches into his pocket and hands her a tiny origami bird made out of palm leaves.

'For you,' he says. 'Dhivehi kabili. It brings good luck.'

Cara stares at it. No one has made her anything for years. Not since Alexa used to come back from primary school with some kind of painted clay pot or pasta-bead necklace. Her eyes well up. 'It's beautiful. Thank you.'

Zach appears behind them.

'We'll be out in a second,' he says, pushing the door half shut so Devi is left outside.

'Ready, sweetheart?' he calls out.

Alexa finally appears from her bedroom wearing a long blue sundress. She holds on to Zach's arm as they walk out to the buggy. Cara hangs back, closes her fingers over the palm-leaf bird, crumpling it into a ball as she slides it into a pocket of her dress and shuts the door behind her.

9. 3 days 10 hours left

Cara is woken up by what sounds like raised voices. Her heart thuds as she rolls over in the pitch dark to check the time. It's only after she can't find her bedside table that she remembers where she is, piecing together her thoughts like the bits of a jigsaw. On holiday. In the Maldives. *Safe*. Her head swims as she squints into the blackness, tries to find her phone. There is a loud thump, like someone tripping over a piece of furniture, then silence.

Her hand finds the lead of her charger and she pulls her mobile up from the floor. Three a.m. She only went to bed four hours ago. The open-air Seabreeze restaurant had been buzzing with guests when Devi dropped them off, the whole place lit by candles set along the edge of the wooden deck that stuck out over the water so they could watch the fish swimming around below them. Zach had picked a table on the opposite side of the restaurant to Ryan and Cindy, and Cara had watched them ask a succession of waiters to take their photo during every course. She can still taste the giant prawns, the size of small lobsters, caught fresh earlier that day and griddled on the barbecue.

Marc had hung around after they'd finished eating, quizzing Zach about his business, and her husband had lapped up the attention, as usual, Marc's laugh louder and more exaggerated each time Zach spoke. Zach had even taken his glasses off so Marc could try them on. Gave the same spiel she'd heard so many times before about how no one could tell they were made of recycled bullet casings. About how investing in eco-friendly products was the way forward; a chance to be highly profitable and save the planet at the same time.

Zach hadn't been like this when they first met. But then, neither had she. She wonders whether being *just a mother* for sixteen years – her mother-in-law's description – has left her resentful that she has nothing else to focus on. Perhaps if she hadn't given up her job, if she'd kept something back just for *her*, rather than the ad hoc administrative work she does for Zach that she fits around Alexa being at school, she'd feel she had something valuable to contribute to the conversations that crop up in situations like this. When someone asks what she does and she admits to being a stay-at-home mum, she is immediately rendered invisible, as if having a child has stripped her of any skills she once had, let alone winning her any acknowledgement for the multitude of new ones she's developed while Alexa has been growing up.

Who wears glasses made of recycled bullets? Zach thinks it's cool; he calls it 'a conversation starter', but as far as she's concerned, it's just a bit weird. *Bullets from where?* He'd said shooting ranges, but how does he actually know, and who would want to be associated with anything like that?

She'd followed Alexa as she got up from the table, leaving Marc pouring Zach another glass of whiskey; her husband in his element as the centre of attention. Alexa had said she was going back to the villa: the only place she could get wi-fi. Cara had been about to ask if she could come too but had hesitated, unsure if she would sound too needy. Maybe her daughter just wanted some space.

Alexa had squeezed Cara's hand and looked back at Zach before walking away down the path, and Cara couldn't help wondering whether her daughter had been having the same thoughts about Zach as she had. *Such a show-off.* She'd felt a lump in her throat at the thought that she'd allowed an opportunity for them to connect slip through her fingers.

Cara had stepped out of her shoes and made her way across the powdery white sand, the clear night sky lit up by myriad stars. She had never seen anything like it. At home, they were only visible as the odd pinprick of light if you really searched for them, even when there weren't any clouds. Here, they filled the sky in a gigantic arc that curved above her head.

She'd been paddling in the shallows when she spotted a silhouette further down the beach. A man holding two lengths of chain with what looked like round balls attached to each end, whirling them over his head to form different shapes. He'd moved his body at the same time, bending down on to his knees and then standing back up again, never letting go. Devi. She'd watched, fascinated, something in her stomach tightening at how he looked without a T-shirt on. Ripped abs, unlike Zach, whose fixation on running and swimming has made him lean, like a whippet. Eventually Devi had seen her and stood still, staring in her direction. She hadn't moved, despite the tug in the bottom of her stomach that had urged her forward, feeling it would somehow cross a line, despite the fact that her husband was sitting in a restaurant only metres behind her. She'd wanted to wave, but hadn't, and he'd picked up his chains and walked away, leaving her alone on the beach.

Is it Alexa she just heard? She's not sure. Maybe it's someone outside on the jetty. She sits up slowly and slides out from beneath her white sheets, Zach lying motionless beside her, his mouth slightly open. The dark polished floorboards feel cool against the soles of her feet. She holds out her phone and uses it as a torch as she feels for the handle to open her bedroom door. The living room is empty. She walks over to the sofas, conscious of the grains of sand beneath her feet that she's carried back with her from dinner. The door to Alexa's room is shut; darkness spills out through the small gap at the bottom.

A pale blue glow emanates from a large panel of glass that has been inserted into the floorboards. Spotlights under the villa switch on at night, turning the water below a luminous blue-green colour. She peers at it, rubbing her bare arms where the air-conditioning has made her skin rise up in goosebumps. An unmistakeable dark shape slides into view beneath the glass. A shark. Sleek and grey, with a black tip on its fin. Cara shivers. It swims backwards and forwards a few times across the illuminated gap, and she watches it until it disappears, a thudding in her chest.

The villa is silent. The front door is locked; no one can get in without a key card and she can see hers, Zach's and Alexa's lying on the coffee table.

She walks back to her bedroom and lies down in bed again, trying to ignore the grains of sand that scratch against her shins. Zach turns over, still half asleep, his salt-and-pepper designer stubble forming a dark shadow on his face. He reaches out, puts his arm around her waist, and she lies still, not wanting to wake him.

She doesn't recall him coming in last night; she must have drifted off before he got back. As she shuts her eyes, she remembers what she saw in the restaurant when she came off the beach. Zach sitting at the table where she'd left him, a glass in his hand. But it wasn't Marc who he was raising a toast with; Marc was nowhere to be seen. The person sitting next to Zach in the seat she'd vacated, holding a champagne flute and laughing with her husband, had been Skye Elliot.

10. 3 days 3 hours left

The glass doors that lead out from Alexa's bedroom on to the decking at the back of the villa are rectangles of solid blue behind her curtains the following morning. She slides them open to find her mother stretched out on the hammock by the plunge pool, a copy of *The Beach Party* in her hand, the paperback bestseller she'd picked up in WHSmith at Heathrow.

'Where's Dad?' she asks, fiddling with the cord of the waffle dressing gown that resort staff had hung on the back of her door.

Cara hesitates. 'Gone for a workout and a swim in the pool. And then he said he's going to see Marc. Apparently, he wants to get a look at the new desalination plant.'

Alexa bites her lip. 'I thought he was supposed to be having a break from the business? If he's just going to work, then we could have stayed at home.'

Cara doesn't answer, and Alexa feels her mother appraising her from behind her sunglasses.

'Were you and Dad arguing last night?' Alexa wants a reaction, for her mother to stop being so diplomatic. Her dad had agreed not to work on this holiday; why is she defending him by not discussing it?

Her mother sits up, making the hammock swing from side to side on the deck, removes her sunglasses and lowers her book on to the rope netting.

'Dad and I are fine,' she says.

But the telltale blankness behind her eyes reveals that she's lying. Alexa wonders why her mother insists on treating her like a child. As if she is too fragile to cope with the truth, despite everything they've been through.

'I was already asleep by the time he got in,' Cara says. 'I thought I heard something in the night too. Did I wake you up moving around?'

'No.' Alexa pulls her phone out of her dressing-gown pocket and glances at Snapchat, flicks through the photos of Holly's party, bored of the conversation, of her mother's attempts to fob her off. She changes the subject, an attempt to return to neutral ground. 'Have you had breakfast?'

Cara turns away to look out over the blue ocean, and Alexa follows her gaze; a calm smoothness all the way out to the reef in the distance, where Alexa can see small waves breaking on the surface of the water.

'I thought you wanted a lie-in,' her mother says. 'If you want something, you can order room service. They do the most amazing breakfasts on floating trays. You could have it in the plunge pool.'

Alexa looks at her phone, something cold trickling into her stomach at photos of Charlie with his arms around Sophie.

'Are you OK?' Cara asks.

'I'm great,' Alexa snaps. 'I'm having such a brilliant time, stuck here miles away from all my friends with no one to talk to.'

'I'm sorry if you –'

'Oh my god, Mum, stop patronizing me. You sound like your therapist. I still don't get why I couldn't have just stayed at home.'

Something hot and bitter floods through Alexa's veins. 'You know why . . .'

'Just forget it.' Alexa steps off the deck and back into her bedroom. 'When Dad comes back, tell him I've gone snorkelling.'

She pulls on her bikini and sprays herself with factor thirty in the outdoor shower area before throwing on the white cover-up that she'd bought on ASOS with her mother's American Express card to match Sophie's, something non-sustainable from a company she knows both her parents disapprove of, and slams the front door of the villa on her way out.

She sits on the sand and tries to pull on her flippers. The tips of her fingers throb as she stretches the tight black rubber over her feet. A mask and snorkel lie beside her in a net bag emblazoned with the Asana Fushi logo. The staff at the diving centre who she'd chatted to for a while said this side of the island was the best place to see the most fish. She'd lied and told them she'd already swum out to the reef yesterday afternoon, to avoid getting a long lecture on water safety. She can see where the water starts to turn a darker shade of blue – it's not even that far. The drop-off is further out, where the water turns almost black and the reef shelves away into the ocean as steeply as a cliff face.

The beach is empty. All the guests must either be at breakfast or shagging in their villas on the other side of the island. Alexa spits into her mask and bends down to rinse it out in the sea before pulling the strap around her head. The powder-white sand is almost too bright to look at without her sunglasses as she wades into the water, the tender skin on her leg stinging in the salt.

The water only comes up to her knees for the first fifty or so metres. It's warm, like a bath, and crystal clear – Alexa can see straight down to the bottom, where the current has shaped the sand into ripples: a sea within a sea. When it finally reaches the tops of her thighs she crouches down and lowers her face on to the surface, takes a couple of breaths to check her snorkel is working, the sound of the air being sucked in and blown out of the plastic tube echoing in her head.

Her chest tightens as she experiences a flutter of panic that she's not going to be able to breathe, that she won't see something swimming up behind her, *that she's on her own and can't escape*, but she forces herself to focus on kicking her legs and moving forward. You can't let what happened define the rest of your life. Isn't that what her dad had said? She wants to believe he's right, but her eyes well with tears when she thinks about it and she has to blink to clear her blurred vision.

The reef is further out than she thought, but the water is still shallow and she thinks she could almost touch the bottom if she stood up. Small mounds of coral start to appear beneath her, tiny orange fish swim around the delicate fronds and then vanish as she puts out her hand to touch them. She raises her gaze to check she's heading in the right direction and tries not to let her flippers touch the fragile structures, like the man at the diving centre had instructed.

He'd said to wait for high tide, and something about staying within the markers, coloured poles that stick out above the surface of the water, but as Alexa raises her head out of the sea again she can see she's almost made it to the reef.

She knew she could do it.

The coral becomes denser, patches of grey and green that cover the white sand. This would once have been a mass of different colours, but it's been bleached, like so many other reefs in the Maldives, and is now mostly dead, with only the odd burst of yellow and pink.

She pulls herself through the water and an agonizing pain shoots across her hip. She looks down, unable to touch the bottom to stand up, but she can't see anything. Her skin feels as if it's on fire. She splutters as seawater floods in through the top of her snorkel and, as she gasps for air, it drops out of her mouth.

Fucking hell that hurts.

She turns on her back in the water, trying to float, *it hurts it hurts it hurts,* but can't catch her breath. She pulls off her mask and it sinks down on top of the coral as she rubs her eyes to stop them stinging.

She tries kicking her legs to swim against the current, to get back to where it's shallow enough to stand up, but each time she moves the pain gets worse. She can't move. *What the fuck just happened? Why does it hurt so much?* Alexa squints, trying to see the beach; it's only about three hundred metres away, but it may as well be three hundred miles.

11. 3 days 2 hours left

'Has anyone taken another fan to villa seven?'

Marc's tone is tinged with weary exasperation as he addresses the staff in the meeting he has requested in their quarters, a purpose-built prefabricated building situated in the centre of the island, out of sight. The guests never visit here; the signposts direct them towards the paths near the beach, overlooking the ocean.

Always keep them focused on the money shot.

He observes the people standing in front of him in the heat, their faces shiny with sweat. There's no CFC-free air-conditioning here, not even in the dormitories, where they are packed in like sardines.

'Is number seven the villa with the Americans?' Devi asks. 'Mr and Mrs Miller? I took them one this morning – do they want another? They'll have four in there with the two we already gave them last night. I don't understand why they need so many – I checked the air-conditioning and it's all working fine.'

Marc takes one of the white flannels off the pile of freshly ironed linen in front of him and dabs at his damp forehead.

'Mr Miller says his wife requires a breeze in the room at all times. Evidently lowering the temperature of the air-conditioning doesn't have the same effect. At Asana, our customers' needs must always be our highest priority. Let's make sure we get another one taken in there, please.' He smooths back a strand of hair that seems to have escaped the generous handful of pomade he slicked through it this morning. 'And what are all these doing here?'

He points at a heap of towels and cushions on the floor.

'We've had to change them,' Devi says. 'Mrs Miller says she is allergic to the colour orange. She also has an intolerance to nuts, cow's milk, soya milk, strawberries, dust mites and several other things. She's given me a list.'

Marc clenches his fists and shuts his eyes briefly as a ripple of laughter runs around the room. *That couple is going to be a bloody nightmare.* The thought slips out before he can stop it, and he tries to tuck it away with the other things he keeps in the back of his head, folding them over and over like pieces of paper until he can pretend they aren't really there at all.

'Mr and Mrs Miller expect a certain level of service from the Asana Fushi resort, and we will endeavour to match their particular requirements,' he says. 'I'll talk to them at dinner and explain that although our electricity here is largely solar powered, we would appreciate it if they could try not to use it excessively, but, in the meantime, please let me know if they ask for anything else.'

He smiles at the staff, an attempt to demonstrate empathy with the tricky situation they face with guests like these. One of the disadvantages of working in the unparalleled-luxury market is having to deal with some of the most demanding people on the planet.

Pause for maximum effect. Isn't that what they'd said on his most recent training course?

He hesitates, lowers the tone of his voice.

'And as I'm sure many of you are already aware, we've also got an Australian eco-influencer staying with us at the moment in villa nine. Skye Elliot.'

Marc looks at the blank faces staring back at him. He doesn't want to admit he hadn't heard of her either until the publicist from the magazine running the feature called him. Then he'd looked her up – almost three and a half million followers on Instagram. The ability to catapult any brand she raves about into the spotlight, and practically bankrupt anything she expresses a dislike for.

He picks up the magazine he brought into the meeting with him, flips over a few of the pages and holds up a photo of a woman with blonde hair tied up in a messy bun, her face freckled from the sun. 'This,' he says, 'is Skye Elliot. She's here to write a feature on Asana Fushi. Everyone – I repeat, *everyone* – is to make sure they know exactly who this woman is and that they give her anything she asks for at any time. She's got several tattoos down her arm, which makes her easy to spot, and it's her thirtieth birthday today. I'm organizing a low-key celebration this evening – a few bottles of Bollinger and some petits-fours. We'll rope off a VIP area in the Murika restaurant for her and a few selected staff will serve them. I'll let you know the details later. Any questions?'

Heads shake in the airless heat.

'She's allowed access to all areas in the resort, and I'd be grateful if you can make an effort to keep your staff quarters immaculate for the duration of her visit.'

His phones buzzes, and he glances at the screen. Not another message from Lilia. *Does she ever stop?* He told her he's signed the divorce papers and sent them back to the solicitor – what more does she want him to do? As if he doesn't already have enough on his plate.

He moves his feet slightly further apart, adjusts his stance to stop himself swaying, wonders if he's going to pass out. It's stifling in here, and he hasn't been keeping sufficiently hydrated. He doesn't like staff meetings at the best of times, but having Skye scrutinizing everything he does has put him on edge.

'I also need to let everyone know that we had a rather disappointing review on Tripadvisor,' he says. 'Two stars, which obviously brings down the resort average. Apparently, Mr and Mrs Petrov didn't like the geckos in their room. Now, I realize there's not much we can do about that, and I have replied to reassure them that the creatures are totally harmless and eat the mosquitoes, but we do need to try to make an extra effort.'

'To do what?' Devi asks.

Marc swallows.

'To ensure our guests' needs are always met,' he says. 'Our bookings are still down on pre-Covid levels and we need to get them back up. Otherwise . . .' He trails off.

There's a shuffling of feet, and he can sense the uneasiness at the prospect of fewer visitors and the possibility of redundancies. He claps his hands for silence.

'Skye Elliot has also said she wants an honest opinion on the resort from the other guests, so please don't discuss that she's writing a magazine feature. Not even between yourselves in Dhivehi. Most people staying with us at the moment are British, Russian or German, but there's always a chance someone might understand what you're saying.'

Marc walks out of the room, leaving the soiled flannel

he used to wipe his forehead to be picked up by one of the cleaning team. He heads back to reception, remembering to smile at the guests he meets along the sandy path; his standard platitudes of *lovely day, fantastic weather, don't forget your sun cream, hope to see you in the bar later* falling out of his mouth despite his brain being elsewhere.

He checks no other staff are around before he logs on to his computer and opens a folder that contains details of all the publicly filed accounts for ZH Investments Limited, together with dozens of articles about Zach that he had pulled off the internet shortly after the Hamiltons' booking was made a few months ago.

Marc knows quite a lot about Zach Hamilton. And Zach has no idea quite how useful this information has been.

12. 3 days 2 hours left

The yoga teacher walks across the wooden floor of the pavilion and stands beside Cara's mat. She can't be much older than twenty and is wearing a crop top that shows off her toned abs.

'To come out of downward dog and into cat pose,' she says, 'just bend your knees until they reach the ground. Make sure your hands are shoulder width apart, then arch your back and lower your head.'

Cara follows her instructions, her arms shaking as she adjusts herself into the correct position, conscious of Cindy on the mat next to her, who has clearly done these kinds of classes before. She's even wearing a sodding sweatband.

'We'll do this four times, everyone,' the instructor says. 'Remember to take slow breaths between each move; copy my inhalations and exhalations.' She doesn't take her eyes off Cara while she's speaking.

Why isn't she watching anyone else in the class?

Cara wipes a layer of sweat from her palms on to her Silou London eco-sustainable leggings. The bifold doors that run the length of one side of the yoga pavilion give a view straight out over the blue ocean. Several potted palms have been placed at either end of the doors and their arched, green fronds flutter in the CFC-free air-conditioning. The surface of the water looks perfectly still; more like a swimming pool than the sea. A thatched parasol stands on the white sand beside the small path that leads up to one of the beach villas; beneath it are two empty teak sun-loungers, neatly folded orange towels embroidered with the 'AF' logo laid on top of the cream cushions.

Maybe she should have gone snorkelling with Alexa instead of coming here. Or maybe not; her daughter can't seem to bear spending time with her at the moment. On the one hand, Cara is desperate to appease her in an attempt to keep the channels of communication open between them, but at the same time she has been sorely tempted to slam the villa door firmly in her face more than once on this holiday already. The fractures in their relationship have been expanding for a while. Alexa didn't use to be a daddy's girl, but she's turned into one recently, and Cara is terrified it's her fault. They used to be so close. She'd do anything to get that back. Should she give her space? Not give her space? Her therapist told her that Alexa needed time, that she wasn't ready to hear the apologies Cara kept holding out like a handful of sweets, begging her to take one.

'And now we're going to go into child pose,' the yoga teacher says. 'Sit back on your heels and sink down so your chest meets your thighs and lower your forehead on to the mat, keeping your hands stretched out in front of you.'

Cara does as she's told. She always has. Her friends tell her she's easy-going, but she thinks that's just a more flat-tering way of saying she's compliant. Zach had suggested she give up her job as cabin crew after Alexa was born because she'd found it difficult to cope, so she'd done it. And she'd carried on doing the things other people wanted her to do without really thinking about it because, in the end, it made life easier. She ate the broccoli her mother-in-law served up every time they went round for Sunday lunch despite the fact Cara had told her a dozen times she hates the stuff. She sorted out Zach's diary and travel arrangements because he told her she made fewer mistakes than his assistant. Alexa needed a lift back from some party at midnight, so she'd drag herself out of bed in her pyjamas and then drive several miles out of her way to drop Sophie back too. She's become a pushover. *An easy target.* And look where it's got her.

She can sense the yoga teacher beside her, checking she's in the right position. She wonders if Zach has finished his tour of the desalination plant with Marc. Whether there will be time for her to go back to the villa and curl up on their king-size bed by herself before lunch. She can't seem to shake the feeling of exhaustion that has spread through her body in recent weeks, burrowing deep into her bones.

The doctor had run a few tests and said there was nothing physically wrong with her. She'd told him she was waking up in the middle of the night and couldn't go back to sleep so he'd prescribed Temazepam. She kept the pills in her jewellery box, where Zach never looks, had even brought a couple of packets out here with her *just in case*, but she doesn't want to take anything that might dull her brain or slow her responses.

There's no way she's letting herself be vulnerable again.

Zach had suggested going back for sessions with the therapist she'd seen when she was diagnosed with postpartum depression after Alexa was born. Her mother-in-law had insisted for weeks it was just the baby blues, something every new mother suffered from, and that she should try to pull herself together, especially as Zach was having to work so hard with the business. After three months, when she was still crying for most of the day, she had decided to ignore her mother-in-law's advice and gone to see someone.

It had helped back then; she had been driven by a determination to get well, to become the mother she wanted to be for her daughter, the person she knew still existed behind the layer of fog that had enveloped her, stopping her seeing or feeling anything. She'd described it to her therapist as a creeping numbness that had slowly receded, one session at a time, until eventually she could smile when Alexa grinned at her, could pick her up without feeling a terrible sense of dread.

This time around, she's not sure therapy is the answer. She hasn't been completely truthful with her therapist. What choice does she have when she can't find the right words to admit what she's done? She hasn't told Zach the sessions aren't helping. Why would she? The sessions are a chance to get out of the house; away from everything. *Away from him?* The thought slips into her brain before she can stop it.

'So, now, I want you to adjust yourselves into the mouse position,' the yoga teacher says. 'Slide your arms around so they are tucked in down by your side, your palms face up, your forehead still touching the mat.'

Cara shuffles herself around; her body doesn't fold nicely like Cindy's does, or the bodies of all the other women in the room. They are all slim with tanned limbs that flex in a way hers don't seem to, no matter how hard she tries.

Ever since peri-menopause kicked in, she has only to look at a slice of bread and she puts on half a stone. Her whole body shape has changed; there's a roll around her stomach that never used to be there, and the circumference of her chest beneath her bust line has expanded to the point where she's had to buy new bras. She gets into position but can feel drops of perspiration slipping down her cleavage.

'And breathe.'

The yoga teacher is now standing behind her. Cara's heartbeat starts to race. She doesn't like this position. She shouldn't have come. She thinks about the origami bird Devi gave her. She'd taken it out of the pocket of her dress this morning, tried to smooth out the crumpled leaves. Imagines herself flying away. The taste of freedom.

The teacher bends down and puts her hands on Cara's back, pushes her hips lower on to her thighs. A few months ago, Cara would have welcomed the release of tension, but now she has to force herself not to stand up, shove the teacher away from her and hold her against the wall of the pavilion by her throat.

Get your fucking hands off me.

She repeats the words silently to herself, inside her head. Just like she did back then. Still as impotent as ever. She feels a tear slide down her cheek and on to the mat. Tries to brush it away quickly before Cindy notices. Not *defenceless*, as her therapist keeps telling her. *Useless*.

And the worst thing is, Alexa knows it.

13. 3 days 1 hour left

Zach watches Marc unlock the door of the desalination plant, a white-painted concrete building hidden behind the diving centre and camouflaged by undergrowth. He steps inside, relieved to be temporarily out of the heat, and waits for his ears to adjust to the steady hum of the air-conditioning while he glances at the rows of pipes and machinery that cover the surface of one wall.

'It's CFC-free,' Marc says.

Zach nods. 'Impressive.'

It's what Marc wants to hear, and he needs to keep Marc happy. His mother always used to say he was more savvy than Steve Jobs when it came to spotting a business opportunity. But then she'd also told him that anything less than a grade A at school was unacceptable and that he'd never be half the man his father was.

'Isn't it? We test the water for quality and pH levels every hundred litres, and it's mineralized and chilled before it gets delivered to the guests. We were getting through over a thousand plastic bottles of water a day in the resort before we had the system installed. Now we don't import any.'

Zach raises his eyebrows. 'Amazing.'

He watches as Marc walks over to examine a readout on one of the machines, his face still flushed, despite the drop in temperature.

'I was chatting to one of the other guests, Ryan Miller,

about it last night,' Marc says. 'I think he works in the same field as you. Ethical investing? Is that right? You fund environmentally friendly projects?'

Zach nods. Ryan bloody Miller is turning out to be a pain in the arse. Zach doesn't remember him from the sustainability conference – he's usually good with faces but, with three hundred attendees, he can't be expected to recall every one. He looked him up online last night and immediately recognized the name of his company. ZH Investments had outbid it for a recent project. A decision, with hindsight, that Zach wouldn't make now, given what he has since found out.

'This kind of thing must be right up your street, then,' Marc continues. 'Do you know, we have double the number of visitors in the Maldives than a decade ago? It's no wonder there's a strain on the water resources. Almost one and a half million tourists last year. Most of the resort islands have plants like this now, or are getting them, but the islands where the local population live and the tourists never visit are still lagging way behind.'

'So you think there's an opportunity to roll out this kind of thing elsewhere?' Zach deliberates over his sentence, wanting Marc to think this is the first time he's considered the idea.

Marc nods. 'Absolutely. Get in early and there's the chance to make a lot of money. And I mean a lot, especially with the tax breaks for foreign investors. We're talking high seven figures.' He hesitates. 'Ryan said it sounded right up his street.'

Zach rubs the stubble on his chin, the possibility of high seven figures too tempting to resist. The answer to his prayers.

'My company has a lot more experience than Ryan's with this kind of thing,' he says. 'We're more profitable, have more access to capital and are more established. Maybe have a word with your contacts, see what they think, and then we can talk more about it.'

Marc glances at his watch, then puts his hand on Zach's shoulder.

'Will do. Shall we head back, then?'

'Yes, we probably should.' Zach feels his phone vibrate in his pocket as he steps back, moving away from Marc's hand. 'Cara will have finished whatever activity she was doing this morning. Yoga, I think.'

'Well, if your wife is joining in with the activities here, I think it's only fair that we organize something for you as well.'

'I don't know,' Zach says. 'I'm not really a –'

'Big-game fishing.' Marc's face lights up. 'You'll love it. I'll set something up.'

Zach can't bring himself to tell him that he hates boats. Any kind of swell and he starts feeling seasick.

'I think Cara and I are supposed to be diving tomorrow.'

'Oh, that's a shame,' Marc says. 'Ryan sounded keen when I suggested it.'

Zach hesitates, feels an opportunity start to slip through his fingers.

'How about the day after?'

The smile reappears on Marc's face. 'Great. I'll make all the arrangements. The last guy I took out caught a mahi-mahi. A thirty-pounder.'

'Wow.' Zach attempts to sound enthusiastic, despite the fact he's never heard of a mahi-mahi. Marc locks the door behind them, his keys jangling as he squints in the sunlight.

'Are you heading straight back to reception?' Zach asks.

Marc nods.

'I think I'm going to wander back the long way along the beach,' Zach says. 'Get a bit of exercise.'

Marc proffers a handshake. Zach accepts it, flinches slightly as their damp palms slide against one another, feels Marc hold on a little longer than necessary. Zach waits for him to head off in the direction of reception before he pulls out his phone and reads the message on the screen.

Are you going to do what we agreed? Or would you rather I told her?

Something cold slithers through his stomach. He thinks of Cara in her yoga class, her limbs stretched, muscles taut. He types a message back.

It's not as simple as that.

A prickle of sweat slides down his back as he waits for a response.

Nothing.

He swallows, then types out a text before turning off his phone.

I'll sort it. Just give me a couple of days.

14. 3 days 1 hour left

Skye already has fifty-five thousand likes for the picture of her breakfast that she posted less than half an hour ago – French toast with pieces of mango grown in the resort carved into flower shapes, interspersed with slices of dragon fruit. She hadn't eaten it, of course, all she's had is an espresso, but she knows it's an image that will cause a small voice inside her followers' heads to question how she manages to eat like that every day while staying a size eight. Creating a spark of envy is a trick she's learned; it guarantees instant clickbait for maximum interaction and likes.

As long as people are focusing on her life, she doesn't care if they hate their own. She's not stupid. She knows her followers are the ones who bring in advertising revenue and that without them she wouldn't be able to make a difference in areas that really matter to her. Her altruistic brand relies on a certain kind of dark capitalism in order to survive, one that she's more than happy to buy in to. She serves up content her followers aspire to; so what if it doesn't always reflect reality? Her environmental causes are the ultimate beneficiary, which has to be a good thing, even if she has to ignore the voice in her head that whispers *but so are you*.

She'd cropped and filtered the photo to make the food look even better than it had done on the plate, ensuring it blended aesthetically with the rest of her grid before adding the hashtags #Homegrown #Natural #Ecolife, and now her followers are all trying to guess which resort she's staying at before she does the big reveal tomorrow.

After an exfoliating body scrub followed by a massage with essential oils carried out on the privacy of the deck of her overwater villa by one of the spa therapists, for the last hour she's been doing the less glamorous side of her job: sitting inside a beach villa with one of the cleaners looking at the various products he uses, as well as the range of toiletries provided by the resort, checking the ingredients to ensure they don't contain any chemicals that will disappear down the plughole and pollute the water or the resort environment. To be fair to Marc, in this respect Asana does seem to be sticking to its promises.

But just using environmentally friendly products isn't going to persuade her to give Asana a rave review in the magazine feature. Skye prides herself on being more than just another influencer, paid to say she *adores* whatever it is she's been given to talk about. Her followers expect more of her than that. She's capable of digging below the surface and finding out information that will allow people to accurately judge this place on its environmental credentials. The magazine might be happy with a quick tick-in-box exercise, but she's not. She wants to make a *real* difference, and her long chat with the cleaner has thrown up something she knows Marc would be horrified to see in print. Something that could cost him this job. She's still reeling from the revelation.

Surely the cleaner had been exaggerating?

She knows how quickly rumours can spread amongst staff in close quarters. And how they're not always true.

A shiver of apprehension and excitement runs down her spine as she wonders if it is. She needs to be one hundred per cent sure before she puts anything on social media.

She mutes notifications on her phone as she walks out of the beach villa, along the small path through the green scaevola bushes, out on to the beach and down to the water. One of the guests she talked to last night had mentioned there was seagrass growing in the lagoon, and she wants to know if the staff are pulling it out. Although she sympathizes with the need for aesthetics – after all, she'd be nothing without beauty – this particular plant absorbs carbon dioxide and provides food for green turtles. By deliberately removing it to keep the bottom of the lagoon as pristine white sand, it breaches Asana's eco-friendly ethos.

She stands in the shallows, looking for evidence to video, when she sees it. A shape floating on the water. Someone snorkelling? There isn't the familiar length of tube sticking up out of the water. She puts her hand up to shade her eyes against the brightness. It looks like a person, but they don't seem to be moving and she definitely can't see a snorkel. She wades out a bit further, suddenly realizes what she's looking at, strips off her T-shirt and shorts, throws them back on to the beach and begins to swim.

She cuts through the water, keeping the pole markers either side of her. The tide is still low and she doesn't want to risk slicing herself on the coral. The body is just beyond the markers indicating the start of the reef, but she can reach it by swimming out and then coming back in over the drop-off. She focuses on her breathing, wanting to shout but knowing her voice won't carry that far.

Panicking will only make things worse.

She braces herself as she swims along the channel that leads out through the coral into the ocean. Small waves splash against her face and she feels the current pull on her legs; not strong enough to stop her swimming, but enough to slow her down. She takes deep breaths, trying to fill her lungs with as much oxygen as she can, but the stillness of the figure is worrying her. She doesn't know if she'll be able to reach them in time. If it might already be too late.

It's at that moment that Skye sees the shark, its grey body undulating through the water in slow motion. She peers down into the depths, but without a mask on, it's difficult to see anything against the green of the corals.

A scream pierces the silence. Skye pulls herself more quickly through the water and the shape morphs into someone recognizable as she reaches them. The girl she met last night. Zach Hamilton's daughter.

'Stop moving,' Skye says, grabbing Alexa's arm.

'I can't . . .' Alexa's teeth chatter as she struggles to get the words out.

'Lie on your back and float. I've got you. You're fine.' Skye swims around behind her and puts her hand under Alexa's head.

'There's a shark . . .'

'There are loads of sharks,' Skye says sharply. 'You're swimming over a reef. They're completely harmless. Blacktip or whitetip reef sharks, usually. A whale shark if you're really lucky, but they usually stay further out. Nothing here is going to hurt you.'

She looks at Alexa's flippers. 'Where are your mask and snorkel?'

'My mask got water in it so I took it off . . . I think it sank.'

Skye grits her teeth. 'You didn't stay between the markers like they told you to at the diving centre, did you?'

Alexa doesn't reply.

'And I bet you didn't keep your flippers off the coral, either. Are you hurt?'

'Something bit me,' Alexa says.

'Where?'

She points at her torso. 'On my hip.'

Skye adjusts her grip on the girl's body and Alexa lets out a small yelp.

'Does it feel like it's burning?'

'Yes. Like it's on fire.'

'It looks red. I think you've been stung by something. Probably just fire coral. They can sort you out at the medical centre.'

Alexa's eyes fill with tears.

Skye softens her tone of voice along with her grip.

'Come on. It's not far to the beach. I'll take you in over the reef, but you need to stay floating on your back so we don't scrape against anything else. OK?'

Skye feels Alexa's head move against her hands as she nods. She starts to swim, pulling Alexa through the water with her. She couldn't have engineered a better opportunity to meet her properly if she'd tried. She wants to get to know everything about Zach Hamilton, and Alexa, with all the inside knowledge on her father, is going to be just the one to help her.

15. 3 days left

Cara examines her face in the bathroom mirror. Her mother stares back, and she has to blink several times before she disappears.

How can she be turning into her mother already?

She traces her finger over the fine lines that branch out from the corner of her eyes, permanently ironed-in creases that grow deeper by the day, despite the retinol she smothers on every night. Her three-monthly Botox injections have kept her forehead smooth, although she wonders if she should start leaving more time between appointments; her skin has developed an unnatural sheen, stretched and frozen into place. Zach doesn't have to worry about any of this. Men are allowed to age; women are somehow supposed to achieve the impossible and stop at around forty.

She doesn't feel old. She's only forty-nine, and most people would guess she's at least five years younger than that. Not like her mother, who had always looked at least ten years older than she actually was. But the effort and cost involved to maintain the status quo grows greater with every year that passes. She's not stupid. She knows money has the greatest impact when it comes to holding back time, and it's not something she intends to give up in a hurry. Plenty of women would kill to be in her position – a good-looking husband, a big house, a nice car, several holidays a year.

But would they be prepared to make the same sacrifices to keep it?

There's a sharp knock on her villa door and she jumps, grips the edge of the sink, her heart thudding in her chest. *Breathe.* There's another knock and she walks over to the door, hesitates, unsure whether to open it.

'Mrs Hamilton?'

'Devi?'

'Can I come in? It's about your daughter.'

For a few seconds Cara's heart plummets towards the ground and shatters into dozens of tiny pieces.

Not again. Please don't let anything have happened to her.

Vignettes of horror runs through her head: Alexa lying on the sand not breathing, her wet hair spread out around her head like seaweed, face devoid of colour; Alexa being carried up the beach, her leg ripped open, red droplets falling like rain on to the white sand. Cara has always hated blood. She had to shut her eyes before putting plasters on Alexa's knees when she was little.

I shouldn't have let her go snorkelling on her own.

Another knock.

'Mrs Hamilton?' Devi repeats.

Cara presses down the brass handle and the door swings back to reveal him on the doorstep.

'What is it? What's happened to her?'

Devi steps over the threshold and ushers Cara towards the sofa.

'She's fine, Mrs Hamilton. She just scraped herself on some coral, but she's had to go to the medical centre. I did try to get hold of you, but you weren't answering your phone.'

Cara frowns as she picks up her mobile. Ten missed

calls. *Oh God.* She'd forgotten she'd muted it when she went to her yoga class.

'Why didn't you try my husband?' Cara tries to clear her head of the memories of what happened before, the way Zach had looked at her.

'We did, Mrs Hamilton, but we couldn't get hold of him either.'

'Zach's with Marc,' she says. 'He went to see the desalination plant.'

Devi nods slowly but doesn't speak. He looks down at the floor, his fingers clasped together but still moving.

'What is it?' Cara says. 'What aren't you telling me?'

Devi looks at her. He has the longest eyelashes. A perfectly round mole on his left cheekbone.

'Mr Geddes came back to his office about half an hour ago. Perhaps your husband went out again, to the restaurant, or to the pool?'

Cara tries to think, but her head swims, thoughts flowing like liquid. She's sure Zach hasn't been back to the villa since he left this morning, but maybe he has, and she'd been asleep. She'd laid down on their bed for a while after her yoga class, but can't remember actually drifting off. Why isn't Zach answering his phone? He's usually glued to the bloody thing.

'I need to go and see Alexa,' she says, searching around on the floor for her flip-flops. 'I should have been there for her.'

Devi stands up, puts his hand on her arm. His palm is cool and she feels a calmness spread over her skin.

'You are a good mother, Cara,' he says. 'This is not your fault. Alexa is fine. Her injury isn't serious. You cannot always be with your child; you cannot watch them all the time. You have to give them space to grow. And then they will fly away and thrive on their own.'

She notices the tiny flecks of gold in his green eyes, knows he's telling the truth, and wishes she could believe him. She wants Alexa to fly away at some point, as then she'll have done her job properly, but she doesn't want her to go just yet. She needs time to fix the pieces of their broken relationship back together.

Devi takes his hand off her arm, reaches into his pocket and takes out a fish he's woven out of palm leaves and hands it to her. She holds it up by the looped handle and it twists around like a Christmas-tree decoration.

'You don't have to make things for me,' she says.

'I know. But I want to.'

His fingers stroke hers briefly as he takes it out of her grasp and hangs it on one of the picture frames, where it spins in the breeze from the air-conditioning.

'Do you like it?' he asks.

'It's lovely.'

He smiles. 'I'm glad. Shall we go and find Alexa?'

He brushes past her and Cara notices his aftershave smells just like the one Zach used to wear. She experiences an urge to reach out and touch him, but before she can move he's already stepped out of the door, replaced by a heat that rushes in and squeezes her heart like a fist.

16. 3 days left

Zach has seven missed calls on his phone. *Shit*. For a moment, he sees flashing lights, hears sirens and a piercing scream. *Stop catastrophizing. Lightning doesn't strike in the same place twice.* It wasn't his fault. It's what he's told himself so many times he almost believes it, but something niggles in his brain like a persistent fly that won't go away.

He begins to jog along the sandy path from the beach across the island towards the medical centre, adrenaline flooding his body. What if Alexa needs hospital treatment? Could they fly her out? How far is the nearest decent hospital? His mother's words about being stuck in the middle of nowhere echo in his head. Maybe she was right. Maybe they shouldn't have come here in the first place.

'Alexa?'

She's walking beside Skye, wearing a branded resort T-shirt that's several sizes too big for her, holding the bottom so it doesn't come into contact with her skin.

'Alexa?' Her name comes out as a gasp. He runs religiously at home every morning, but now he can't seem to catch his breath. The heat eats up every bit of moisture here between 11 a.m. and 2 p.m., and when he's not standing under the shade of one of the palm fronds that branch across the path he can feel the sun burning his skin. Alexa finally looks over in his direction.

'Thank God you're OK,' he says.

'Finally picked up your voicemails, then?' she asks.

'I was on a tour of the plant with Marc,' Zach says. 'I didn't have any signal.'

'Luckily Skye was kind enough to stay with me when neither of my parents cared enough to answer their phone.'

'What happened?' Zach asks.

'I got stung by fire coral and couldn't swim back to the beach. Skye rescued me.'

Zach looks at the woman standing beside his daughter. Remembers her laughing as they raised a toast together last night in the restaurant. They'd moved on to champagne after finishing off Marc's bottle of whiskey.

'I was in too much pain to speak so Skye explained it all to the doctor and sorted everything out,' Alexa says to him. 'She was brilliant.'

Skye laughs. 'I'm just bloody glad I happened to be out on the beach. Never a good idea to go snorkelling on your own, Alexa. It was great to spend a bit of time with you, but let's do less dramatic next time? As I said, if you fancy helping me film something for YouTube, I'd love the company. I'm in villa nine – give me a shout.'

Skye smiles and Zach watches his daughter grin back. Despite her injury, she looks the happiest he's seen her since they arrived.

'I should go,' Skye continues. 'I've got some more research to do for this article. No rest for the wicked, eh?'

She winks at Zach, pushes her blonde hair back off her face.

He swallows. 'Thanks for looking after Alexa. Perhaps we could catch up at some point. I mean, if you've got time?' he adds. 'I think there's a way we can leverage off each other. You're obviously an expert on the publicity side of things, and my investors are always on the look-out for new opportunities. Some of the projects you're involved in could be right up their street.' He lifts up his glasses, wipes a line of perspiration off the bridge of his nose.

Skye smiles. 'Sure, that would be great. The American guy who's staying here was talking to me last night about doing something similar as well.'

Zach tenses. 'Ryan Miller?'

Skye nods. 'Yeah. The guy with the baseball cap, that's Ryan, isn't it? Anyway, I'm more than happy to chat – just ping me a text or something. Alexa's got my number.'

Zach nods. He can see his daughter staring at him accusingly, knows this is what he promised not to do on holiday, but it's an opportunity he can't afford to miss.

'I'll look forward to it,' Skye says. 'See you later, Alexa.'

He walks with Alexa along the path, past one of the gardeners, who is raking leaves that have fallen from the overhanging branches and putting them in a wheelbarrow.

'What do you want to meet up with Skye for?' Alexa asks. 'It's not like you're into social media stuff. She's pretty much the only person in this resort who is anywhere close to being someone I'd like to hang out with.'

'It's just business,' Zach says. 'She's got so many followers, if we collaborate I can raise the profile of ZH Investments using her social media channels.'

Alexa fiddles with her stud earring, the piercing still sore from where she caught it on the strap of her mask. 'I'm going back to the villa. See why Mum didn't bother to answer her phone either.'

'Your mother will be in a right state when she finds

out what's happened,' Zach says. 'This holiday is supposed to be a –'

'I know she's struggling,' Alexa interrupts. 'You don't have to try and make excuses for her. But it's not exactly easy for me, either.'

'What happened was very traumatic,' Zach says slowly. 'For everyone. We're all dealing with it in different ways. At least you have Charlie to talk to about it.'

'I *did* have Charlie,' Alexa mutters.

Zach frowns. 'Have you two fallen out?'

Alexa doesn't reply.

'I'm sure you'll sort it out.' He goes to put his arm around her shoulders, but she shrugs him off and looks at the reef in the distance.

'I think I'm going to break it off with him,' Alexa says.

Zach shivers, despite the heat. 'Why? I thought you really liked him?'

'I did. But things change. And anyway,' she adds, 'don't pretend that you actually care. You weren't keen on me seeing him to start with. You only went along with it because his dad invested in your company.'

Zach feels his cheeks colour, glances behind him to where he can see Skye disappearing along the path. Alexa's right. He is having to lie about a lot of things right now. Sometimes the end justifies the means, and if he were to tell her the whole truth, he knows she wouldn't ever speak to him again.

17. 2 days 23 hours left

Cara watches Devi head outside the villa to where the buggy is parked on the jetty. She can see that the flowers he draped over the seats last night have wilted in the heat and their coloured petals are starting to fade like a Shibasaki watercolour painting.

She's about to follow him, but the feeling in her stomach mirrors the palm-leaf fish he gave her that is spinning in frantic circles in the warm breeze coming in through the open door.

She needs to go and find Alexa, but something makes her feet stay where they are.

It's your job to keep her safe.

And you've failed. Again.

A humming noise vibrates in her head, and she experiences the same sensation she had in the seaplane on the way over here. A need to get away, an acute sense of danger, despite there being nothing she can see or hear.

You're safe.

She tells herself this, reaching out to hold on to the doorframe as dizziness threatens to overwhelm her. The humming gets louder and she covers her ears as something small and fast like a tennis ball whips past her face and then disappears. The noise isn't coming from inside her head at all. It grows fainter, then louder again as the object returns and hovers in the air a couple of feet away from her face, as if it is staring at her.

The numbness she's felt before begins to creep up her body. She can see Devi getting back out of the buggy, his eyes wide in concern. She tries to pull the door shut, forgetting her other hand is still holding the frame, and the dark wood closes on her fingers.

The white-hot pain blurs her vision and she lets out a shriek as she slides to the floor.

'Hold on to me.' Devi's voice is calm, and she feels one of his arms around her waist as he helps her up and on to the sofa.

'Just stay still.' He disappears and comes back with a wet flannel filled with ice cubes from the mini-bar and places it gently over the tips of her fingers.

'I think they're OK. Your index finger caught the worst of it. I don't think anything's broken, just bruised.' He gives her a brief smile and she smiles back, despite her eyes welling with tears. 'It was just a drone,' he says. 'Some of the guests hire them and fly them around to get photos of Asana Fushi from the air. They're not supposed to use them on the jetty though, only on the beach. I'll talk to Marc about it. Can I get you anything? A glass of water?'

Cara shakes her head. 'I'm fine. The ice is helping.' She lifts up the flannel and grimaces as she looks at the blood oozing out from under one of her nails. 'I need to go and see Alexa.' She starts to get back up, but Devi puts his hand on her arm.

'Just give yourself a minute,' he says. 'Don't rush. Alexa will be fine.'

She looks at him.

'I keep having these dizzy spells,' she says. 'It feels like something terrible has happened, or is about to happen.' She wipes her face where a tear has escaped down her cheek.

Devi puts his hand on her arm.

'Did something terrible happen?' he asks.

Cara doesn't meet his gaze.

'Terrible things always happen,' she says. 'They're part of life.'

He nods. Doesn't attempt to contradict her or tell her she's overreacting. Cara feels the numbness that had been creeping up her legs recede, sinking back into the ground like water. She realizes she's been more honest with this man she barely knows than she has with her therapist.

'I really do need to go and see Alexa,' she says.

Devi lifts up the flannel and wraps it around her index finger.

She needs to pull herself together. She's been here before, already has the T-shirt. She had so much therapy after Alexa was born, had fought to get well and put that episode of her life firmly behind her. But control over her mind and body seems to be slipping away from her all over again.

She knows what sparked it all off.

What she doesn't know is whether it's going to get worse.

And what if she does something terrible again?

18. 2 days 22 hours left

Zach edges past the buggy that is parked in front of their villa. He hopes the sushi platter and large Diet Coke he's just treated Alexa to has taken her mind off her injury. She doesn't seem like she's in pain as she pulls out her key card and frowns as she holds it up to the pad by the door.

The sound coming from inside is unmistakeable. A man's voice. Shouting.

Zach picks up one of the golf umbrellas from the stand by the front door and Alexa flinches as she sees its sharp metal tip.

'Stay here,' he says.

She nods.

'Hello?' he shouts.

He can hear a knocking sound as he walks past the coffee table towards the bedroom. The door has been flung open. The muslin drapes on their four-poster bed are tied back neatly, but the pillow on Cara's side of the bed looks creased. Her bedside lamp with its base carved out of driftwood is still switched on and Devi is standing outside their bathroom.

'Mr Hamilton –'

Zach lowers the umbrella. 'What are you doing in here?'

'It's your wife, Mr Hamilton. We were going to the medical centre to find Alexa, but Cara trapped her finger in the door when we were leaving. She said she was going to run it under the tap, but then she locked herself in the bathroom and now she isn't answering.'

Zach strides across the room and knocks on the door a couple of times.

'Cara?' There's no answer. 'Open the door.' He looks at Devi. 'How long has she been in there?'

'Only a few minutes. I was just about to call you.'

Alexa appears in the bedroom doorway.

'Thank you, Devi,' Zach says stiffly. 'I'll take things from here.'

'Should I get someone to help? I can call Maintenance to come and unscrew the lock if you need to –'

'That won't be necessary.' Zach fishes around in his pocket and holds out a ten-dollar bill.

'Mr Hamilton, I don't –'

'Just take it. Please. I appreciate your discretion.'

Devi stands rooted to the spot while Zach tucks the money into the chest pocket of his shirt.

'Mrs Hamilton will be fine,' Zach says smoothly. 'I'll take care of it. Can you come back and collect us at seven for dinner? Thank you so much for your help.'

Zach hears the electric motor of the buggy start up. He looks at Alexa and wonders if she has the same sick feeling in the bottom of her stomach as he does.

'Go and sit outside on the decking,' Zach says. 'I'll be out in a minute.'

Alexa walks across the wooden floorboards in the living room, past the coffee table with its vase of flowers, and avoids stepping on the glass panel in the floor. Zach watches her grab her AirPods before she slides open the bifold doors, then shuts them tightly behind her. She lowers

72

herself carefully into the hammock and firmly presses her earbuds into her ears.

Zach knocks on the bathroom door again.

'Cara, open up. Talk to me.'

Silence.

'It's just me, Cara. Devi has gone and Alexa is out on the deck. Can you open the door, please?'

There's a shuffling, then Zach hears the sound of a bolt sliding back. He pushes open the door to see Cara sitting on the closed toilet lid. She holds up her finger, the tip wrapped in a flannel.

'You know what I'm like with blood,' she says. 'I thought I was going to pass out.'

'Is it badly hurt?' Zach asks.

She shakes her head. 'I don't think so. Just throbbing.'

'Alexa's fine, by the way,' he says.

'Why didn't you answer your phone?' Cara asks. 'Devi was trying to call you.'

'I was with Marc,' Zach says. 'I didn't have any signal. Where the hell were you?'

'You weren't with Marc,' Cara says. 'Devi said Marc was back at reception.'

'Devi doesn't know what he's talking about,' Zach says sharply. 'Why did you let Alexa go out by herself in the first place? You know she's never snorkelled before.'

'She's sixteen and she can swim, Zach, for heaven's sake. I didn't know she needed to be supervised. She doesn't want me going everywhere with her.'

Zach lets out a snort of exasperation.

'And I think we both know why that is.'

Cara looks at him, her face white.

'Jesus, Zach. It was an accident.'

'Sorry.' He leans down and cups his hands around her face. 'I'm sorry. That was out of order.' He kisses her forehead and then pulls away. 'I'm just stressed. I've got a lot on my plate at the moment.'

Cara takes the flannel off her finger, drops it in the laundry bin and stands up, then closes her eyes and leans against the bathroom wall for support. Zach puts his hand on his wife's forehead, feels how hot her skin is. Wonders if she's had too much sun. He slides his arms around her and draws her into an embrace. Her heart flutters, like a bird trying to escape.

'I know how stressful these past few weeks have been for you,' he says. 'You've got to use this holiday to rest. We're going diving tomorrow, I'm going to organize that private picnic for us, and I'll ask Devi to book you and Alexa into the spa for an afternoon. I want you to relax. Chill out.'

He looks at his wife. She seems so fragile now. She hadn't been when they first met. His mother had said she was a fighter, rough around the edges, someone who would need to smarten up if she wanted to fit in with the rest of the Hamilton family. And she had. No one would ever know Cara had grown up on the fifteenth floor of a tower block. There'd been that wobble for a few months after Alexa was born, but he'd thought that was all sorted.

'Alexa knows what happened was an accident,' Cara says. She presses her mouth against his ear. 'And you know it wasn't just my fault. It was yours too.'

19. 2 days 21 hours left

He hadn't said anything when Vincent called him this morning and told him to come here – he knows to get on with the job and not ask questions. It's one of the reasons he's lasted on the team as long as he has – but now he's beginning to wonder if this really was such a good idea.

His Mercedes is parked just down the street. Far enough away not to be picked up on either of the two CCTV cameras attached to the side of the building. He saunters towards his vehicle, keeps his head down, mirrors the pace of the people around him, blends into the crowd. His speciality. He opens the door of his car, slides on to the leather upholstery, takes off his baseball cap and drops it on to the passenger seat, runs his hand over the stubble on his head.

The office isn't the type of building he normally spends his time in. Usually, it's somewhere far less salubrious. Concrete tower blocks with the lifts out of order, the staircases reeking of piss. Cheap rented properties which have been turned into cannabis farms, the windows boarded up, plastic sheeting covering the walls. This place was luxurious in comparison. All glass and mirrors. Dozens of ring lights embedded into the ceiling boards. Comfy sofas arranged around a high-gloss black coffee table – the kind that shows every fingerprint. Some sort of plant display below the wide stone reception counter; like the ferns Marie has in their garden. He'd felt out of place as he walked past other employees coming in and out of the building dressed in suits, his trainers squeaking on the wooden floorboards.

He'd hoped coming in after the morning rush hour would mean that the reception was less busy, but he wasn't that lucky. When he'd finally got to the front of the queue, he'd given the woman his usual spiel as he held out the parcel — asked whether anyone had ever told her how much she looked like Jessica Biel and, to be fair, on this occasion he hadn't actually lied — there was a vague resemblance — but her face had remained neutral, no sign of the smile he can normally elicit.

She'd refused to give him what he wanted. Told him she couldn't breach their strict confidentiality rules. Not even if he asked nicely. And she hadn't smiled once.

Now he's got to take the news back to Vincent, and he can already imagine how it's going to be received. He picks up his phone and distracts himself by scrolling through reels on Facebook, something Marie showed him how to do the other day, keen to put off the moment as long as possible.

20. 2 days 20 hours left

'Mrs Hamilton?' The villa appears empty when Devi steps inside. The cleaners must have already been in to do their late-afternoon clean as the smell of biodegradable coconut polish lingers in the air. He allows the front door to click shut behind him, puts his master key card back in his pocket.

'Cara?' he says again.

The cushions on the sofa have been plumped up and rearranged, the fresh fruit on the wooden platter on the table has been replaced. All the glasses that were half full of various beverages have been emptied, washed up and replaced above the mini-bar, which has been restocked with different vintage wines, soft drinks, popcorn and hand-made salted caramel chocolates.

He'd done this job for over ten years before being promoted to a butler. He knows exactly how it works. Back then he'd been expected to sort out the villa in under an hour first thing in the morning, including a thorough clean of the bathroom, followed by another check-over in the late afternoon, and then a turn-down service when the guests were at dinner. He'd learned to be invisible. A skill that has proved exceptionally useful.

Before he started, he hadn't realized how much mess people could make in twenty-four hours. Guests came away with enough clothes to wear for a year and then distributed them in piles all over the floor. He had folded them, or hung them up, and the same process would be repeated for the duration of their stay. And clothes weren't the worst of it. Not by a long way. Used condoms, soiled sanitary towels; he'd always left the bathroom until last in the hope that the products he'd use to clean the sink, bath and floor would remove the layer of filth and disgust that sat on his skin. And when they went home, some of the guests didn't even bother to leave a tip.

They already had so much, more than they could ever need, but they didn't value it. And as guests were so often careless, when something went missing, it was rarely noticed. On the odd occasion when it was, and a fuss was made, the item in question could be made to reappear after a thorough search of the room. Along with the guest's profuse gratitude in the form of a hefty tip, which he always puts away for his wife and daughter.

'Cara?' Devi peers into the master bedroom, but there's no sign of anyone. The glass doors that lead out to the decking from the Hamiltons' bedroom are open. Guests interrogate the staff about their eco-friendly policies but then proceed to leave all the lights on and the air-conditioning turned up full blast with the doors open.

He can see Cara lying on one of the sun-loungers. Designer sunglasses on and her hair pulled back off her face with a silk scarf. No sign of Zach or Alexa. He walks past the bed that the cleaners have re-made; sheets pulled tight, smoothed down and tucked under the corners. He glances at the pillows: three of them on each side of the bed for maximum comfort, the filling and thickness chosen by the guest before they arrived. Everything looks just as it should.

He walks over towards the decking and Cara sits up, turns around.

'Devi?'

He smiles. 'I hope I didn't disturb you.'

'No, it's fine.' She takes her cover-up from where she's hung it over the back of her lounger and pulls it on over her red swimming costume. 'I was just catching some sun.'

'Mr Hamilton not here?'

'He's gone to see Marc. Something about a big-game fishing trip. I'm going for a massage a bit later, and Alexa is with Skye, I think.'

'I just came to check to see if you were OK after . . . earlier,' he says.

Cara glances at her finger, the tip a blue-black inky colour. 'I'm fine.'

Devi hovers by the doors.

'You can sit down if you want.' Cara pats the lounger beside her and he moves into the space, the smell of his aftershave making her skin tingle.

'Do you have a family?' she asks.

'I have a wife, Asma, and a daughter,' he replies, surprised. Guests rarely ask him about his life.

'What's your daughter's name?'

'Imani. She's four.'

Cara smiles. 'A few years before she hits the nightmare teenage years, then.'

A flicker of emotion runs across Devi's face.

'Do you want to see a photo?' he asks.

Cara nods.

Devi pulls out his phone, sits down on the lounger and scrolls through photo after photo of a tiny girl with huge eyes. Cara feels a pulling sensation in her stomach. She remembers Alexa at that age. Her little hand constantly reaching for her own, holding it tightly.

'She's not well,' Devi says. 'She has thalassemia; she has to have a lot of medical treatment. It's why I am here working and not at home with my family. It's common in the Maldives, but my wife tells me Imani's condition has flared up again recently.'

'How often do you get to visit them?' Cara asks.

He shrugs. 'Usually twice a year. It's difficult, as I'm the only one who can do the fire show.'

'I saw you on the beach.'

He grins. 'I know. You need to come and see the actual show. I promise you, it looks much better when everything is alight.'

'You should ask Marc for time off,' Cara says.

Devi looks down, clasping his hands. Marc never gives the staff extra time off and, even if he did, Devi can't afford to take it. He wants to tell her that her Roberto Cavalli cover-up would pay for dozens of medical trips. It must have cost more than he earns in a month. She has no idea.

'Maybe I will,' he says. 'I'm glad you are feeling better. I've booked a table for you in the underwater restaurant at seven o'clock tonight.'

'You're very kind.'

Devi smiles. He reaches into his pocket and takes out a small turtle fashioned out of wire and a beer-bottle cap.

'For you,' he says. 'I find if I have something to hold when I get worried, it helps.'

Cara stares at him as he presses it into her palm. Her fingers reach out and touch his, so lightly that at first he isn't sure if he's imagining it. Desire flares inside him, a heat that makes his skin burn as Cara wraps her whole hand around his. He thinks of Asma, of their hurried, fumbled couplings when they actually get to see each other and Imani is asleep. They don't touch like this any more. And it's been months since he's seen her. Too long. There's a moment when he knows he should look away, stand up and get off the lounger, but instead he reaches out and strokes her face.

Cara leans forward and closes the gap between them as she kisses him, leaning backwards on to the cream cushion as she pulls him towards her. His hands move across her body, stroking every inch of her skin. The turtle drops on to the decking with a clinking sound, slips through a gap between the wooden slats and falls into the sea.

Fifteen minutes later, Devi lets himself out of the villa, checks his shirt buttons are properly fastened and smooths down his hair. He's rarely flustered; close encounters of a sexual kind aren't usually part of his weekly routine – nothing like that has ever happened with a guest before.

The heat of his desire lingers as he scrolls through the photos on Cara's Facebook account while walking back to the staff quarters. Her stunning period house with its antique furniture and a view over fields, a grey Tesla model X, her with her husband and daughter, the three of them eating out at dozens of different restaurants. He thinks of Imani, of the clinic where his wife took her for her most recent blood transfusion, of the paint peeling off the walls and the dark circles under the doctor's eyes.

A flicker of guilt passes over his skin when he thinks about Asma, but what's done is done. And now he's had a chance to think about it, Cara might prove very useful.

21. 2 days 20 hours left

Alexa sits down on the beach, lets the white sand run through her fingers like sugar; millions of fragments of coral ground down by the sea into tiny pieces. A swing hangs motionless from a wooden bar in the ocean ahead of her, the Asana Fushi name and logo carved in large wooden letters above it. A perfect photo opportunity. She can see Skye's overwater villa in the distance, further along from hers on the jetty, but when she knocked on her door a while ago she hadn't answered, and despite wandering around the whole island, Alexa hasn't been able to find her.

The sun is beginning to slip down towards the horizon, the surface of the sea calm, rippling slowly like a layer of blue silk. The heat is more pleasurable now, less intense than earlier; a deep warmth rather than burning hot on her skin. The red weal on her hip has faded to a pale pink colour and the pain has gone, leaving only a faint prickling sensation if she touches it.

She checks her phone. A message from Charlie.

We shd talk when ur back.

The knot that has been sitting in Alexa's stomach since she saw the photos of him and Sophie at Holly's party tightens slowly, like a coiling snake. She wonders if he's with Sophie at this very moment. She knows exactly what he'll say if she speaks to him, and it hurts as much as if someone had cut a hole in her chest.

She gets up off the sand, brushes away the tear that slides down her cheek, walks into the water and feels it lap against her legs like a warm bath. The bleached wooden jetty sticks out in the turquoise water on one side of her, her family's overwater villa protruding above the sea on brown wooden stilts. She can see Cindy and Ryan on the white bicycles that belong to each villa making their way along the boards, pausing every now and again to look over the edge at something in the sea. She wades out a bit further, amazed that she can still see her feet just as clearly as if she were standing in a swimming pool, the sunlight on the water making criss-cross patterns on her legs. Charlie might be a total dickhead, but he's not here, experiencing this, and she is, but the thought of him with Sophie at Holly's party still burns.

She'd told Skye about the photos she'd seen when they were waiting for the doctor in the medical centre. Skye's reply in her Aussie accent had been direct – *Fuck him, Alexa. Men just aren't worth it. I've been single for a couple of years after the last guy decided he wasn't keen on my tattoos and, honestly, it's been the best time of my life. What do you need a bloke for?*

Alexa couldn't answer. Because Charlie made her feel loved? Because she wanted just one thing in her life that wasn't as fucked up as much as everything is at home? She's not even sure Skye would understand that. She lowers herself slowly into the water, stretches out, shuts her eyes and floats on her back, letting the feeling of weightlessness take over her body, relishing the silence.

She remembers her mum taking her to Bournemouth when she was little; one of the many things they used to do, just the two of them, days full of warmth and laughter, outings that have tailed off in recent years. She'd loved splashing in the surf, eating mint-chocolate-chip ice-cream on the beach, but it's only after being somewhere like this that she can see what she was missing. No dark yellow coarse sand covered in sharp pieces of dried black sea-weed, no one shrieking beside her, no hordes of sweaty bodies squashed in next to one other, their towels laid out no more than a foot apart. Compared to that, this is paradise.

After a few minutes floating on her back, she rolls over on to her stomach, puts her feet back on the sand. The water only comes up to the top of her thighs and she wonders how much further she can wade out before she's forced to swim. The reef is still visible in the distance, marked by the water changing to a dark blue colour. She looks across at the line of overwater villas, identical cubes of luxury with thatched roofs rising to a point in the centre.

Theirs is the third one along the jetty from the beach, and she's far enough out in the water so she's almost parallel with it, can see between the two wooden fences that have been put up at either end of the decking to provide extra privacy from their immediate neighbours.

It's her mother's swimming costume she sees first, a splash of red against the cream cushion. It takes her a few seconds to realize what she's looking at. Her mother is lying on her back. Devi is leaning over her, his face so close to hers it looks like they are touching. She starts to turn away, her cheeks burning, wanting to erase the vision completely from her brain, but the image plays back in a loop in her head.

Were they kissing?

Don't be ridiculous.

The realization won't compute in her head; a sum that doesn't add up.

She turns back, torn between not wanting to know and needing confirmation. She squints. Devi has disappeared. Her mum has picked up a book and is reading.

There's no way Mum would do that.

She repeats the words to herself as she turns away and pulls herself through the water, using front crawl to get away from the jetty as fast as possible, squeezing her eyes shut as she swims.

She can try and convince herself as much as she wants but, deep down, she knows exactly what she just saw, and she wonders what her dad will do if she tells him about it.

22. 2 days 19 hours left

Devi walks through the vegetable garden on his way out of the staff quarters, past the dappled shade of the banana trees and the bright green stalks of lemongrass with their citrus scent that gets more pungent in the evening. Another one of Marc's great ideas. Guests love thinking their food is made with produce grown on the island. But the reality is that much still has to be imported to keep up with their demands.

You should ask him for time off. Cara's words echo in his head. He glances at his phone, sees a flurry of WhatsApp messages from guests.

Can I get a facial booked for tomorrow?

Table for 4 at restaurant at 8 p.m. Room 132.

Villa floor covered in sand. Needs cleaning.

When he'd started as a butler, guests had to find him in person to ask him to do something. Now, he's on call twenty-four seven. Requests can come through at four in the morning. Few people say please. Fewer say thank you, even after he's achieved the seemingly impossible. Personal submarine trips, champagne towers on the beach, luxury yacht cruises, and designer wedding dresses transported to the resort in their own seaplane.

Marc owes him some time off.

He begins to run along the path. He'd been the fastest runner in his village when he was growing up, the fastest on his island at twelve, and, at eighteen, the fastest on the atoll. He likes to think about what he could have achieved if he'd had the chance to compete properly as he speeds up his pace, his bare feet kicking up the sand on the path behind him. He enjoys feeling the thrum of his heartbeat, the metallic taste in the back of his throat when he really pushes himself. It reminds him that he's still alive.

He slows his pace as he approaches reception. The guests don't want to see him running. Marc has chastised him before. People think there's an emergency. They start to panic. Devi's tips depend on him being invisible; on him fixing issues with the minimum of fuss. A slightly different skill set will be required to get what he wants from the Hamiltons.

He knocks on the door of Marc's office and turns the handle.

Marc looks up from behind his desk.

'I'm sorry to bother you,' Devi says, 'but my daughter isn't well. I wondered if I could take a couple of days off to go and see her.'

He's pictured himself saying it over and over again on his way here. Each word a foot pressed into the ground. Hard. Forceful. Solid.

Marc clears his throat. 'It's really not the best time, Devi. We're very busy at the moment.'

Marc doesn't have a family and a daughter to support. He'd told them his wife had gone back to France to spend time with her family, but that was months ago and there's been no mention of when Lilia will be back. The staff have got a sweepstake running, and the overwhelming majority don't think she'll ever return.

'Was there anything else?' Beads of sweat glisten on Marc's forehead despite the fan that is hanging from the ceiling, spinning around so fast Devi can barely see the blades.

'No,' Devi says, his nostrils flaring. Two days. Not much to ask. He's never requested time off. Not in the whole time Marc has been here. And he's the one who helped to show Marc how to run the resort in the first place. He heads back up the path to the staff quarters, his fists clenched. He's heard the rumours whispered between the staff about their boss. That Marc is hiding a dirty secret. He takes out his mobile and flicks through his contacts, dials the number and waits for the line to connect. He hesitates briefly before he speaks into the silence.

'I think there's something we might be able to help each other with,' he says.

23. 2 days 18 hours left

The glass roof and walls of the underwater restaurant are shaped like a semicircular tunnel and radiate a deep blue glow as the waiter shows the Hamiltons to their table. Dozens of fish swim all around them: baby reef sharks, parrotfish, yellowtail wrasse and other small tropical ones Zach doesn't know the name of, all suspended in the cerulean hue. God knows how much it cost to build.

As he pulls out a chair for Cara to sit down, he wonders if he's done the right thing coming to eat here. It was supposed to be a treat, but his wife is already looking at the enclosed space with apprehension and Alexa hasn't stopped complaining the entire walk over here.

'Hi, you guys!'

His body tenses as he realizes that Ryan and Cindy are sitting at the table opposite them. Cindy waves, and he smiles briefly, then lifts up his menu and hides behind it.

'There's nothing on here I fancy.' Alexa looks at him as if she expects him to magic a new dish out of thin air. Her lips are set in a hard line he is becoming very familiar with.

Cara studies the wine list. He wonders whether it's a deliberate tactic to avoid the Millers, or Alexa. One wrong comment by either of them at this point and the whole evening is going to go pear-shaped.

'I'm sure they can do something else if you ask for it,' Cara says. 'What would you like?'

Alexa looks at her, daggers across the table.

'I'm not hungry.' She points at the glass ceiling above them. 'It doesn't look very safe, does it? How do they know it's not going to break?'

Cara glances upwards and Zach sees her run one finger across her eyebrow in the way she always does when she's stressed.

''Course it won't break. Don't be ridiculous,' he says sharply.

Cara shuffles in her seat, one foot tapping against the floor.

'I'm not being *ridiculous*,' Alexa snaps back. 'There's a shitload of water outside. It must weigh a ton. The glass only needs one weak point –'

'Alexa!'

Cindy and Mark turn around and gawk at them. Zach flushes.

Count to ten. Breathe.

'Can we just try and enjoy this meal, please? Your mother and I –'

He breaks off as Alexa rolls her eyes.

'What?' she asks.

'You know what. Lower your voice, please.'

Alexa picks her napkin up off her lap and throws it down on her empty plate.

'I don't know *what*, actually. It feels like I'm trapped inside a sodding aquarium. I'm going to find Skye. I'll see you back at the villa later. You two will have a much better time without me, anyway. Perhaps you can tell each other all about what you've done this afternoon.'

She glares pointedly at Cara as she pushes her chair out

from under the table with a loud squeak. Zach smiles at Ryan and Cindy, who have stopped talking to each other and are now clearly glued to his family's conversation.

He looks at Cara as Alexa flounces out of the restaurant.

'Aren't you going to try and stop her?' he asks.

Cara shakes her head.

'She can get room service later if she wants something. Now you see what I have to deal with when you're at work. I love her more than anything, but when she's like this she's fucking infuriating.'

Cindy leans over and taps Cara on the arm.

'I don't mean to intrude,' she drawls, 'but I couldn't help overhearing. If you're struggling, one of my friends had real issues with their daughter and said family counselling really helped. We're lucky – our Riley seemed to sail through the difficult stage.'

Zach glances at his wife, sees spots of colour appear on her cheeks as she takes a sip of water.

'Thanks for that advice,' she says. 'But I think we're all good.'

Cindy smiles. 'Happy to help.'

'I'm glad I'm not at home to have to deal with it. Thank God for business, eh?' Ryan winks at Zach, who smiles flatly before he turns away, making it clear the conversation is over.

Zach reaches for Cara's hand, but she pulls away.

'I am trying, you know,' he says.

'A bit of an effort for a couple of weeks isn't going to cut it, Zach.' She lowers her voice to avoid Ryan and Cindy overhearing. 'And before you tell me you have to look after the business, I already know that. I'm talking about you actually being present and taking an interest in Alexa, and me, for the small amount of time when you *are* around. Not spending time networking or checking your phone.'

Zach doesn't have a chance to reply before the waiter appears.

'I'll have a glass of Veuve, please,' Cara says. 'We're celebrating the fact that my husband and I have an evening alone without a hormonal teenager. In fact, forget the glass. We'll have a bottle.'

'Didn't your therapist advise you not to –'

'It's one evening, Zach. You're the one who keeps telling me to chill out.'

The waiter glances at Zach, who hesitates, then nods. She's right. It is only one night. But he doesn't want her using the excuse of a hangover to pull out of their diving trip tomorrow. He's already got everything arranged.

The waiter returns, pours out two glasses, tiny bubbles rising up in the pale amber liquid. Cara lifts hers and clinks it against his.

'To our holiday,' she says, taking a sip.

He smiles. Glances across at Ryan on the next table, who raises his glass in a silent toast. Zach narrows his eyes as he raises his glass back.

'Yes,' he replies. 'And to life-changing experiences.'

24. 2 days 17 hours left

Alexa walks along the jetty, the wooden boards lit up by the full moon as well as the lanterns. Away from the restaurant and bars, there's no sound other than the waves lapping against the sand. The heat is softer now, and the fish below her are more active, their dark silhouettes flitting backwards and forwards in the shallows. She walks past her villa, carries on until she reaches number nine. When there's no answer after she knocks on the door, she tries the handle.

Skye is sitting on the sofa in the living room with her back to her, wearing a pair of headphones, her bare feet up on the coffee table. Several candles and five vases full of flowers stand on the various surfaces, their heady fragrance filling the room. Skye's laptop is open and she's watching herself in one of her videos on YouTube. Alexa gazes at her on the screen; even without the sound she can see Skye has an air of confidence that tells the world she doesn't give a shit.

Alexa taps her on the shoulder, the ink of her octopus dark beneath her fingertips. Skye gasps as she rips off her headphones and whirls round to face her.

'Jeez, Alexa. Don't creep up on me like that.'

Alexa bites her lip. 'I did knock.' She glances at the laptop screen as Skye pushes it shut. 'I didn't fancy eating with my parents so I wondered if you wanted to hang out?'

Skye glances at her desk, hesitates.

'Don't worry if you're busy.' Alexa starts backing up towards the door. 'It doesn't matter.'

Skye shakes her head.

'Nah, you're welcome to stay. I've got a couple of things to finish, but I'm almost done, and then we could go and watch the fire show?'

Alexa slumps down on to the sofa, refuses to let herself think about Devi and the last time she saw him. Her mother told her he was the one who performed in the show.

'Are you working on the magazine article?' Alexa asks as Skye writes something in a notebook.

'Yes. Just making some notes. And researching some stuff for a group who are trying to restore the coral reefs around here. I'm going to put together a short video about it. See if there's anything that can be done to help.' She flicks a few strands of hair out of her face. 'Marc needs to agree, of course.'

'Why wouldn't he?' Alexa asks.

Skye shrugs. 'He doesn't want me doing anything that inconveniences the guests. I don't think he really understands the urgency of my work. If we carry on the way we're going, by 2050 the oceans will contain more plastic than fish. Did you know that?'

Alexa shakes her head.

'You're lucky to have a dad who takes an interest in this stuff,' Skye adds.

Alexa thinks of Zach in the restaurant, then of her mum lying on that lounger, and feels as if she's trying to swallow something spiky that's stuck in her throat.

'My family isn't as perfect as you think, you know,' she says.

Skye looks at her. 'No one's perfect. But at least your dad's making an effort to do the right thing.'

Alexa shrugs. 'It's part of my dad's brand to be eco-friendly. He isn't always like that.' She hesitates. 'He doesn't spend much time at home.'

Skye frowns.

'How come?'

Alexa hesitates. 'He's always working. Doing stuff for the business. Sometimes I think he forgets Mum and me even exist.' She hesitates before adding, 'First World problems, I know.'

Skye shrugs. 'Everyone has crap to deal with. It's just different crap. You don't fancy following in your dad's footsteps, then?'

Alexa slides out of the Gabriela Hearst sandals she'd stolen from her mum's wardrobe and puts her feet on the sofa, the bottom of her dress slipping up her legs.

'I don't know what I want to do when I leave school. Uni probably? Travel?' She runs her finger over her nose ring. 'There's nothing I feel that passionate about. I envy you for that. There's lots of things I'd like to tear down, but I don't know if there's anything I want to build up.'

She feels a loosening in her stomach after she's spoken, then pulls down the bottom of her dress as she catches Skye glancing at her scar.

'I had an accident a couple of weeks ago,' she says quickly.

Skye nods, almost as if Alexa hasn't spoken. Alexa wishes she could stay here and didn't have to go back to her villa. She can talk to Skye about anything, and she doesn't pry, doesn't insist on knowing all the drama, unlike her friends at school.

'I'd travel if I was you,' Skye says. 'You can't beat seeing the world. So many gorgeous places, different cultures, it makes you realize how precious this planet is. Anyway, I'm all done,' Skye announces, shutting her notebook and putting down her pen. 'Shall we go and watch the fire show? They do a later second performance, don't they?'

Alexa bites her lip. 'I'm not sure I want to.'

Skye frowns. 'Why not? It's supposed to be amazing.'

Alexa flushes, peels off a piece of her gel nails.

'What?' Skye says.

Alexa doesn't reply.

Skye smiles. 'You can trust me, you know.'

'It's Devi,' Alexa says. 'I think I saw him with my mum, earlier.' She hesitates. 'Like, *with* my mum. Together. On a sun-lounger.'

Skye frowns. 'What, shagging? You're kidding me?'

Alexa swallows the lump in her throat, shakes her head.

'Not shagging, but it looked like they were snogging.' Why should she be embarrassed about it? She wasn't the one on the lounger.

'Please don't say anything to anyone,' she adds. 'I haven't decided whether to tell my dad.'

Skye draws her fingers across her lips.

'Sealed,' she says. 'But if you want my advice, I'd stay out of it. Let your parents sort it out.' She hesitates. 'Things aren't always what they look like, you know.'

The image of the lounger flickers through Alexa's head. *It was exactly what it looked like.* She can't begin to decide what she thinks of her mother, but it's clear Devi is taking advantage of her. A total sleazebag. She shakes the scene away, trying to blank the details in her head.

'I'm going to go back to my villa,' Alexa says. 'Chill out for a bit. I don't fancy socializing tonight.'

'Are you sure?'

Alexa nods.

Skye shrugs, runs her hands through her hair. 'OK. How about you come over tomorrow morning and we'll record something for my YouTube channel.'

Alexa nods.

They both stand up to leave, but Alexa hesitates at the door, envelops Skye in an unexpected hug before following her out on to the jetty, wrinkling her nose at the overly sweet floral smell that seems to have soaked into her skin.

She tries to block out the feeling she's overshared, that she's just handed Skye an unexploded bomb and it's only a matter of time before she detonates it.

25. 2 days 16 hours left

Cara slips into a chair in front of the raised circular stage on the beach, her senses fuzzy after the bottle of champagne she's just downed with Zach over dinner. Other guests are already seated in the darkness, waiting expectantly for the show to start. The sea is an expanse of blackness ahead of her, tiny dots of white lights from other islands winking in the distance.

Zach had said he needed a few minutes to sort something out with Marc, but she has a feeling she'll be sitting here for a while on her own. It's typical of her husband. He'll promise the world, but never follows through. Unless it's business. She has to hand it to him; in that respect, he knows what he's doing. ZH Investments has grown exponentially over the past few years, profits tripling year on year. It's given them a lifestyle she never thought was possible. But it's come at the expense of their relationship, which although she doesn't want to admit it even to herself, is a mess.

She knows he's been seeing someone else. She's not stupid, even if he thinks she is. He'd come home in the early hours a few months ago, the smell of her perfume on his skin as he'd slipped into bed beside her. Since then, his 'meetings' with Victoria, the company finance director, have got later and more frequent, and he's constantly on his phone. Cara had chosen to ignore it, hoped it would fizzle out, like most of these things do. Several of her friends have been through something similar and their marriages have come out the other side, worse for wear but still functioning.

She'd been desperate to maintain the facade, clinging stubbornly to a notion that marriage provided an air of respectability. Not to mention, in her case, a deep cushion of financial security. She had been patient. Waited. Dropped hints; some subtle, some less so. None of which Zach had chosen to pick up on, any attempt to discuss the situation batted away with feeble explanations. She'd hoped coming out here on this holiday would give them a chance to talk properly, to spend some quality time together. And if necessary, for her to issue an ultimatum. But as the holiday draws on, that's looking more and more unlikely.

She hadn't planned what had happened with Devi this afternoon. There had been no forethought. A moment of madness. Curiosity as to what she was missing out on rather than a desire for revenge. She found him attractive, had wondered if he'd felt the same prickle of electricity that she did when she looked at him. He seems to *see* her so much more clearly than Zach does. But more than anything, she'd wanted to know what it would feel like to rewind, to experience the intensity you only ever get right at the very start of a relationship, before kids and life get in the way. To not have to think about what groceries she needed to pick up, whether she'd remembered to fill in the form Alexa needed for school, whether she'd got that last load of washing out of the machine. She'd wanted to see if it felt like it had with Zach in Sydney all over again, but it hadn't. And thankfully she'd stopped before it went too far. A passionate kiss and a bit of a fumble. Guilt scrapes at her insides and she shifts position in her seat. The music starts and the audience begins to clap.

After Devi had left, she'd thought those fifteen minutes would be something that she could bury for ever, something no one else would ever find out about. Not Zach, and certainly not Alexa. But now there is an uneasiness swilling around the bottom of her stomach; she's been naïve. Alexa's comments in the restaurant feel less raw after a bottle of Veuve, but Cara is sure her daughter saw her with Devi, and if she did, it's only a matter of time before it comes out.

26. 2 days 16 hours left

Skye spots Devi standing on the beach as the guests walk across to where the stage has been set up for the fire show. She feels a wave of sympathy for Alexa; she hadn't expected to like the girl. In some ways, Alexa reminds her of herself at that age, an angry teenager pissed off with the whole world. Having to go on holiday with fucked-up parents can't be fun, although Alexa must have got it wrong about her mother having a fling. Skye wouldn't kick Devi out of bed, but Cara's got far too much to lose. Zach seems like a great guy. She remembers how he'd insisted on leaving the restaurant on that first night, despite her entreaties to stay and have another drink; how she had watched him weave his way down the path back towards the jetty and his villa.

'Ms Elliot?' Devi walks towards her before she has a chance to join the other guests.

'Marc asked me to look out for you,' he says. 'I believe it's your birthday today?'

Skye nods, trying to blank out the image of him and Cara together that flashes into her head.

'He's arranged a few drinks in the bar after the performance and would be delighted if you could join us.'

'That's very kind,' Skye replies. 'I'd love that. So, is there a show every night?' she asks, wanting to say something to fill the awkward silence that is broken only by the faint sound of music coming from the back of the stage in the distance.

'Two or three times a week,' he says. 'That way there's a chance for everyone to see it.'

'Do you wear that?' she asks, pointing at his hoodie.

Devi shakes his head, and she catches a glimpse of his green eyes in the glow of the lights that have been strung across the bushes.

'I need to change into the uniform Asana gave me,' he says. 'It's with all my other stuff in a storeroom next to the restaurant so I don't have to trek backwards and forwards from the staff quarters with it every night.'

Skye hesitates, wonders if this would be a good opportunity to get some photos. Include a 'behind the guest entertainment' angle in her article.

'Can I see?' she asks.

She follows him as he heads around the side of the restaurant and opens the door to a small room about the size of a cloakroom. Various pieces of equipment hang from metal hooks along one wall: metal chains, ropes knotted and twisted into different-shaped cubes and balls. He takes a pair of black trousers, a tunic with an AF logo emblazoned on the shoulder and a pair of gloves from a hook on the door and holds them up.

'This is what I wear.'

'They look great. Can I get a photo of you in here? A behind-the-scenes shot? Magazine readers love that kind of thing.'

Devi grins broadly.

'Don't pose,' Skye says. 'I want to get one of you looking natural. It's more authentic.'

Devi puts the clothes back on the hook, picks up one of the cubes and throws it into the air.

Skye smiles as she takes a couple of photos with her phone, then stares at the results on the screen. With a bit of editing, they'll be perfect for the article or an Insta post. She's captured his face perfectly; can see his look of concentration, his long eyelashes, the mole on his cheekbone.

She feels her top stick to her skin in the heat. She's got what she needs, and past experience has taught her it's never a good idea to be stuck in a confined space with a man she doesn't really know.

'It's actually pretty airless in here,' she says. 'I'm going to grab a seat and I'll come and find you after the show?'

Devi nods, throws another cube in the air as she walks out.

27. 2 days 15 hours left

The pop music coming through the speakers makes the sand vibrate beneath Skye's feet. Devi has three dancers with him on stage and performs trick after trick, juggling flaming batons and lighting up the darkness with poi suspended from metal chains. Skye doesn't take her eyes off the way his body flexes with each move. She can see why Cara Hamilton liked what she saw.

'Not bad, is he?' Ryan Miller leans over and shouts in her ear as the troupe finish to a standing ovation. Skye grins and smiles back.

'Amazing. I wonder how long it took him to learn how to do that?'

Ryan shrugs. Cindy is on her feet beside him, whistling her appreciation.

Skye hesitates. 'I'm having a few drinks for my birthday after this. Would you and Cindy like to come?'

Ryan nods as the guests begin to file off across the sand. 'That would be great. We'd love that, wouldn't we, Cind?'

His wife nods, still clapping.

'There's an area reserved in Murika,' Skye says. 'The fusion restaurant. I'll see you in there. I just need to have a quick chat with Devi.'

Ryan follows her to the end of the row as she leaves her seat, leaving Cindy still applauding.

'What I told you last night,' he says, lowering his voice. 'I've had it verbally confirmed by someone else.'

Skye looks at him. 'Really?'

He nods. 'So you'll do what we agreed?'

'What we agreed,' she replies, 'was that you'd get proof. Conclusive. Not hearsay. I need that before we go any further.'

'But if –'

Skye cuts him off. 'Proof, Ryan,' she says. 'Then we'll talk next steps.'

She walks away and waits by the restaurant until Devi comes off the stage, carrying an orange bucket hat full of notes.

'Are you ready for your birthday celebrations?' He holds up the hat. 'I'll come over in a minute. I just need to take this back to my room first. I can't afford to lose my tips.'

'I'll come with you,' she says. 'I can ask you some questions for the article I'm writing at the same time.'

He looks at her, raises his eyebrows.

'If you want,' he says.

They head off down the sandy path, turning off on to the narrow track that leads to the centre of the island. Lights spill out from inside the prefabricated rectangular building, illuminating the path in front of them.

'Did you enjoy the show?' Devi asks.

Skye nods. 'You were brilliant.'

He grins as he opens the main door of the staff quarters and points down the corridor.

'My room is off there,' he says. 'But you can wait here if you want.'

Skye hesitates, torn between not wanting to follow him into his bedroom alone but knowing she won't get a better opportunity to see where the staff sleep. A chance to get some more photos for her magazine feature. She taps her pocket to check she's got her phone with her.

'I'll come,' she says.

The dormitory is cramped, five beds lined up on each side of the room with barely enough space to walk between. The walls are painted yellow as if to distract from the miserable lodgings, and there's a small bedside table beside each bed, on top of which is a neat pile of the occupant's personal belongings.

An ancient fan on the ceiling pushes the hot air around the small space. Skye sits down on Devi's bed and looks at a photo Blu-tacked on the wall of him holding a young girl who is grinning widely back at him.

'Your daughter?' she asks.

He nods.

A battered paperback sits on top of his bedside table, its pages bent and misshapen as if they've got wet and dried out again. She picks it up, revealing his passport lying on the table underneath, and reads out the title.

'*The Holiday*,' she says. 'Any good?'

'Yes,' Devi says. 'A guest left it here. You can borrow it if you want.'

He opens the drawer of his bedside table, pushes the hat containing the notes and coins inside, then walks back over to the door.

'Shall we go and see what Marc has got ready for you?' he asks.

Skye hesitates.

'In a second,' she says, flicking through the pages of the book. 'First, I think we need to have a chat. I got your message, Devi. Tell me, just how do you think we can help each other?'

28. 2 days 10 hours left

Cara wakes up when it's still dark. Her sheet is tangled up in a bundle at the bottom of the bed and the mattress underneath her is damp; a wet stickiness against her burning skin.

Zach is snoring beside her, his mouth open. She slides out of bed, pours herself a glass of water from one of the resort bottles in the mini-bar fridge and downs it in one go. She shouldn't have had that much champagne. Her night sweats are bad enough already without the added palpitations that now flutter beneath her ribs. A thrumming as if something is trapped and about to burst out. She'd thought she was having a heart attack the first time it happened but knows if she waits, *breathes through it*, it will recede.

Zach doesn't stir as she walks out into the living room, which is lit by the glow from the underwater lights beneath the glass panel in the floor. Alexa's room key is lying on the table. She remembers hearing her come in; a mother's instinct never to fully fall asleep until her child is home safe. She double-checks her room anyway, peering into the darkness at the figure lying on the bed, before silently shutting it again.

Three fifteen. Now she's awake, she knows she won't be able to go back to sleep, even if she could ignore the sound of Zach's snoring. The joys of menopause. She slips off her damp nightdress and pulls on a T-shirt and shorts before letting herself quietly out of the villa. It's still pleasantly warm, but the slight breeze on her skin makes her shiver with pleasure. Oversized glass lanterns placed at intervals along the wooden boards light up the length of the jetty, and she revels in having the beach completely to herself.

She wonders if she can strip off and go for a swim, feel the water against her skin. Do something that makes her feel alive. She can't explain things like this to Zach. He'd watch her, think her behaviour was evidence she is unstable.

Do it.

She discards her clothes and wades into the shallows, revelling in the water, which still feels like a warm bath, even at this time of night. She turns around as she hears the sound of voices and sees two silhouettes further down the beach. She screws up her eyes, but it's too dark to see clearly. From their animated gestures, it looks like they're having some kind of argument. She crouches down in the water, desperate not to be seen, her heart beginning to thrum in her chest.

You have every right to be here.

She has no desire to be discovered naked, but her shorts and T-shirt are too far away to reach. Her pulse speeds up and her mind flashes back to that evening and the creeping numbness returns to her legs. Paralysed, just like she was back then. Unable to do anything, despite her brain shrieking at her to do something, to run, to move. She holds her breath, sinks down until she's as low as she can get in the water and prays they won't come any closer.

One of the figures paces backwards and forwards. *Is that Ryan Miller? What's he doing out here at this time of night?* She begins to shiver, hoping she's hidden by the shadows of the jetty. He's with a woman, but she's taller than Cindy. *Is it Skye?* She's not sure, but it looks like they're arguing; he's got both hands out in front of him, gesticulating wildly, and she's shaking her head. Their voices float over in the darkness, their words unintelligible.

Finally, they move, disappearing up one of the paths through the vegetation. Cara listens, every sense on heightened alert, but there's no sound apart from the waves breaking on the shore.

She waits until cramp makes her legs scream in agony before forcing herself to stand up. She grabs her T-shirt and pulls it over her head, then hobbles as fast as she can along the jetty back to her villa, her breath coming in gasps, her key card out of her pocket and ready in her hand long before she reaches the door.

The back door stays firmly shut. The man gives it another shove, harder this time. Maybe he's losing his touch. He used to be able to get one of these open in under thirty seconds, but he's already been here for ten minutes and there's no sign of it budging. He wiggles his credit card between the frame and the lock, swallows his frustration as the handle still won't turn, then finally – at fucking last – it gives way, his card slipping through the gap.

He waits, bracing himself for the shrill sound of an alarm to slice through the air at any moment, but there's nothing. Maybe they didn't bother to turn it on. He looks closely at the yellow box attached to the brickwork. Or perhaps it's a fake. Now he looks more closely he can see there aren't any wires coming out of it. Just a flashing light that must be powered by a battery. He's surprised. He wouldn't have thought they'd have risked it after what happened.

He goes inside, slowly so as not to knock into anything, shines his torch around in the darkness. They've moved the furniture around since he was last in here. New armchair. Nice colour. He could do with one like that. He reaches out and touches the edge of the silver photo frame that's propped up on the desk in the study with his gloves. All three of them together in one of those black-and-white arty shots, like the ones Marie insisted on getting last year. Cost a bloody fortune. Happy families. Or at least it looks like they are there, but photos never show the whole truth.

He flips through the various pieces of paper lying on the desk, but they don't tell him anything he doesn't already know. He carries out a quick search of the bedrooms, then the sitting room and the dining room, but there's nothing in any of them either.

Now what? It's not up to him. He's not paid to make those kind of decisions. He's done what Vincent asked and now he just has to report the bad news. After last time, there's no way he's doing it in person. He gets out his mobile and dials the number.

30. 2 days 2 hours left

Zach steps off the main jetty and on to the diving boat, relieved to be out of the sun. The long wooden vessel has been converted from a traditional dhoni, everything painted in blue and white, including the roof, the tips of the bow and stern curved up towards the sky creating its distinctive silhouette.

His arms are piled high with the scuba equipment he collected earlier from the diving centre and he shakes his head as one of the staff offers to take it.

'It's fine, I can manage.'

The man shrugs and points him towards one of the benches that are positioned along either side of the cabin.

'You sit?' he says. 'Help yourself to fruit.'

A number of low tables covered in linen tablecloths with the Asana Fushi logo have been set up in the centre of the boat. Zach looks at the pieces of fresh melon, pineapple, mango and kiwi impaled on kebab sticks lying on metal platters but doesn't take one. The smell of diesel makes his stomach turn over. He tries to keep his eyes on the line of blue that forms the horizon as it moves up and down with the motion of the boat. The travel-sickness tablets he'd taken this morning had better bloody do their job. He glances at his watch.

'How long will it take to get to the reef?' he asks.

The man from the diving centre takes hold of Cara's hand and helps her on board.

'Around forty minutes. It's not too far. Are you sure you don't want some help with all that, Mr Hamilton?'

Zach adjusts his grip on the wetsuits and weight belts and shakes his head.

'I'm fine, honestly.'

He should have insisted they get on last. He wants to get going, not hang around staring out to sea through a shimmering haze of engine fumes. Four couples are still standing on the jetty, chatting idly, and he can hear the familiar drawl of Cindy's accent. Zach had bumped into Ryan in the diving centre and his heart had sunk. He doesn't want to talk business, doesn't want to hear about Ryan's latest successful project. He wants this to be a chance for him and Cara to reconnect.

He was relieved when she said she still wanted to come. Normally after a few glasses of champagne Cara needs a lie-in, but she had been up and ready before he was even dressed. Alexa hadn't stirred when he'd poked his head around her door; a silent mound under the white sheet. God knows what time she'd got in last night.

He remembers what his daughter said yesterday about splitting up with Charlie and a chill runs down his spine. Charlie's dad, Vincent Pearce, is his biggest investor, and not someone he wants annoyed. He's well aware of what Vincent is capable of if he doesn't get what he wants.

Ryan finally steps on to the deck and sits beside Cara, dumping his diving equipment on top of Zach's.

'Your daughter not coming?' Cindy asks.

Cara smiles, shakes her head.

'She's not into scuba diving.'

'We always get Riley to try stuff she hasn't done before,'

Cindy says as she sits down beside Cara. 'Don't we, Ryan? It's important that kids try new things, push themselves outside their comfort zone. We'd have never ended up being cabin crew if we hadn't done that, would we?' She taps Cara's thigh, and Zach feels his wife shuffle closer to him.

'I guess not,' Cara says flatly.

'Wasn't it just the best job?' Cindy continues. 'You used to love it.' She observes Zach and frowns. 'You sure you're OK there?'

Zach grimaces. Cara leans forward, picks up a bottle of water out of the crate full of ice and hands it to him.

'Don't look at me,' she says. 'Keep your eyes on the horizon.' She turns to Cindy. 'Sorry, he gets seasick.' She hesitates. 'You might want to move down the bench a bit.'

Zach doesn't actually feel that nauseous, but it's a great excuse for him not to have a conversation with either of the Millers. He wonders if Ryan knows he's going big-game fishing with Marc tomorrow, whether he's talked to Skye again. For about the tenth time on this holiday, he wishes Ryan hadn't come to Asana at all.

The contents of his stomach settle as they move away from the jetty, the rocking motion of the boat steadying as they pick up speed.

Zach watches his wife scrape her hair off her face and gather it back into a ponytail as the boat cuts through the water, the warm breeze a relief after the close humidity on the island. Asana Fushi shrinks to a small green dot in the ocean behind them as they head out towards the reef. He hears the familiar ringtone of a mobile and automatically reaches for his pocket before Cindy pulls her phone out and proceeds to hold a conversation at a volume that can be heard by everyone else on the boat. He'd left his in the villa, like he promised Cara he would. Under his pillow. Switched off.

A man sitting a few feet further down from him wearing a pair of neon-yellow trunks runs his hand lovingly over the bump that protrudes from his partner's stomach. Zach brushes away the beads of perspiration that have formed on his forehead.

He reaches forward, puts his empty bottle of water in the trash bucket. He should never have got involved. It was only supposed to be a one-night stand, an encounter that could be explained away the following day by too much alcohol, something that went too far in the heat of the moment after a business dinner. But Victoria – or *Tori*, as she always signs off her texts – had clearly had other ideas. A week after that first tryst, she had come into his office, pushed his Aeron chair-on-wheels away from his desk and slid herself on to his lap before he'd had time to object, her hands unbuttoning the new chinos Cara had bought him a few days earlier.

He'd been so fucking stupid.

Cara smiles at him, picks up the wetsuit lying by her feet and starts to put it on. He needs some headspace so he can work out what to do about Victoria without ending his marriage or ruining his business. The last thing he needs is to be slapped with a lawsuit for unfair dismissal.

As the boat slows down, the loud roar of the engine quietens and the smell of diesel returns. Cara lifts up her hair and turns her back towards him.

'Can you zip me up?'

He pulls on the strap to fasten her wetsuit, watches as her skin is swallowed up by the neoprene. He remembers how much she used to love him running his fingers down her back, how he used to be able to make her shiver with pleasure. He can't remember the last time she'd asked him to do that. When he climbs into bed next to her now, all she wants to do is sleep. He still has needs. He just should have been more careful. A lot more careful.

The diving instructor signals that they should start putting on their scuba gear. Zach feels a flutter beneath his ribs, a moment of hesitation as he attempts to separate his and Cara's things from the pile of items Ryan has dumped on the deck.

Zach picks up one of the regulators with its pressure gauge, black plastic tubes spread out like giant spider's legs, and hands it to a member of the crew, who connects it to Cara's tank. It's been ages since he and Cara dived together, years since they got their PADI qualification. The crew member finishes with Cara's tank and starts on Zach's as he pulls on his wetsuit.

The instructor squeezes washing-up liquid into their masks and rinses them out in a bucket of water. The driver cuts the engine and the boat sways in the water, the swell out here more evident as the horizon bobs up and down more vigorously, producing an unpleasant sloshing feeling in Zach's stomach. He hates this bit. He wants to get into the sea as fast as possible but has to stay where he is and listen to the safety briefing.

The divemaster finally finishes talking and Zach shuffles over to the side of the boat, his fins clasped in one hand. He sits down and slides his feet into the tight black rubber fins before looking back at his wife of nineteen years, who has been hijacked by Cindy again, and swallows the acid that rises up in his mouth.

Does he really want to do this?

One of the staff lifts the harness containing the diving equipment on to his back and does up the straps before helping him to his feet. Zach stands up, inflates his BCD, puts his hand over his regulator and mask to hold them in place and steps off the boat into the water.

He checks his buoyancy and treads water while he waits for Cara and the others. The visibility here is excellent; he can see everything ahead of him for about thirty metres when he dips his head underwater. He runs through what he's going to do next and tries to slow the stream of bubbles coming from his regulator.

Calm down.

He watches Cindy laugh at something Cara says before Cindy steps into the water. His wife takes hold of the instructor's hand and lets him perform a few last checks of her equipment. Something in Zach's stomach twists, but he knows it's too late to back out now. In forty-five minutes, it will all be over.

31. 2 days 1 hour left

Cara's hangover seems to be getting worse rather than better. The fruit kebab hasn't helped – her stomach is a swirl of acidity. The thought of sticking a regulator in her mouth and breathing in air that has had every drop of moisture removed makes her break out in a layer of sweat beneath her wetsuit.

Zach said the diving centre had offered to fill their tanks with nitrox – a higher percentage of oxygen and less nitrogen to reduce the chance of decompression sickness – but he'd decided to stick with the normal mix as they weren't going below twenty-five metres. She doesn't care what she breathes as long as it gets her safely to where they are going and back on the boat.

She'd felt relieved when Zach stepped off into the water. He's been stressed about this trip all morning; hadn't been able to stop jiggling his knee while he was sitting beside her, had clenched his jaw when Cindy's mobile rang. After almost twenty years of marriage, she knows all his tells, but he doesn't know hers at all. What she did yesterday with Devi is written all over her skin if he only looked closely enough, but he seems blind to the nuances he was once attuned to, hasn't noticed the red hives that still itch on the side of her neck despite the anti-histamine tablets she'd taken earlier.

The divemaster beckons her over and she steps forward,

the last of the guests still on the boat apart from the pregnant woman. She pulls her fins on to her feet before her harness is lifted on to her back, the straps clipped into place, and slides her mask over her head, the rubber strap catching in her hair. Needles prick her scalp as she disentangles the strands. The seal is tight against her face, too tight, and she knows she should stop and loosen it or she'll end up with deep grooves in her skin when she takes it off, but the divemaster tells her to get into the water and she doesn't want to hold the others up.

She holds her regulator in her mouth as she steps off the side of the boat, the coolness of the ocean flooding into her wetsuit a welcome relief after the heat of the sun. She stops kicking, deflates her buoyancy-control device to check it's working, then swims over to where Zach and the others are waiting.

He joins his thumb and index fingers together in a loop and she mirrors the action back to him. The divemaster checks everyone is ready and indicates they should start their descent. The reef is a burst of colour here. A forest of coral of different shapes and sizes teems with thousands of brightly coloured fish. Crimson fronds shaped like the skeletons of huge leaves spread themselves out in front of her, delicate veins branching out from a central limb in intricate patterns that remind her of lace doilies.

Larger fish appear. Parrotfish – sapphire blue with splashes of purple and yellow, the sound of their beaks as they graze on the coral like someone clicking their fingers next to her ear. One of the other divers points out the snout of a moray eel poking out from a crevice, its jaws open as they swim past.

Cara can just make out Cindy's slim silhouette ahead of her. She seems to remember their time at United so much more clearly than Cara does. Was she always so annoying? Had she been in First Class, with Cara, or in economy? She's sure they never shared a hotel room. She hadn't made much of an impression on Cara at the time – giggly and a bit irritating, from the little she remembers, but maybe she's just projecting what she feels about her now. Cindy swims further away, disappearing into the blue.

Where's Zach? He's supposed to be her buddy, to swim next to her. A wave of irritation surges through her. She can't follow anyone until she's equalized the pressure in her ears; it currently feels as if someone is stabbing them with a knife. She ascends a few feet, pinches her nose and tries again. She finally achieves the same popping sensation she used to get at work when the aircraft took off.

More marine life. Surgeonfish with royal-blue bodies and bright yellow stripes down their backs. Pennant coral-fish coloured like zebras with long, trailing fins that remind her of swallowtail butterflies.

Zach is further away now, and she can feel a knot form in her stomach. She checks her pressure gauge. Just over 120 bar. Her tank is still over half full. She can hear the bubbles escaping from her regulator, faster now as she takes deeper breaths. *Relax.* He'll slow down and turn around in a minute.

She had been hoping to see a whale shark, but she's no longer sure this would be such a welcome sight. The knot in her stomach tightens at the thought of anything that size swimming towards her or coming up behind her out of the deep blue. The water begins to feel colder and she wonders how much longer they're going to be down here.

Why doesn't Zach just fucking slow down?

She kicks her legs to catch up, feels her fins propel her through the water. Suddenly, her mouth fills with air, even though she hasn't taken a breath. Her cheeks expand, puffing outwards, her skin stretching until her eyes water. She pulls out her mouthpiece. The second stage of her regulator is producing a constant stream of bubbles that rise up in a trail towards the surface.

Oh God. It's gone into free flow.

She turns it over in her hand so the mouthpiece is facing downwards, but the bubbles don't stop.

Don't panic.

She tries to remember what they were taught about free-flowing regulators on her PADI course, but it was years ago. Her mind has gone blank. She tries hitting the black plastic with her hand, but the bubbles continue to flood out.

The knot moves up from her stomach to beneath her ribs. If she opens her mouth to breathe through the bubbles, she's terrified she'll end up swallowing water. Choking.

She can't do it.

And she can't see Zach.

Swim.

She lets go of the regulator and lets it dangle by her side as she pulls herself through the water, desperate to reach the first diver ahead of her. The knot expands in her chest, like a balloon that's stretched until it's about to burst.

Turn around. Please help me.

The pressure in her lungs is too much to bear. She lets her breath out, a few bubbles escaping from her mouth at a time, putting off the moment when she's going to have to inhale until the last possible second.

There's a high-pitched humming in her head. She stretches out to grab hold of the diver in front of her. Just a couple more metres. Her vision begins to cloud over, swirls of black appearing at the edges of her mask as her hand connects with a rubber fin.

The diver begins to turn around and Cara lets out the remainder of her breath in one go, a string of bubbles appearing out of her mouth. Her wetsuit feels as if it has been filled with a layer of ice. She doesn't understand what she's looking at. The man staring at her isn't wearing a scuba mask. His face is the same one she saw four weeks ago. Narrow eyes, thin lips, his scalp visible through his shaved hair.

He's come back.

He moves towards her, and Cara deflates her buoyancy-control device, lets herself float up with the stream of bubbles. She knows this is the wrong thing to do, that unless she stops to decompress, her lungs will explode. The humming gets louder. Blackness spreads over her mask as she shuts her eyes.

She can feel fingers digging into her shoulders. Zach's mask is a few inches away from hers, and he's staring at her and holding a mouthpiece in her mouth. His thumb and index fingers are pressed together and she nods as she gulps in lungfuls of air, holds her hand up in a response. He puts his thumb up, indicating the boat, but continues to hold on to her harness and points at her mouthpiece, then himself. Cara realizes he's given her his octo so she can breathe; a second source of air attached to his tank.

He starts to ascend, and Cara holds on to his arm, still gulping air. He flattens his hand and lowers it to tell her to slow down, then scrunches it into a fist, telling her they need to hold their position for the first decompression stop.

The rest of their group pause their ascent and float alongside her. Ryan watches her, the whites of his eyes visible through his mask. He looks as petrified as she is.

Why the fuck did Zach swim off and leave her?

Bubbles are still appearing out of her malfunctioning regulator, disappearing up towards the surface, but the stream has slowed and she knows if she looks at her pressure gauge the needle will be in the red, her tank almost empty.

The divemaster indicates they should start moving again, and she rises towards the surface. She focuses on controlling her breathing, won't let herself think about the man's face.

He can't be real.

Zach should have stayed with her, but he didn't. He was the one who persuaded her to come on this diving trip, had picked up their equipment from the diving centre, given her that specific regulator. And now she can't help wondering whether her husband did something to put her in this situation in the first place.

32. 2 days left

Alexa picks up another fragment of broken coral and attaches it with a cable tie to the metal frame sitting in the tank of seawater beside the diving centre. The structure reminds her of an upside-down version of the hanging basket outside their front door at home.

'Like this?' she asks.

Skye stands opposite her, filming her with her phone.

'That's great,' she says. 'I just want a few more shots that I can edit together to show how the resort is trying to help regenerate the reef.' She pushes a strand of blonde hair out of her face. 'But don't feel you have to do this. Wouldn't you rather be sunbathing or something?'

Alexa shakes her head as seawater drips down the front of her T-shirt, a welcome relief against the heat.

'I don't want to go back to our villa at the moment. My parents are pretending they aren't ignoring each other, but you can cut the atmosphere with a knife.'

Skye raises her eyes. 'Tricky. Can you just hold up that piece of coral for me again? Do you mind if I get you in the photo as well?'

Alexa frowns. 'I'm sweating buckets and look like shit.'

Skye smiles. ''Course you don't. You look great. And I'll tag you, of course. Go on, my followers will love it. "Daughter of eco-friendly millionaire helps sustain coral reef on vacation."'

Alexa hesitates, but before she has a chance to object, Skye takes a couple of shots.

'That's great.' Skye grins at her. 'Just hold the frame up a bit higher and I'll get one more.'

Alexa tries to smile, but her lips feel tight as she lowers the frame back into the tank.

'Brilliant,' Skye says. 'I'll add the voiceover later.'

Alexa can't help noticing the gleam in Skye's eyes. The same look she sees in her dad's when he's talking about money. She starts to wish she hadn't let Skye take the photos at all.

Skye hesitates. 'Did you tell your dad what you saw? Is that why they're arguing?'

Alexa shakes her head.

'They had a row on their diving trip. Mum's regulator malfunctioned and she's blaming him.'

Skye frowns. 'Is she OK?'

'Yeah.' Alexa glances down at her shin. 'As much as she ever is. I'm supposed to be going to the spa with her later this afternoon. But I'd rather just hang around here with you.'

Skye moves around to the other side of the tank, where, with the sun behind her, she morphs into a silhouette. Alexa puts her hand up to shade her eyes, thinks of the Snapchat message from Charlie she picked up this morning in response to her message last night telling him it was over.

Whatever. Was ab to say same thing to u when u got back anyway.

Her cheeks flush. She wants to tell Skye about it, hear her dismiss Charlie the way she did before, replace the emptiness inside her with something that makes her feel she doesn't care any more.

'Do you get on better with your dad?' Skye asks.

Alexa hesitates.

'Recently, maybe.'

'His business sounds like it's doing well.'

Alexa squints, unable to see Skye's expression.

'It should be, the amount of time he spends on it.'

'Are all the projects he invests in successful?'

Alexa shrugs. 'I presume so. He makes a lot of money.'

'He's said he wants us to collaborate,' Skye says. 'I help raise the profile of his company in return for him recommending projects I support to his investors. There's another guy staying here, Ryan Miller. His business is similar to your dad's, and he wants to do the same thing. I can only choose one to work with, so I want to make sure I pick the person who will give me the best opportunities.'

Alexa bites her lip. 'My dad isn't stupid. He'd only do something like that if he knows it's worth his while.' She hesitates. 'Look, I don't want you to feel you have to work with him just because we're friends.'

Skye doesn't reply and Alexa sees something flicker across her face.

'We might be friends, Alexa,' Skye says slowly, 'but this is business. I never let my friendships interfere with that.' She turns away, looks at her phone, and Alexa feels a lump in her throat. Skye tuts. 'It's too bright to see my screen properly. Let me just check I've got everything I need and then we can go and get a drink or something.'

Alexa stares at Skye's octopus tattoo as she disappears into the diving centre, examines the skin on her fingers as she waits for her to come back, the tips wrinkled from the length of time they've been in the water. Her gels are starting to peel off. She wonders if the spa could do a manicure rather than a massage. That way she won't have to talk to her mum at all. She can't get the memory of her and their butler out of her head. Did she really see what she thought she saw? Or was her brain playing tricks on her, filling in gaps with things that lurk in her imagination?

After a few minutes, her shoulders are starting to burn. She shakes the seawater off her hands and scrapes her hair back into a messy bun. It's rough and brittle from the salt-water and her fingers get caught in the knots as she goes to find Skye in the diving centre.

She is sitting on one of the chairs, poring over her phone. Alexa clears her throat, but Skye doesn't move, her eyes glued to the screen.

'Did you get the shots you needed?'

Alexa wonders if Skye has even heard her. As she walks closer, she can see that a video is playing, tinny voices coming out of the speaker, none of which sound like hers.

'Skye?'

Skye stands up, her face white, swipes what Devi has sent her off the screen and sticks her phone in her shorts pocket.

'They look really great. Thanks so much for doing that.'

She smiles, and Alexa can see why she's so good on social media. She can radiate charm in an instant. Alexa doesn't smile back; something between them has slipped off-kilter. She's not stupid. It's blatantly obvious Skye wasn't looking at the photos of her at all.

33. 1 day 22 hours left

Marc can tell by the way the woman is staring at his shirt that the damp patches under his arms have seeped through the material. Normally, he goes back to his room to change at lunchtime, taking the opportunity to have a fifteen-minute siesta and catch up on some of Lilia's never-ending messages. But today, he hasn't had a chance to do either of those things. He's been stuck in reception. Dealing with demands from what feels like an endless stream of guests. He's sick of their ridiculous requests, the sound of his own voice and the bland reassurances he's convinced none of them are swallowing.

No, I'm sorry, but it is not possible to keep a turtle in the bathtub. Yes, that is still the case even if you fill it with seawater.

I realize we have agreed to provide you with a white wedding, but we cannot arrange for a snow machine to get here by tomorrow. And even if we did, I think it's highly unlikely it would work in ninety-degree heat.

No, there is no reason to think that the current tornado in the Bahamas will affect the Maldives. The two places are 16,000 kilometres away from each other. I've been in touch with head office, and your tour operator, as you requested, and they have confirmed there is no reason to be concerned. Their advice is to continue enjoying your holiday.

We will certainly make every effort to see dolphins on your boat trip this evening, but we can't promise they will appear at 8 p.m. to coordinate exactly with your marriage proposal.

Absolutely, I understand your concerns. The bite does look itchy, but it is difficult for us to ensure that your room is always one hundred per cent free from mosquitoes, especially if you leave your patio doors open with all the lights on when you go out in the evening.

Marc smiles at Ryan and Cindy Miller, who are sitting in front of him. Cindy has just asked for an extra set of pillows and wants to know exactly how the snorkelling equipment is sterilized between each use. The fans above him are on, but the reception area feels hotter than ever. Gusts of warm air buffet him as the blades turn in continuous circles, the pages of the notepad on his desk fluttering in the breeze.

Cindy drones on, and on. Marc fights to keep a smile on his face as he notices that the edges of the white petals of the kaaminee phool in the vases on the glass tables are beginning to turn brown. He can see half a dozen things that he needs to get the staff to address, but until the Millers leave him alone, he's stuck in his seat.

He swallows a yawn, widens his grin at the same time in an awkward attempt to hide it as Cindy continues to talk, reassures her that yes, the ice in the mini-bar is made of bottled water, and no, they've never had any reports of anyone suffering from the Zika virus in the resort.

She finally runs out of things to say and gets up to leave. Marc sinks into his chair, rubs the back of his neck in relief. *Please let them be the last.* He's fed up with this job, has been for a while. Zach Hamilton has come to Asana Fushi at just the right time.

Earlier, Zach had sat opposite him in the same chair as Cindy, his Reef flip-flops tapping against the marble floor. He'd wanted to know if the wi-fi connection could be improved; his daughter had been complaining about it.

Not without significant investment in the infrastructure, Marc had wanted to say. But, of course, he hadn't. He had nodded sympathetically and spewed out polite platitudes while wondering why Zach's precious daughter couldn't manage without her bloody phone for more than two minutes. Now, he runs his hand over his head, slicks back a strand of hair which has come unstuck.

He looks out of the reception area to the white sandy beach and the sea beyond. The surface of the lagoon is like a swimming pool today, almost flat in the breathless, sultry heat. Skye has left a message asking to talk about the seagrass situation, amongst other things, but she's going to have to wait. He can't afford to do anything at the moment that might annoy the guests and risk his job. If he doesn't come up with the alimony payments, God knows what Lilia will do. Contact the owners? Tell them about what she called his *deviant* habit? He wouldn't put anything past her. The sooner he can get out of this bloody resort and set up somewhere on his own, preferably in Europe, away from this tropical climate that he can't move in without breaking out in a sweat, the better.

At least he's got Zach to agree to the big-game fishing trip. Tomorrow afternoon. A chance for the two of them to chat without any distractions. He knew that pretending Ryan was interested would be enough to persuade Zach to come. He and Zach have so much more in common than Zach would like to admit, although he understands exactly why Zach wants to keep it quiet. But once Zach realizes he can trust him, Marc hopes they'll be able to have a very frank discussion about possible business opportunities.

Marc has learned that when one door closes in life, another one usually opens and, tomorrow, he intends to make sure that's the case.

34. 1 day 21 hours left

Cara is shown into the serenity spa changing room by one of the attendants. The floors are terrazzo with marble hues, the walls and roof painted an off-white; the entire building exudes a sense of calm. Pieces of carved wooden art sit discreetly on plinths and each room is filled with several aromatherapy diffusers containing the exotic scent of ylang-ylang.

The attendant shuts the wooden door behind her, its surface carved to resemble tree bark. Cara shuts her eyes and runs her fingertips over it, wondering if Alexa is going to turn up. She hasn't had a chance to talk to her daughter properly since Alexa made those barbed comments in the restaurant, and she's dreading another confrontation. She rips opens the small paper bag the receptionist has given her, takes out the pair of slippers emblazoned with the Asana Fushi logo and slides her feet inside, questions running through her head as to whether she really needs slippers at all when she's only going to take them off again in a few minutes.

She hangs her designer dress in the locker, one of several she hired from Hurr, to satisfy Zach's insistence on sustainability, especially for this holiday. She wraps the white cotton waffle robe around herself, threading the belt through the loops. She's not wearing the paper pants they've given her; she hates the way they rustle against her skin as she moves, sticks them in the pocket of her robe instead. The music coming through the speakers is a mix of birdsong, waves and pan pipes. It's supposed to be relaxing but isn't easing the anxiety that swirls in her stomach.

Where is she? Cara glances at the clock. Alexa was supposed to meet her here five minutes ago. *Should she just go in by herself?*

The door of the changing room swings open, hitting the wall. Cara winces.

'I got held up.'

She wonders if all teenagers are the same, their world shrunk to a place where everything revolves solely around them.

Would it really kill her to just apologize?

'There's a robe for you on the bench,' Cara says. 'And they said to remove all your jewellery.'

Cara can tell from the way Alexa shoves her clothes in a pile and bangs the locker door that now is not the time to start a discussion about what happened last night. She wishes Zach hadn't booked this session in the first place. She doesn't want to have to lie still while someone runs their hands all over her. She'd have been happier sunbathing on the deck.

She looks at Alexa's flat stomach and the belly-button piercing that Cara hadn't even realized she'd had done, unsure whether that's included in the jewellery instructions. She's not supposed to take the helix one in her ear out for another three weeks. Something else Alexa did without telling her, something else Cara has held back from commenting on to keep the peace.

Alexa stands in front of one of the mirrors and tries to unfasten the thin gold chains around her neck. Cara digs her nails into her palms, wondering what the masseur will think if she sees the crescent-shaped imprints in her skin. *Hurry up, Alexa.* The minute hand of the clock on the wall completes another circle. *How many of those bloody things has she got round her neck?*

'Ready?' she asks.

Alexa rolls her eyes. 'Does it look like I'm ready?'

Cara looks at her, feeling an intense heat flood her body. She's trying. And Alexa throws it back in her face. Every time. *Fuck you*, she thinks. *Fuck you.*

'I don't know, Alexa. That's why I'm asking the question. Can you just stop being so antagonistic for once?' She takes a deep breath. 'Is there something you want to say to me? Because if there is, just come out and say it.'

Cara's eyes meet her daughter's in the mirror. She realizes she can't remember when they last looked at each other properly, face to face. Probably not since the accident. She can tell Alexa is furious, but there is a sadness beneath the anger in her eyes that Cara wasn't expecting. It stabs her straight in the heart as the spa music continues to tinkle around them. She wonders if it is too late to pull off her robe, get dressed and run back to the villa.

Alexa finally unclasps the last chain around her neck, slides the handful of metal into the pocket of her shorts and sticks them into the locker.

'There's nothing to say, is there?' she says. Cara can hear the hopelessness in her voice as she adds, 'You can't change what happened.'

Alexa looks down at her leg and Cara feels a prickly sweat

break out across her cleavage. She deserves everything Alexa throws at her. It was her fault. She did that to her. No wonder her daughter hates her. She should never have got in the car, should have looked before she reversed out of their driveway. If she hadn't been in such a blind rage, she would have seen Alexa come out of the front door and step on to their gravel driveway. But she'd only heard the sickening thud, followed by her screams. She can still hear them now, sounds that will be engraved on her brain for eternity.

'I'm sorry,' she says. 'I know I've said it before, Alexa, but I really am truly sorry. If I could go back and change things, you know I would, but I can't.' Her eyes well up.

Alexa hesitates as if she's weighing something up, and Cara holds her breath as her daughter takes a step forward and reaches for her hand.

'I know it was an accident, Mum. I know shit just happens sometimes.' She points at the red line on her skin. 'And the seawater has made it loads better. I bet it won't even scar.'

A tear runs down Cara's cheek as she puts her arms around her daughter's shoulders and embraces her. The stiffness seems to slide out of Alexa's body as she hugs her back for what feels like the first time in for ever. Cara shuts her eyes. Breathes in the smell of her hair, her skin. Wishes they could stay like this, that she didn't have to let her go.

Alexa opens the tree-bark door, and Cara follows her into the treatment room that has their names written in italics on the door. Cara walks towards the massage table. Her hands are slippery with emotion as she undoes her robe, hangs it up on the hook on the wall, lies down on the table and pulls the towels over her, conscious of her wobbling thighs and soft midriff compared to her daughter's taut body.

'Are you and Dad talking again?' Alexa's voice sounds muffled from where she lies on the other side of the room.

'We're fine. I was just a bit shaken up after what happened on the dive.'

'It wasn't his fault, Mum.'

'I know.' Cara adjusts her position so her face fits over the hole in the massage table. She can see the bowl of water filled with floating pink and white petals below.

There's a pause before Alexa speaks.

'Dad is trying, you know. If he hadn't been there when I got injured, I don't know what we would have done.' Cara wants to say that if he hadn't been there, they never would have argued, and the accident would never have happened in the first place. 'You need to think about what you're doing, Mum. Anyone out swimming can see you on those sun-loungers, you know.'

35. 1 day 20 hours left

Zach switches his phone to silent. He could block Tori, but if she takes offence and quits her job he'll be screwed. Not only would his business be without a finance director when he's never needed one more, but he could also face a potential claim for constructive dismissal, not to mention a paternity case. He needs to try and cool things down, back away from the situation; let her down gently.

He never should have started it in the first place. His life with Cara isn't perfect, but he loves her and he's not simply going to throw it all away and start again. He's worked too hard for that. He'd promised Tori that he'd tell Cara about the baby while they were away, but he has no intention of doing that. Legally, Cara owns fifty per cent of the business. She'd worked full-time for him as his PA when he'd first set it up, could argue she was instrumental in making the business a success. If he tells her what he's done, he could end up losing half of everything he's worked for. And if she gets a good solicitor, probably a lot more than that.

And he can imagine what his mother will say. She's devoted her life to ensuring the Hamilton name has never been associated with so much as a whiff of scandal. She adores her only granddaughter and her initial dislike of Cara has developed into a grudging tolerance. She might not disown her only son, but he knows what she'll say, can hear her clipped voice in his head: *I suggest you fix it, Zach. And fix it now.*

He takes a few steps towards the bushes at the side of the sandy path as one of the resort's electric buggies pulls up alongside him.

'Can I give you a lift, Mr Hamilton?'

It takes him a few seconds to recognize Devi behind the wheel.

'Thanks, but I'm going to walk.' He taps his Apple Watch. 'I need to get some steps in. Been slacking for a few days, and it's been letting me know. Too many open rings.'

Devi smiles. Zach doubts the butler even understands what he's talking about. Apple might have taken over the Western world, but they still have a way to go out here.

'It's a health app,' Zach says. 'Lets me know if I'm not getting enough exercise.' He hesitates as Devi continues to smile at him. 'I'm going to head back to the villa via the beach,' he adds.

'Have fun, Mr Hamilton,' Devi says. 'Be careful, the sun's still pretty strong. I think your wife had the best idea – stay in the shade on your deck.' Devi holds up his hand in a wave as the buggy pulls away with a familiar whine.

Zach wonders if Cara has finished in the spa. Whether it's helped her to relax. He shouldn't have suggested going diving. He'd hoped it would be a way to reconnect, remind her of something they used to do together. But the trip had been a disaster – he hasn't seen Cara that terrified since Alexa was bundled into the ambulance.

He'd only left her for a moment, had just wanted to see the lionfish Cindy had been pointing at. He'd thought Cara had seen it as well, its lethal brown-and-white spines waving around like giant feathers in the water. He'd presumed she was following him until he'd turned around and seen her panicking, trying to head for the surface. Thank God he'd managed to reach her in time to pull her back.

The divemaster had continued to insist that the equipment had been safety-checked by at least two of the crew before they'd left Asana Fushi, despite Zach's stream of expletives when they got back to the boat. Ryan had seemed almost as shaken up as Cara, his face ghostly white when he'd pulled off his dive mask, and Zach had noticed how quiet he'd been all the way back to the resort. One of the other divers said he'd seen something similar happen before on a previous holiday – a malfunction due to grains of sand stuck in the respirator mechanism. Odds of a million to one, but sometimes accidents just happen.

Too many accidents seem to be happening to them recently.

His Reef flip-flops dig into the sand as he walks, and he can feel his feet burning. Devi was right: the heat is even more intense today. He kicks off his shoes, picks them up and jogs down to the edge of the ocean, feels an instant relief as his soles touch the wet sand before sinking into the water. He wades in further until he's ankle-deep, imagines what it would be like to be stuck out here without any shade. He'd burn alive in no time.

He can just about make out the overwater villas in the distance through the shimmering heat. He adjusts his sunglasses and wipes the sweat off his nose, remembers the state of Marc's shirt when he'd left him in reception. Those dark patches. Pale blue isn't the best colour to wear out here.

He wishes he didn't have to go fishing with him tomorrow. But he needs Marc's contacts. Marc knows the owners of the hotels that don't yet have desalination plants and which ones need financing to get them installed. He could start an environmental initiative across multiple islands, and if he manages to get Skye involved it would generate a huge amount of publicity. ZH Investments would have a pipeline of new business for months, if not years. Enough money to fix all his problems. A much-needed plan to get the business back on track.

If he gets Marc hammered, he might tell Zach what he needs to know, but if he doesn't, Zach is going to have to offer him something in exchange. Probably a job. Something he can later retract. It's obvious the man is desperate for one. He's dropped enough unsubtle hints and is always slapping him on the back, buying him drinks. He'd even come into the gym when Zach was weight training and offered to spot him. Zach just needs to work out exactly what he's going to say.

His pulse quickens as he feels his phone vibrate. If he's completely honest, it's not Tori he's most worried about. Her WhatsApps are irritating, but if he can get this deal with Marc done he can pay her off. As he knows only too well, everyone has a price. He'll be able to persuade her that having the baby isn't a good idea – for either of them. And if she insists on going ahead with it, he'll tell her he has no interest in helping to raise another child but will pay his fair share so long as she agrees to keep his name off the birth certificate.

But Tori's messages aren't the real issue. They don't fill him with the same ice-cold fear as the others he's been receiving.

If Cara or Alexa find out about those, they'll never forgive him.

36. 1 day 19 hours left

Skye knocks on the door of the dormitory. She had walked into the staff quarters feeling like an intruder. The ugly prefabricated beige structure looks out of place here, like something left over from the 1970s; nothing like the other traditional wooden buildings that the guests use with their thatched roofs and immaculate decor, and certainly not something she's about to post on her Insta. She wouldn't have considered coming at all if Devi hadn't asked to meet her. She clasps the paperback she borrowed from his room tightly in her hand, an excuse to be here if anyone asks what she's doing.

Devi opens the door and peers into the corridor, steps back to let her inside.

'No one's around,' he says. 'They're all out doing jobs.'

Skye stands in the small space between the rows of beds, not sure where to sit, finally perching awkwardly on the end of his mattress.

'I got the video you sent me,' she says.

He nods. 'And?'

'If it shows what I think it does, then –'

'It does.' He cuts across her before she can finish.

'How long has it been going on?'

He shrugs. 'I've known for a while. It's hard to keep anything a secret around here. Staff talk, even when they're told not to, you know?'

Skye hesitates. The magazine will be interested if she can get hold of visual proof. It's the kind of thing that will create a splash with her followers. She knows how much they love being the first to find something out. But she's also waiting to hear back from Ryan. If what he said is true, then she'll have evidence of something more meaningful and far-reaching than Devi's claims, and anything she's ever featured on her channels. Something that could go properly viral. A way to move away from her 'eco-influencer' label and into more serious topics. A Netflix series – that's what she wants next. It's what she deserves. It's not that she doesn't believe in the environmental causes she espouses – she does – but she hasn't spent all this time building up tens of thousands of followers not to try for something bigger. Multiple income streams and an even bigger platform were the goals from the start. Maybe the fact that Alexa hasn't proved as useful as Skye thought she could be won't matter after all.

'The problem,' she says to Devi, 'is that the quality isn't good enough. It's too fuzzy, even after editing, so I can't use it on my channel.'

'If you want something clearer, then I know how to get it,' he replies.

She looks up as the sound of voices floats along the corridor outside.

'I thought you said there was no one else here?' she whispers.

Devi holds up his finger to his lips, walks over to the door, shuts it behind him as he slips into the corridor. Skye stands up and walks around the dormitory, her flip-flops making a slapping sound on the tiles.

She glances at Devi's bedside table and returns his book to where she'd found it. His passport is still there. She picks it up and opens the red cover embossed with a palm tree, moon, star and two flags. Devi Abdul Jahan. Born 13 July 1985. Thirty-eight. In the photo, he looks serious, staring straight ahead into the camera. But his face shape seems different. His nose is more aquiline. And he has a moustache. She looks more closely and something cold unfurls in her chest. The man looking back at her has brown eyes. Not green. And his skin is smooth, flawless. No mole on his cheekbone.

This man is not the Devi she has just been talking to. So who the fuck is he and why has Devi got this passport?

Footsteps echo along the corridor. She shoves the passport back and pretends to look at her phone.

'It was just one of the cleaners,' he says as he comes in. 'Forgot something from the laundry room.'

Skye smiles, hopes he can't hear her heart thudding in her chest.

'Alexa told me she saw you with Cara Hamilton,' she says.

Devi looks at her.

'I mean *with* her,' Skye says. 'Is that true?'

He hesitates. 'I thought we were here to make an agreement. About information that I have, which you need.'

His face doesn't give anything away. Skye notices him continuously rub his thumb and forefinger against one another, but his expression stays exactly the same, a polite smile and nothing more.

'We are,' she says. 'But if I do this, what are you going to get out of it?'

'Why does that matter to you?' Devi asks. 'You still get what you want.'

'I'm genuinely interested.'

Skye studies him, the quiet man with the green eyes that don't match his passport. Something slides across the bottom of her stomach as he speaks.

'Let's just say sometimes there is a need to shake things up a bit,' he says. 'I know what I'm doing, don't you worry about that. You just need to make sure you do too.'

37. 1 day 10 hours left

The man checks his watch. Harrelson is late, again. He prefers work-ing alone, dislikes these types of jobs, when he has to take someone else with him. When he's on his own, he can trust his instincts, doesn't have to take anyone else into consideration. He has enough experience to know when something isn't quite right; a feeling deep in his gut that tells him things are off.

Taking someone else means more chance of a mistake. And there's been too many of those recently, too many near-misses and things that should have been spotted earlier, although he knows Harrelson would disagree. But then Harrelson disagrees with most things. The guy is a hothead; always the first to start an argument and, quite frankly, a fucking liability.

He'd given him two weeks when he'd first started. Vincent doesn't usually tolerate loose baggage. But it turns out he's Vincent's nephew, so he's still here, two months later, a thorn in his side that he can't get rid of. In life it's not what you know, it's who you know. His dad told him that when he'd left school, and he hadn't believed him at the time. He thought it would come down to how hard he worked, but now he realizes just how true it is.

When he's by himself, he can't blame anyone else if it all goes to shit. This time it'll be down to Harrelson as well, and he doesn't trust Harrelson as far as he can throw him.

He glances at the house he's parked in front of, wonders if he's going to have to get out of the car and knock on the door. Fucking hell, Harrelson, if we agree eleven o'clock, you should be out at eleven. Sharp. Not hanging around for some more Netflix and chill with your girlfriend.

He's about to switch off the engine just as the front door opens. Harrelson walks towards him, a stupid grin on his face, bloodshot eyes staring out of his puffy face. Great. He's clearly had a few drinks as well. Just what he needs. He clicks the button to open the doors.

'All right?' Harrelson asks.

The man nods. He's not, but he's not about to tell Harrelson that. It'll just make the situation worse, and they should have left ten minutes ago.

'Get in,' he says. 'Let's go.'

38. 1 day 9 hours left

Zach rolls over in bed, slides his hand over the sheet into the space where his wife should be. Cara isn't there. He fumbles to find the light switch; after only three days here, his subconscious hasn't yet learned the exact position of the objects in this room. He squints as his eyes adjust to the brightness. She's definitely not here. And the sheet is cold; she clearly hasn't been here for a while.

He slides his legs out from under the covers, walks over to the bathroom, pushes open the door and turns on the light, but there's still no sign of her. The frosted-glass compartment that houses the toilet is unoccupied. He peers through the glass door to the outdoor area. Five paving stones set into the sand lead to a raised stone plinth surrounded by greenery, the rain shower suspended above. No Cara.

He picks up his Apple Watch from the side of the sink where he must have left it last night, his fingers clumsy with sleep. Four a.m. The plastic strap slithers through his fingers and the watch falls face down on the marble tiles. There's a loud tap as it hits the floor. He can see immediately that the glass is shattered, dozens of thin white lines spreading out across the face from the point of impact, like a deranged spider's web.

'Shit.' He whispers the expletive under his breath and leaves the watch on the bathroom shelf. It might technically still be working, but it's useless. He can't even see the bloody time.

Alexa's bedroom door is shut as he walks into the living room; his daughter is clearly fast asleep. He stands over the glass panel in the wooden floor, the ripples on the surface of the luminescent turquoise water beneath him changing the smooth motion of the fish into jerky, unnatural movements.

Where the fuck is his wife?

He slides open the glass doors that lead out to the deck, the heat after the chill of the air-conditioning smothering him instantly like a blanket.

Thank God for air-conditioning.

Still no sign of Cara.

There is a heavy stillness in the air that unnerves him, an eerie silence, apart from the lapping of the waves. The sea stretches away to the horizon, an inky-black colour, and his stomach turns over at the thought of swimming in it now, at night, unable to see what's below him, of the terrors that lurk in the darkness.

Wouldn't she have left him a note or something to tell him where she was going? It's not like the bar or any of the restaurants will still be open. Everything shuts here by one thirty. He closes the glass doors behind him and goes back into the villa, tiptoeing across the polished floorboards in the living room so as not to wake Alexa.

One of the key cards to the villa is lying on the pile of magazines on the coffee table. Zach lifts it up, flicks through the magazines, moves the wooden fruit platter and the half-empty bottle of suncream to one side. The other key card isn't here. Cara must have taken it.

He glances across at Alexa's room. Should he wake her? Not yet. He doesn't want to worry her. This is the last thing she needs. He picks up the notepad with the Asana Fushi logo printed at the top and scribbles a short note before pulling on the T-shirt and shorts lying on the bottom of his bed.

Alexa, couldn't sleep. Just popped out to get some air.
Call me if worried. Dad x

Another lie to add to the others he's told recently. A small voice in his head asks what he's going to do if he doesn't find Cara. What if she tripped on the deck, hit her head? Fell in the sea? *Or something worse?* Her visits to her therapist don't seem to have been helping as much as he thought they would.

Anger bubbles beneath the surface of his skin. His mother warned him Cara would be hard work before they got married, that her background was too different, that she was an outsider who wouldn't be able to adapt to the Hamilton ways of doing things. He'd taken no notice at the time, but he's beginning to see what she meant.

He lets himself out of the villa, being careful to hold the handle so the door clicks shut quietly. The jetty is empty, lit up by floor lanterns placed on the ground at regular intervals, the patches of light in the water they cast filled with wriggling dark silhouettes of fish. Easily bright enough for Cara to see where she was going. He shivers and quickens his pace.

There's a woman standing with her back to him a few hundred metres away. She's paddling in the shallows, holding up the bottom of her dress, her long hair falling down her back.

Thank God.

He steps off the end of the jetty and starts to walk towards her. The water by her feet is filled with tiny lights; it's as if the stars have fallen into the sea. Each time she moves, they glow more brightly. Bioluminescence. He's heard of it – a phenomenon caused by plankton in the water when they are disturbed by oxygen – but has never seen it before. The woman laughs as she swirls around, watching the glittering display.

'Cara!'

She turns around at the sound of his voice and a man appears behind her. Zach realizes with a gut-wrenching jolt that it isn't his wife at all.

Shit.

He holds up one hand in an apology, then turns and heads back up the beach towards the jetty.

Now what? Should he go to reception and find someone to help? What if Alexa wakes up and doesn't see the note? He'd left it on the floor in front of her bedroom door, but it's easy to miss, especially if she's walking around in the dark.

Fucking hell. What is Cara playing at?

He's going to have to wake Alexa up. Explain the situation, and then they can both go and look for her. Call reception and get them to search for her too. The more people involved, the more ground they can cover. It'll be quicker and more effective than trying to do it on his own.

He starts back along the jetty, unable to drag his eyes away from the shimmering lights in the water. *Did Cara see these? Decide to go for a swim?* He looks out over the lagoon but, apart from the phosphorescence, it's merely a pitch-black expanse in which anything could be hiding.

He holds the key card up to the pad at the entrance to the villa and hears the familiar click before he pushes open the front door. As he steps inside, it's the distinctive smell of her perfume that makes something inside him go slack, a feeling of weightlessness at the realization that he's found her. Orange blossom, jasmine and rose. Gardénia by Chanel.

He reaches for the light switch, but before he can turn it on something hits the side of his head. Hard. He staggers backwards and puts his hands out, squeezes his eyes shut to try and get rid of the high-pitched whine that permeates his brain. The glow from the glass panel in the floor begins to fade, narrows to a small point, and then there is nothing but darkness.

39. 1 day 8 hours left

'Mum.'

Someone is shaking her arm.

'*Mum.*'

Cara opens her eyes. There's an odd metallic taste in her mouth. She runs her tongue over her teeth, wishes she had a glass of water. Zach is sitting on the floor next to her, his head in his hands, his back against the villa door.

'Zach?'

Her voice comes out half whispered, and he doesn't answer. Doesn't even look at her.

'Zach?' She repeats his name, but he still doesn't respond. It's as if she hasn't spoken. 'I'm so sorry. I thought you were someone else.'

She didn't mean to hurt him.

'What did you do?' Alexa digs her fingers into Cara's arm. Cara tries to pull away, but Alexa doesn't let go.

Cara looks at the chaos around her. The wooden platter that was on the coffee table, along with the net that covered it, is overturned on the floor, pieces of mango and papaya scattered by her feet like yellow Lego bricks. A model's face contemplates her accusingly from the crumpled cover of a magazine.

Her daughter's brown eyes are wide with fear. Cara's stomach flips as she remembers the last time Alexa looked at her like that, blood oozing from her leg on to their gravel drive, the smell of exhaust fumes in the air around her. She shakes her head, trying to clear the dizziness that has settled inside it.

'I couldn't sleep,' Cara says. 'I went for a walk along the jetty and then read out here when I came back. I didn't want to wake you.' She looks at Zach. 'I saw the handle of the door moving and I panicked. I thought . . . I thought someone was trying to break in.'

'You knocked me out.' Zach's voice is croaky.

'I had no idea it was you. I'm so sorry. I thought you were asleep.'

'I woke up,' Zach says, 'and realized you weren't here. So I went outside to try and find you.' He presses one hand against the side of his forehead and winces. 'Jesus Christ, Cara.'

She swallows, her mouth dry.

Her daughter is still staring at her, and she feels a hot flush spread across her face. *She doesn't believe you.* Alexa takes her hand off Cara's arm. Cara can feel Zach watching her intently, as if he thinks she's going to make a sudden movement towards him.

'Is it bad?' Cara asks.

He takes his hands away from his head and she can see a lump.

'How did you not realize it was Dad?' Alexa asks.

Cara doesn't answer. Her body feels slightly off-kilter, as if it doesn't belong to her. She looks at her feet, recognizes the red gel varnish that covers her toes, checks the brown birthmark is still there on her ankle. She sees a glance pass between her daughter and her husband, something that pushes her away, placing her firmly outside their tight circle.

'Mum?' Alexa says. 'Are you OK?'

'I'm fine.'

That glance between the two of them again.

Zach rubs his forehead. 'I was hoping this holiday would help you relax, but I don't think . . .'

'I'm fine.' Cara blocks out the image of the man with the shaved head swimming towards her on the dive, his piercing eyes looking into hers through the water.

'You say that, but you're not, are you?' Alexa says.

'I don't think . . .'

'We need to talk about it, Mum. You discuss it with your therapist, but *we* don't talk about it. You, me and Dad. I know you're still stressed about it, and . . . and it's making you do stuff you'd never normally do.'

Cara feels a wave of guilt slosh around her insides.

Please don't say anything. Please.

'I know how awful it was,' Alexa adds. 'I was there too, you know.'

Cara had thought they were going to die. That evening haunts her nightmares. The sound of the doorbell, the thud of the front door being slammed back against the wall, the three men in balaclavas pushing past her, one of them grabbing hold of Alexa as she tried to run away.

'They dragged us up the stairs, put cable ties round our wrists and ankles and pushed us into the bathroom, then took the key out of the door and locked it from the outside.' Cara's voice trembles as she tries to block out the memories of the smell of the man's cheap aftershave mixed with sweat. The feel of his hands on her skin. Alexa screaming.

'You told me,' Zach says quietly.

She hasn't told him that she still wakes up in the middle of the night, her sheets damp with sweat. For a few terrible seconds she thinks she's back in their bathroom with her ear pressed against the door, desperately trying to hear what their captors are saying.

Zach raises himself off the floor, winces as he stands up and turns his head from side to side.

'Alexa's right,' he says. 'You haven't been the same since the break-in.'

'You weren't there,' Cara snaps back. 'You have no idea how terrifying it was. I thought they were going to –'

She breaks off, her voice choked.

Zach reaches out and squeezes her hand.

'I wish I had been there. I could have protected you. And Alexa.'

Cara clenches her jaw. She'd done her best. Doesn't keeping their daughter safe every day for the first sixteen years of her life count for anything? She covers her face with her hands.

'I just keep hearing their voices in my head,' she says. 'And I know that if they hadn't broken in, we wouldn't have been arguing about the insurance a couple of weeks later and I wouldn't have stormed out of the house.' She looks up at her daughter's face. 'And I wouldn't have ended up hurting you.'

40. 1 day 8 hours left

Zach reaches for Cara's hand.

'We know you didn't mean for it to happen,' he says finally.

'I still hear them too,' Alexa says. 'The way their footsteps got louder as they came up the stairs. Their voices outside the door.' She fiddles with her helix piercing as she looks at her dad. 'After Mum managed to cut my cable ties with a disposable razor, we thought about trying to smash the bathroom window and climbing out on to the roof, but there wasn't anything we could use to break through the double glazing. And we were terrified they'd hear us before we managed to get out, and do something worse.'

Zach runs his hand over the lump on his forehead. He'd thought Cara had found out about Tori. That she'd attacked him in anger. But it's not that at all. He felt his chest expand with relief, but there's a part of him that wishes Cara did know. One less thing to hide. He's tired of trying to juggle everything but knows he can't let go of any of the balls. If one falls, they'll all come down.

'We had no idea where they were,' Cara continues, her eyes welling up. 'Sometimes we could hear voices downstairs, but we didn't know whether one of them was still sitting outside the door, listening to us whisper.'

Zach's hands are trembling. He still can't believe what his wife and daughter went through. It's the kind of thing he's used to seeing in films, not something that would happen in their house.

'I'm so sorry,' he says.

Cara blinks away tears.

'At least if the police had found them, I'd know they'd be locked up somewhere. I could feel safe. But they could be anywhere. They could come back at any time. Every time I go back to the house, I'm terrified they'll be waiting for me. I wake up at night, thinking I can hear noises downstairs.'

Zach looks at her. 'They wouldn't risk coming back.'

Cara hesitates a moment then says, 'Wouldn't they? You can't say that, Zach, because you have no idea. Did they get what they came for? They barely took anything. Didn't even ask about the safe. I know the police said they must have panicked and left because that Amazon delivery driver knocked on the door, but they aren't even sure about that. And I saw one of them through the bathroom window when they ran out, for heaven's sake. Without his balaclava. What if he saw me?'

Zach feels his face flush. Cara's right.

'I know it was awful,' he says, 'but we just need to try and move forward.'

'*We?*' Cara says. 'This isn't about you, Zach. You didn't go through that ordeal. You were safe and sound, miles away in your high-security office. You have no idea how fucking terrifying it was.' She hesitates. 'We thought they were going to kill us.'

Cara scrapes her hair off her face, gets up, puts the wooden platter back on the coffee table and starts picking up the fruit. Alexa leans down to help her. Zach notices the marks left behind; light patches on the polished wood where the acid has stripped away the colour. He rubs the back of his neck as his wife walks into their bedroom. The sky outside the glass doors has turned a pinky-orange colour, a dim light pushing away the darkness.

His phone vibrates in the pocket of his shorts, and he tenses instinctively. He's developing a Pavlovian response to the bloody thing.

The messages are getting more frequent. Any time of day or night. His wife and daughter have been through their own hell, but he's made a promise he can't back out of, and dread sits like a stone at the bottom of his stomach at the thought of what he's going to have to do to fulfil it.

41. 1 day 6 hours left

Alexa can't get back to sleep. The muffled sound of her parents' voices drifting through her bedroom wall woke her up a couple of hours ago.

Should she have said something? Told her dad?

She'd been going to – seeing her mum with Devi was surely just more evidence that they should be worried about her mental stability – but there was something about the way her mum had looked at her when they were in the spa that made her hesitate. Her mum is the only one who really understands what it was like. Terror so intense it had made every cell in her body freeze, followed by seething humiliation. Her dad says all the right things, but he wasn't there; he doesn't really know. And maybe she hadn't seen what she thought she had. Maybe she'd just seen Devi at an odd angle and it made it look like something it wasn't. How can she say something that will make her family implode unless she's a hundred per cent certain?

She scrolls through her phone, looks at what Charlie has been posting on Snapchat, sliding the screen slowly to the right to reveal his messages but not far enough for him to see she's opened them. He's not even attempting to make an effort to hide the fact that he and Sophie are now clearly together.

They deserve each other.

She whispers the words out loud but can't make herself

believe them. She wants to be like Skye, to not give a shit, but instead it feels like someone has scraped out her insides, leaving them raw.

She checks Skye's account on Snapchat and Insta, but she isn't active, hasn't been for hours. She sends her a message anyway, asks if she's awake, waits a few minutes, but there's no reply. Her brain won't switch off; even the stupid videos on TikTok fail to distract her. And it's already so hot. She kicks her sheets off to try and cool down.

She can't just lie here. She checks her phone again: 7 a.m. Still nothing from Skye.

Fuck it. She'll go and see her.

She needs to talk to someone. Her head feels as if it's going to explode. She texts her parents and tells them she's going to sit on the beach. She slides out of bed, pulls a mini-dress she'd bought on Vinted over her bikini and throws her suncream, book, towel and phone into a tote bag, before closing the door quietly behind her as she lets herself out.

She can see that the door to Skye's villa is open as she walks up the jetty, a bicycle parked outside, the basket on the front filled with cleaning equipment. She knocks, then goes inside when she doesn't get a reply. A cleaner is mopping the floor of the living room.

'Is Skye here?' she asks.

The cleaner pauses, mid-stroke, and shakes his head.

'Did she say when she'll be back?'

He smiles, shakes his head again.

Alexa bites the inside of her lip, retreats to the jetty and goes to sit on the beach. A heron struts across the sand in front of her, digging its sharp bill into the wet sand at the shoreline. She looks at the red mark on her shin. The salt water has definitely helped it to heal – it's faded to a pink colour from the vivid red it was when she arrived and the puffiness around the edges has disappeared.

She feels the heat from the sun that's emerging over the horizon, turning the sea from a royal blue to an azure colour, and remembers she hasn't yet put any suntan lotion on.

Surely it's too early in the morning to burn?

She should have worn a longer skirt. She saw a woman by the pool yesterday who had white lines in the shape of bikini straps across her back. Her dad keeps telling her how much closer to the equator they are here, how much hotter the sun is than at home, how she needs to be careful. But she knows that it doesn't matter how careful you are; sometimes the worst still happens anyway.

A hermit crab scuttles in front of her, leaving a trail of dots on the surface of the sand before stopping dead and hiding inside its shell. She picks it up and takes a photo, watches its orange claws flail frantically in the air before placing it down again. It disappears into one of the hundreds of tiny holes along the beach just as Cindy jogs towards her wearing Ryan's baseball cap, a pair of sports leggings and a neon-yellow crop top.

'Got to get out early before the heat kicks in,' Cindy says. 'How's your mum doing? Awful thing to happen on a dive.'

'She's OK,' Alexa says.

'Does she ever talk about when we used to fly?' Cindy asks. 'She always prided herself on being the best on the team. She only stopped after she had you.' She takes off her baseball cap and smooths back her hair. 'Got herself promoted to First Class in record time. Did she tell you that?'

Alexa shakes her head.

'You know, that surprises me,' Cindy replies. 'She loved telling everyone at the time.' She smiles, but her eyes are narrowed. 'Anyway, do let her know that I'm only down the jetty if she needs anything.'

'Sure will.' Alexa mimics Cindy's accent without meaning to. She shuts her eyes and lies down, pretends she's sunbathing, waits until she can no longer hear Cindy's trainers hitting the sand before sitting up again. She checks her phone, but Skye still hasn't replied.

Where is she?

Seven thirty is too early for breakfast, and Skye said she wasn't a breakfast person anyway. She'd confided that despite her Instagram posts, a double shot of espresso is the only thing she consumes before lunch. Alexa wonders if Skye has spoken to her dad, whether they've agreed to work together. She knows he's stressed about the business – he's been spending a lot of time on his phone, which is never a good sign. It's another reason she's decided not to say anything about what she saw. She doesn't want to make things any worse than they already are. Splitting up with Charlie might already have made things awkward for him.

She checks her phone once more: nothing. Skye must have gone to the restaurant. She gets up, brushes the sand off the back of her legs and heads along the sandy path in that direction. She walks past one of the gardeners, who is clipping back the bushes. Visitors only get to see the pimped-up version of the island when they're here. They go home believing they have spent a week or so going 'back to nature' but, in reality, nature isn't neat or pretty. It's brutal.

She passes the entrance to one of the beach villas, notices Devi standing in the doorway talking to someone. She shrinks back into the bushes. She doesn't want him to see her, wouldn't know what to say.

She hears a woman's voice, followed by laughter.

'Shh,' Devi says. 'I'll get fired if they find out we've been in here. I need to get the key back to reception before the next guests arrive.'

The woman emerges from behind Devi's shadow and runs her hand through her hair before she steps outside.

Alexa feels as if someone has winded her.

Skye.

Barefoot, her white-blonde hair dishevelled, she blows Devi a kiss as she walks away, carrying a pair of heels so high that even Alexa would only ever be seen wearing them at night.

42. 1 day 5 hours left

Devi hopes he's done the right thing. He'd sat in his dormitory yesterday evening, waiting for the others to come back from their shifts, wanting the buzz of chatter to distract him. It's a big risk. He could lose his job. Everything he's worked for. But his family will be better off in the long run.

Karma. A small voice whispers in his ear, but he dismisses it. What he's doing is for the greater good. *Change doesn't come without sacrifice.* Hadn't he read that in a book somewhere? But he's sick of always being the one to sacrifice something. He's done it for years, has finally had enough.

His phone buzzes.

Can you come now?

Another message from Cara Hamilton. It's eight o'clock in the morning and she only sent the request thirty seconds ago. Asking him to come and fix a blocked sink.

Give me a chance, he wants to write. *I can't always come running the minute you click your fingers.* He doesn't, of course; that would result in a summons from Marc and immediate dismissal. He's seen it happen too many times before. Sometimes it only takes a guest to make a complaint about the way one of the waiters has looked at them and the man will find himself back cleaning rooms, or worse, on a boat to Malé. And Devi is only too aware that he cannot afford to find himself on a boat to Malé, or anywhere else in fact. He needs to stay exactly where he is.

Apologies. I'm on my way.

Cara doesn't reply, but he doesn't expect her to. Any effort at communication on her side, as with all guests, stops the second they've got what they want.

He walks around the edge of the island to the jetty on the beach, submerging his feet and ankles in the crystal-clear water. Staff aren't meant to go on the beach; they are supposed to use the paths that criss-cross the centre of Asana Fushi so as to remain invisible to the guests, but at this time of the morning the resort is quiet and, if anyone asks what he's doing, he'll tell them it's an emergency and this is the quickest route.

When he started working here twelve years ago, the beach was much larger. He would have had to walk across at least another fifty feet of white sand to reach the edge of the ocean. The rate of erosion is getting faster, more sand disappearing every year. Global warming means the sea levels are rising. And it's not just Asana Fushi that's affected. It's every island, in every atoll. The local ones where tourists never visit, where many of the families of the staff live, have been hit worst of all. He's watched Skye's YouTube videos. She'd said recently that 80 per cent of the Maldives will be uninhabitable by 2050, and he has visions of thousands of people being swallowed by the ocean, one after another.

Where will everyone go?

Devi has seen the politicians' speeches about it on television, but, as Skye said, nothing ever changes.

He walks along the wooden boards of the jetty towards the Hamiltons' villa, sees Cindy Miller coming towards him, braces himself for her next request. She reaches out and puts her hand on his arm as he walks past. *Can she get a softer pillow? She's tried the ones Marc sent over, but none of them are any good. Perhaps he can bring a selection, so she can find one that suits her best?* He grits his teeth, assures her that he'll bring some as soon as he's finished this task.

He watches her walk away as he knocks on Cara's door, unsure what to say when she answers. Should he pretend nothing happened? He imagines that's exactly what she's going to want him to do, particularly if her husband is there.

Cara opens the door and Devi fixes his well-practised for-the-tourists smile on his face.

'Thanks for coming,' she says, beckoning him inside. 'The sink floods as soon as I turn on the tap.'

Devi wants to ask why it's so urgent, why she doesn't just use the other one, or the one in her daughter's bathroom, but swallows the question as he follows her through the villa carrying a sink plunger and toolbox. He wonders where her daughter is. And her husband, for that matter. She seems to spend a lot of time on her own.

He runs the tap for a few seconds, then turns it off again.

'Looks fine to me,' he says.

'The basin just overflowed,' Cara says. 'I think it's blocked.'

Devi gets out the plunger, pumps it up and down a few times, then turns the tap on again, watches the water drain away through the plughole.

'I don't think there's anything wrong with it now,' he says. He tries not to think about the images he has of her in his head: her pale skin against her red swimming costume, her hair spread out over the lounger cushion.

'Great.' She presses one hand to her chest as he picks up his toolbox, water from the plunger dripping on to his arm.

'I have a few more jobs to get done, so I should go,' he says, and turns to walk out of the room. He already has a list of over twenty requests on WhatsApp and will have to work until ten o'clock tonight to get everything finished.

'Devi?' Cara says quietly.

He turns around.

'About before.'

He keeps the smile fixed on his face.

Don't respond.

Cara hesitates. 'I mean what happened out on the deck.' She looks down at the floor, refuses to meet his eyes. 'I trust that we can just move on and that we don't need to mention it again?'

He realizes this is really why she asked him to come over.

These people. Who do they think they are?

His face burns as he thinks of Asma; he should have refused Cara's advances. Extricated himself politely from the situation. He wishes he could go and dive into the sea, wash himself clean.

He waits for Cara to look at him, notices the spots of colour on her cheeks.

'Of course, Mrs Hamilton.' His voice is clipped.

'Cara, please.' She smiles as she adjusts the rope belt on her dress.

Devi looks at her standing there in her designer dress, the baguette diamond on her engagement ring catching the light. What she's wearing is likely worth more than his annual salary.

'Do you remember me talking about my daughter?' he asks.

Cara nods. 'How is she? Didn't you say she wasn't well?'

'Imani is still not great, to be honest with you. My wife has been taking her to the medical clinic, but . . .' He hesitates.

If he does this, there will be no going back.

'. . . but it's expensive for us,' he adds.

Cara frowns. 'You have to pay?'

'Not for the treatment itself,' he replies. 'But each time Imani is in the hospital, we have to pay for my wife to travel to Malé, and for accommodation.'

He puts the plunger on the floor, pulls out his phone and shows Cara a photo Asma sent him a couple of days ago. Imani with her nose buried in a pink rose, Finifenmaa, the Maldivian national flower.

'She's very sweet,' Cara says.

Devi puts his mobile back in his pocket.

'The thing is, Mrs Hamilton . . .'

'Cara, please.'

He swallows. 'The thing is, Cara, I'm raising money to cover Imani's treatment costs. And I would really appreciate anything you felt able to give. And, of course, I would ensure what happened stayed confidential. Just between us.'

'I'm not sure if I . . .'

She trails off, realization dawning. Devi waits to see whether his gamble has paid off, whether he needs to make it clearer what he's asking her for. 'Blackmail' is such an ugly word; he hopes he doesn't have to use it.

'I can give you some money,' she says slowly. 'For Imani,

I mean. So your wife can stay with her and not have to worry about the cost.'

Devi nods, briefly.

Cara wraps her arms around herself. 'I need to talk to my husband about the logistics, but I'll speak to him when he comes back later.' She hesitates. 'You're like me, Devi: you'd do anything for your child. I know it's crass to talk figures, but would two thousand be acceptable?'

'Pounds?'

He nods. It would take him six months to earn that amount.

Cara twists her wedding ring around on her finger. 'I'll let you know when I've spoken to Zach.'

She doesn't follow him as he walks out of the villa and steps into the dazzling sunshine. He wonders if it is a sign that things are moving in his favour for once. He crouches down on the edge of the jetty to fasten his shoelace and Cindy Miller walks past him again. He smiles as he says a polite good morning and tells her he's just off to get a selection of pillows for her.

His phone buzzes and he looks at the WhatsApp message.

I'm going to do it. Change doesn't come without sacrifice.

It wasn't a book he'd read those words in at all. The message is from Skye and it's one of her motivational quotes. He just hopes they both know what they're doing.

43. 1 day left

'Looking forward to reeling in something big later?'

Cara watches Marc pat Zach on the shoulder as they eat lunch in Murika. The outdoor tables overlooking the beach are covered in long white linen tablecloths that brush against the sand. Her husband turns around in his wicker chair, a forkful of champakali nimki halfway to his mouth.

'Can't wait,' he replies.

'Great.' Marc points at Zach's face. 'You hit your head on something?'

Zach touches the still-swollen lump with his fingertips.

'Bathroom door. Walked into it in the dark. Looks worse than it is.'

Marc raises his eyebrows. 'Ouch. I'll meet you on the jetty at four. No need to bring anything, I'll make sure the staff have everything ready.'

Cara waits for Marc to walk away, takes a sip of her sparkling water, wishes it was something stronger as she leans back against the taupe cushions. She fiddles with a strand of coir that has unravelled on the edge of her coaster.

'You're still going, then?' she asks.

Zach's plate is almost empty and she's barely touched her turbot. Zach seems to inhale his food, always desperate to move on to the next thing.

'I promised Marc,' he says.

'I've hardly seen you today. You disappeared early for a run and you've been at the pool all morning. We aren't exactly spending much time together.'

'Sorry.' He pushes his knife and fork together on his plate. Cara winces at the scraping sound. 'I thought you wanted to be on your own today,' he adds. 'Catch up on some sleep.'

The mineral water fizzes uncomfortably on her tongue. 'I'm not ill, Zach.'

He hesitates, changes the subject. 'I'll be back for dinner at seven thirty. And tomorrow we've got our private-island picnic so we'll get to spend the whole day together. I asked Marc to sort us out a table at the teppanyaki place for dinner tonight. Will Alexa want to come?'

Cara shrugs. 'I don't know. I'll ask her when I see her. She's been out all morning, but I told her not to go snorkelling unless she had someone with her. Didn't you see her when you were at the pool?'

Zach shakes his head. Cara takes another mouthful and then signals to the waiter that she's finished, despite leaving half of her lunch untouched. The thought of having to ask Zach for money has killed her appetite.

'She's probably with Skye.' Zach blots a couple of drops of sesame oil off the tablecloth with his napkin. 'I'm glad they've been spending time together. I'm hoping some of Skye's ambition and work ethic rubs off on her.'

Cara inwardly raises her eyebrows. They're supposed to be here to relax. Not for Alexa to plan her future career. Sometimes she wonders how she and Zach have stayed married for so long when they no longer seem to want the same things. At least he hasn't mentioned what happened last night. She feels terrible, but Zach's way of dealing with anything difficult has always been to sweep it under the carpet and pretend it never happened.

She swallows. 'I need to ask you something,' she says.

'Yes?'

'It's about Devi.'

For a moment, her husband's gaze clouds over and she realizes he's lost interest before she's even asked the question.

'What about him?' His eyes slide away from hers, searching the restaurant behind her, and she knows he's looking for a waiter to ask for the tab.

'I told him we'd give him some money. His daughter's not well and he has to pay for his wife to travel to the hospital and for accommodation in Malé whenever she needs treatment. I said we could help.'

Zach clicks his fingers, mimes writing with a pen and then holds his thumb up.

'I'll tip the guy when we leave,' he says. 'I'm sure we can add on a few extra quid.'

Cara takes another sip of her drink.

'No, I mean enough to help him properly.'

Zach frowns.

'How much were you thinking?'

She swallows. 'Two thousand.'

'Rufiyaa?'

The waiter puts a black leather folder on the table with a paper slip inside. Zach checks the total, adds a gratuity and then signs his name by his room number. He nods at the waiter, who takes the folder away.

'No,' Cara says. 'Pounds.'

Zach looks at her. 'Don't be ridiculous, Cara. We're not giving that kind of money to a stranger.'

'He's not a stranger.'

Zach briefly shuts his eyes. 'Fine, the man who cleans our room.'

'He's not a cleaner, either.'

Zach lowers his voice. 'Our personal concierge, butler – whatever the fuck you want to call him. I'm sorry, Cara, but no, we are not doing that.'

She opens her mouth to speak, but he holds up his hand.

'Firstly, contrary to what you seem to think, we are not made of money. We can't afford to hand out cash to people we barely know. And secondly, you don't have any idea if what he's told you is true. For all you know, it might be a story he tells all the guests.' He leans across the table, puts his hand over hers. 'I know you want to help him, Cara. And that's admirable. It really is. But I think you need to ask yourself if you're in the best frame of mind right now to be able to make sensible judgements about things.'

She feels as if he's slapped her.

'I've already told him we'll do it.'

He looks at her, and she feels the connection between them loosen.

'Well, you'd better just untell him then, hadn't you?'

Zach stands up and walks away without waiting for her to follow. She watches him go, wonders if the couples who are still eating are watching her, whether they've overheard the argument.

Zach hadn't even blinked when he'd signed for the tab. Eight of those lunches would add up to the same amount that she's agreed to give Devi. She can't afford not to pay him, can't risk what might happen if she doesn't.

She pulls out her mobile, opens WhatsApp and sends Devi a message.

Meet me by the hammock swing on the beach at 9 p.m.

44. 21 hours 30 minutes left

Skye rubs a palmful of Natural Elements suncream over her face and neck. The boutique shop has recently started selling tins of it, something else she'll mention in her magazine article. It's a shame most guests still seem to prefer using the more well-known brands in plastic bottles which can't be recycled and whose contents leave behind 25 per cent of their chemical ingredients in the water. People have no idea of the damage oxybenzone and octinoxate cause the reef – increasing its susceptibility to bleaching and deforming baby corals. She's asked the diving centre to put up a notice about it, but the staff said they needed to check with Marc first.

How will things change unless people are forced to take notice?

She pulls on her rash vest before double-checking she's got everything she needs in her dry bag, scrolls through the contacts on her phone and types a quick message.

Leaving now. Will let you know when it's done.

She picks up her bag – it's heavier than she expected – and heads across the beach to the diving centre. Ryan Miller is sitting on one of the guest sofas just inside the entrance.

'I was hoping to bump into you,' he says. 'I've got what you asked for.'

'Really?'

'A hundred per cent.'

'You're kidding me. How did you manage it?'

'I'll tell you once you've seen it. Is now a good time?'

Skye hesitates. 'I've actually got a kayak booked for the next couple of hours, but we can catch up when I get back?'

He pulls off his baseball cap. She catches a glimpse of his pale scalp through the thinning strands before he shoves it back on.

'Did you hear about what happened to Cara Hamilton on the diving trip?'

Skye nods.

'I just wanted to say . . . I had nothing to do with it.' Ryan scratches a patch of sunburn on his shoulder. 'I was drunk the other night on the beach after your birthday drinks. Hammered, in fact. Sorry the conversation got a bit heated. I was only messing around when I said I was going to get back at Zach. I was just sounding off about him avoiding me. That's all.'

Skye studies him. 'If you say so.'

'I'm telling the truth.'

'I never said you weren't. Look, Ryan, I'm only inter-ested in what you said you could get me. Nothing else. Let's just focus on that, shall we? I'll come and find you when I'm back.'

She glances at the coffee table beside him.

'And don't forget your sunnies.'

The staff barely glance at her as she searches through the hangers suspended from a horizontal metal pole at the side of the small room. Most of the life vests are way too big; they've been made for six-foot-tall bulky blokes and will swamp her slim five-foot-five frame. *Don't say they haven't got any left*. She unhooks the last one from the rack, tries it on. It's a bit on the small side when the plastic buckle is clipped shut, but better than nothing. She'd wanted one in blue or black, rather than this lurid neon-orange colour, but hopefully she'll be too far away for him to see her. The nylon is still damp from the last wearer and smells slightly musty, a mix of seawater and men's aftershave. Thank God she wore her rash vest.

She swings the dry bag over her shoulder and walks down to the edge of the water to where several jet-skis, paddleboards and kayaks are lying on the sand.

'*Ba'ajjeveri haveereh*, Miss Elliot!'

One of the staff waves at her, and she waves back, points to one of the kayaks. The man nods and holds up his thumb in response and helps her drag the kayak across the sand and towards the sea. He holds the back to keep it steady while she climbs into the seat and carefully lowers her bag inside. She grabs hold of the paddle as he pushes the kayak to set her off, feels the weight of it in her hand as she floats away from the shore.

Perspiration drips down her forehead as she checks her watch, praying she's timed this right. The sun sparkles on the surface, creating spots of dancing light. She adjusts her sunglasses and lowers the paddle into the shallow water. The kayak glides smoothly across the calm area of the lagoon, but she knows it will be a different story when she gets beyond the reef. The waves are choppier further out and it takes more effort to keep upright. The last thing she needs is to tip over. Her life jacket will keep her afloat, but if the contents of her bag end up in the water, they won't stay dry for long and this trip will be a waste of time.

What does she always tell her followers? Breathe. You've got this.

She loves being in this place. It reminds her of her dad. He had left school at sixteen and worked in construction all his life but spent every spare moment of his free time with her on one of the beaches near where they lived in Sydney. Manly, Narrabeen, Tamarama: anywhere it was possible to surf. She'd been able to stand up on a board since she was five. He'd died two years ago, aged forty-eight. Killed by mesothelioma caused by breathing in asbestos fibres in one of the building sites he'd worked on.

He's the reason she started her YouTube channel in the first place. People need to understand the symbiotic relationship they have with the environment. See that the damage they cause now will only come back later to haunt them. They should do better, take more responsibility. But she's realized that trying to change things from the bottom up takes too long. It's only those at the top, those with the most power, who can really make a difference. At the end of the day, money still talks the loudest. And she'll do whatever it takes to have both.

The kayak cuts through the water as she lifts and lowers the paddle: left, right, left, right. Her shoulders ache as Asana Fushi's beach shrinks to a slim white line. She rests the paddle in front of her and checks her watch again. Any time now. If she's planned this right.

She reaches down and undoes the clips on her dry bag, finds her dad's binoculars and pulls the strap over her head, wishing he was still here to be able to see her do this. He'd support her, she knows he would. He was the one who taught her about Robert Swan, whose famous quote is still emblazoned on the banner of her YouTube channel: 'The greatest threat to our planet is the belief that someone else will save it.' She's just incorporating his philosophy into something that will be more effective in the long run. Sometimes you have to tear down before you can build up; ironically, Alexa had the right idea.

A small cloud passes overhead, a brief respite from the sun. She should have brought a hat. She'd thought there would be more of a breeze once she got out over the reef, but there's hardly any wind at all. She can feel the stillness, can see the horizon shimmering through waves of heat. Maybe that will make this easier. She waits, checks her watch again.

Be patient.

A movement catches her attention, and she looks through the binoculars. A boat is pulling away from the jetty of Asana Fushi. The one she's been waiting for. She wipes the sweat off her forehead and looks again. Marc is standing in the cabin. She adjusts the focus so his face is clearly visible, his slicked-back hair, the pale blue linen shirt he always wears. It's definitely him.

She opens the dry bag again, checks she has everything ready.

The boat moves away from the jetty, staying between the poles that act as markers to stop it running aground on the coral. It should pass by to the left of where she is now if Marc follows the route Devi said he would, but she needs to make sure she's in exactly the right position.

She paddles forwards for thirty seconds, then looks through the binoculars again. She can see several large green refuse bags on the deck.

Not much longer.

As she adjusts the binoculars to zoom in, she realizes

there is someone else on board. Another man. Dark hair, greying at the edges. Stubble. Glasses. Laughing at something Marc has said. Zach bloody Hamilton.

What the fuck is he doing there?

She lets the binoculars drop so they're hanging from the strap and thinks of Alexa, of what this will mean for her.

You don't owe her anything.

She looks again at the boat, half-formed ideas crystallizing into something more solid in her head. A chance to bring down two birds with one stone. A double exposé. It's not what she was expecting, but this is one of those opportunities that comes along rarely in life.

Change requires sacrifice.

It's one of her favourite mottos – and she'd never said the sacrifice had to be on her part.

45. 21 hours left

He'd dropped Harrelson back at his house, given Vincent an update, and is now on his way home, a six-hour drive. There had been a point during the job when he'd wondered if Harrelson had been about to kick off, but he thinks his raging hangover made him think twice and it'd gone without any complications. They had made it to the agreed location despite leaving late and had exchanged the bag in the boot of the Mercedes for another one with different contents. Vincent was happy. Some good news to cheer him up after his failure to elicit any useful information from that receptionist earlier this week.

He makes a video call to Marie when he stops at one of the motorway service stations to let her know he's on his way, sees his son, who is off school with a cold, wave at him from where he's sitting on the sofa playing on his Nintendo Switch, wishes he was there with them rather than driving halfway across the country again.

This feeling of dissatisfaction is something he isn't used to. He knows something hasn't been quite right for the last few weeks, but he hasn't been able to put his finger on exactly what it is. Some of his more recent encounters, which have required a certain level of persuasion, have been playing on his mind. He keeps seeing their faces. Or what's left of them. Marie's content, oblivious to the reality of what he does, and his son seems happy too, although he gets to see him so rarely he can't be completely sure. Maybe that's the problem — the demands of this job mean he's constantly having to travel, is never at home.

There are factors that, up until now, have compensated for it. The money is a thousand times better than anything he'd earn doing anything else; his mortgage was paid off years ago and he gets a brand-new car every few months. But this job isn't something he can just quit and then decide to do something else. Certainly not for the kind of people he does it for. Vincent wouldn't let him.

So, is he just going to carry on doing it for ever?

If he gets enough money together, he could retire. He dismisses the thought as soon as it flashes into his head, but it keeps coming back; a niggle in his brain as the Mercedes purrs on down the motorway, rain lashing against the windscreen.

46. 21 hours left

Cara had stopped in at the boutique on her way back to their overwater villa; all white walls and individual items arranged on floating glass shelves with no prices on display. The kind of place she never would have dared to go into when she was younger, staffed by sales assistants who only had to look at what she was wearing to know she couldn't afford to be there. Today, one glance at her Heidi Klein maxi dress, which no one would ever guess she didn't actually own, and she's offered a glass of Prosecco while she browses. She'd ended up buying a pair of polished shell earrings that she didn't really like and probably wouldn't ever wear because she felt sorry for the woman standing behind the counter. Having to pretend to be nice to people in ninety-degree heat while standing on her feet all day must be worse than being a butler.

She's thinking about whether she can give the earrings to her mother-in-law as a going-home present when she meets Cindy walking down the jetty.

'Bought anything nice?' Cindy points at the small paper bag she's carrying.

'Just some earrings.'

'You can't beat decent accessories,' Cindy says.

'They're not for me,' Cara says. 'They're –'

'You always used to wear expensive jewellery when we flew,' Cindy interrupts, before she has a chance to finish.

'Did I?' Cara knows that isn't true. She'd hardly had any money back then. Had shopped for outfits in Dorothy Perkins and bought make-up from the bargain counter in Boots.

'You always looked so *together*. Perfect. All the crew loved you. A right little Miss Popular.' Cindy laughs, but Cara feels an undercurrent of something sharp and bitter beneath her words. 'How are you feeling now?' Cindy continues. 'After the dive?'

Cara shrugs. 'No lasting effects. Guess I was lucky.'

Cindy's smile twists. 'I guess you were.' An awkward silence follows, and Cara points along the jetty to their villa.

'I should probably –'

'Yes, me too. I've arranged to meet Ryan at the pool.' Cara watches Cindy walk away, a small kernel of suspicion sitting like a hard lump beneath her skin.

Zach has left for his fishing trip by the time Cara gets back. She sits down on the sofa in their living room, welcomes the coolness of the air-conditioning as she texts Alexa.

What time will you be back, and are you eating with us tonight?

She'll be lucky to get a response. If her daughter texts her, Alexa expects an answer immediately, as if Cara has her phone constantly in her hand, poised to respond at all times. But it doesn't work the other way around.

She checks WhatsApp to see if Devi has replied to her request to meet and sees he has sent a thumbs-up emoji. She scans through his Facebook posts, sees photo after photo of Imani, the little girl growing younger as she scrolls back. There's a part of her that empathizes with what Devi is doing. She'd do the same in his situation. Your child comes first, no matter what. Despite Alexa sometimes testing her patience to the limit, there's nothing Cara wouldn't do for her.

Unlike Devi, they haven't had to worry about money since Zach's business took off about ten years ago. Not like when she was growing up. Her mother had stuffed five-pound notes into envelopes in a biscuit jar on the kitchen counter to try and budget for all the bills: electricity, gas, food, petrol, the Kays catalogue, multiple credit cards. A juggling act, moving money from one place to another, putting off paying anything until the last possible moment.

Marrying Zach has allowed her to step out of her old life and into a shiny new one where cash is rarely seen, cards are used for everything, and money exists as a concept, something they can access whenever it's needed. A life in which she isn't always holding her breath, waiting for the next bill to arrive. A bank account that never runs into overdraft, investments in multiple equity funds, school fees, a gardener and a cleaner twice a week, shopping deliveries from Abel & Cole and Waitrose, long-haul holidays three times a year and several donations to various eco-charities to offset their carbon footprint. She is fully aware she has nothing to complain about. But sometimes it doesn't stop her hating her life. And herself – for letting it ensnare her, for being something she can't relinquish.

She looks up at the sound of a ringtone from Alexa's room.

Why hasn't she taken her mobile with her?

She opens the door to her daughter's bedroom, sees the clothes folded up in a neat pile on the chair. She bets the cleaner did that – Alexa would have dumped them on the floor.

She has a horrible feeling that she should have tried to be stricter, should have imposed a set of rules a long time ago, but it's too late for that now. Once you reach a certain point, it's impossible to go back. And Alexa's friends are no different. That's part of the issue. All of them competing silently with the latest iPhone, the most expensive designer trainers, allowances that are so generous it means they are out in different bars with fake IDs every Friday and Saturday night, and booking Ubers on their parents' debit cards to get home afterwards.

Cara knows they have lectures in Alexa's school assemblies on worthy causes; they hold mufti days and donate to various different charities, but getting her daughter and her friends to appreciate the value of money is like trying to get a magnet to stick to a wooden surface. None of the teenagers in the exclusive club Alexa was born into understand what it's like to go without. If they want something, they get it. It's as simple as that.

She can't see Alexa's phone anywhere. It's not on her bed, where her sheets have been smoothed out and tucked in neatly. Or on her dressing table, or her chest of drawers. *Where is it?* She calls her number, waits. Listens. Nothing. The silence echoes around her and she shivers. It can't have been Alexa's phone she heard.

So what was it?

Since the break-in, she hates being on her own. She used to revel in the peace and quiet, but now every sound puts her on edge, sends adrenaline spurting through her veins and flashes of terrifying memories through her brain.

If she shuts her eyes, she can still see the man she'd glimpsed for just a few seconds without his balaclava. She'd watched him pull it off as soon as he got out of their back door, shoving it into his pocket so as not to draw attention to himself. He'd glanced up briefly at the bathroom window and she'd stood frozen, looking back, unable to move. A short buzz cut covered his head. Dark eyes. Or perhaps they weren't dark at all; perhaps her brain had filled in his features and she hadn't really seen him at all. The image slips away before she can focus on the details, morphs into someone else. Sometimes he seems familiar, but she's thought about him so many times, sees him so often in her nightmares, it's not surprising.

The ringtone again. It's coming from under Alexa's bed. She bends down, looks across the polished wooden floorboards. Not a speck of dust, and no phone. She slides her hand under the mattress and along the bedframe, stopping when she hits a solid object. She pulls it out, rumpling the neatly tucked-in sheet.

An iPhone X. But not Alexa's. Zach's.

On the lock screen, covering part of the photo of Zach with his arm around Alexa's shoulders, there's a message. Cara reads it, notes who it is from, and icy tentacles unfurl inside her, freezing everything they touch until she can't breathe. After nineteen years together, she thought she knew her husband. Inside and out. The good and the bad. Not perfect, but then, who is? She blinks, then reads the last part of message again to be certain she hasn't imagined it.

Have you told her yet, Zach? Tick, tock. She's going to find out sooner or later.

The phone asks for a passcode when she tries swiping up. She types in Zach's birthday, but her attempt is rejected. He must have changed it, and she doesn't need three guesses to understand why. She reads the whole message once more, adrenaline pumping through her body, and everything suddenly falls into place, like those red and yellow discs dropping into the grid in the Connect 4 game she used to play with Alexa when she was little.

47. 20 hours 45 minutes left

Alexa stumbles as she lets herself into the storeroom at the back of the diving centre, hits her knee against the wooden door as she takes the almost-empty bottle of Chablis out of her bag. She'd bought it earlier this afternoon, had flashed a smile at the barman and told him it was for her mother. She'd asked him to charge it to their villa and had left the empty chilled glass he'd offered sitting on the counter.

After seeing Skye, she had run back down the path and spent the morning sitting on the beach scrolling through TikTok, tears blurring her vision.

How could she have been so stupid?

She had thought Skye had been interested in her and what she had to say; she had even confided in her. And all the time she must have been laughing at her. And her mum. Devi too, probably – both of them thinking how dumb they were. She wonders how many other guests Devi has seduced, whether it's something he boasts about to the other staff. A competition to see who can pull the most. It wouldn't surprise her. What if her mum had been asleep on that lounger? What if she hadn't even realized what Devi was going to do?

Her whole body burns with humiliation. The memory of Skye walking out of the door, a high-heeled shoe dangling from either hand, flicking her hair and blowing Devi a kiss, keeps replaying over and over in her head.

Why had Skye even bothered to try and make friends with her in the first place?

That's what Alexa can't understand. She'd made the first move, but she hadn't forced Skye to reciprocate. Skye had asked *her* to help her with that video; Skye had asked *her* to go for a drink with her. Alexa hadn't pestered her.

She had wandered down to the lagoon and sat in the warm shallows at the edge, feeling the sting of the salt on the scar on her leg. She'd scooped out fistfuls of wet sand and squeezed them until the grains dug into the soft skin under her fingernails, making her wince, before falling asleep on the lounger.

When she'd woken up, the shock had been replaced by an edgy twitchiness, the memories that had been playing on a repeat loop fading enough for her to contemplate what to do next. She'd walked over to the outdoor cinema, grabbed some popcorn and dozed on the beanbags in the shade, half watching *Shutter Island* flicker across the screen while feeling her blood pulse in time with her heartbeat.

Devi needs to be taught a lesson.

She'd drunk most of the wine by then, swigging straight from the bottle as the film rolled on for the second time, ignoring the looks from the couples sitting on beanbags nearby. Concern? Disgust? She wasn't sure and, either way, she was past caring. By the time Teddy was being taken for a lobotomy, she'd shoved the bottle into her bag and had known exactly what she was going to do.

The storeroom is dimly lit and smells slightly musty. Several old wetsuits hang on pegs on the wall waiting to be recycled, a couple of toolboxes have been left on a workbench and five paddleboards are stacked on top of each other. It must be here. This is where they keep all the water-sports equipment that they use on the beach: the kayaks, the windsurfing boards and the jet-skis.

She squints into the gloom and sees what she's looking for on the other side of the room. She walks over to the red plastic can, unscrews the lid and sniffs. Petrol. She downs the last remaining dregs of the Chablis and attaches the flexible nozzle to the can to form a spout, her hands slipping clumsily while she tries to screw it on. *Maybe she shouldn't have drunk all the wine? Too late now.* She shoves one end of the nozzle into the top of the empty bottle and lifts up the petrol can, her head buzzing with the effort. The clear liquid gradually inches up the sides and she doesn't manage to get the hose out in time before some of it spills over the top on to the storeroom floor. She coughs as the pungent smell fills the space.

She hasn't got anything else to wipe the bottle on, so uses one of the old wetsuits, but the neoprene isn't particularly absorbent and it ends up on her hands. She closes the can and leaves it by the wall, screws the cap on the wine bottle and leaves, checking there isn't anyone outside the storeroom before emerging into the bright sunlight.

The heat combined with the alcohol makes her stumble as she walks across the empty white sand to the sea. She sticks the bottle into the water and tries to wash the smell of petrol off her hands before putting it back in her bag, but it clings to the back of her throat and she can taste it each time she takes a breath.

Wiping her wet hands on her dress, she glances at the messages her mother has left on her phone. The small letters blur in front of her eyes. She can't face the thought of an evening in her parents' company, and she wants to avoid seeing Skye or Devi.

He needs to learn that actions have consequences. She repeats the sentence under her breath as she marches up the beach, one word for each step, until she reaches the restaurant, her mouth dry and bitter from the Chablis. She smiles at the waiters as she makes her way over to the small storage room to the side where Skye had told her Devi keeps his equipment for the show.

A black tunic and a pair of trousers are hanging up on the back of the door, dozens of various stainless-steel chains suspended from hooks on the wall. At the bottom of each chain pieces of thick rope are wound into various different shapes: knot balls, stars and cubes.

And then she spots what she is looking for. Gloves. Long, black fingerless ones that reach up past the elbow with the Asana Fushi logo stitched on the back of the hands. She glances at her watch. Just over three hours to go until the show. She unscrews the cap on the wine bottle and holds one of the gloves over the mouth, then tips the bottle so the liquid soaks into the fabric. Then she returns the gloves to the same position on the shelf and opens the small window a couple of inches to let the smell disperse.

That'll teach him.

48. 20 hours 45 minutes left

The kayak rocks in the slight swell from the breeze that has just started to pick up, a sharp relief from the sweltering heat. Skye braces herself as she tries to keep the camera steady. Usually, she films everything on her phone – it's a more effective way to mimic the feeling of *real life* for her followers – but she needs a more powerful zoom this time to capture what she's after.

She can still see Marc and Zach on the deck of the boat, but isn't sure if they've spotted her. Even if they've noticed her kayak, she's pretty sure they haven't realized she's the one in it. Not yet, anyway. They're too busy drinking. *Does Zach have any idea what's going on?* She wants to believe he doesn't. It violates everything he stands for. She knows there are compromises to be made in every business; she's held her nose and promoted the occasional product she didn't approve of when the money was good enough, but Zach's moral compass appears fundamentally faulty. The odd questionable decision is one thing, but blatant hypocrisy is quite another.

Ryan had told her the rumours circulating about Zach's business the night he'd arrived. He claimed Zach had invested a significant sum in Sheimark, a fast-fashion company which had recently declared profits of fifteen billion dollars. That had been before the explosive Netflix documentary which exposed their appalling record on workers' rights and the high levels of toxic chemicals in their products, but even so. And, of course, their share price had plummeted afterwards. Along with the value of Zach's investment. And then there were the cashflow issues Ryan had hinted at on another of Zach's projects.

She'd thought Ryan was just gossiping. One businessman with a big ego having a dig at another. She hadn't believed that Zach would be stupid enough to do something like that. Cashflow issues were one thing, but throwing money into a company that was the antithesis of everything his brand stood for was quite another. She hadn't wanted to believe it, either. She'd got on better with Zach than she'd expected to. When they'd had drinks together, she could see why Cara had fallen for him. He'd focused solely on her, had made her feel like the only person in the room. The kind of guy she could have seen herself going for, if he hadn't been married.

She'd told Ryan to get proof. Solid, irrefutable proof. What was it Alexa had said? *My family isn't as perfect as you think.* She'd assumed they were just the words of a disgruntled teenager, but maybe there was more to it than that.

Zach looks happy enough talking to Marc at the moment. The two of them can't stop laughing. It turns her stomach. Marc is another corrupt individual taking the guests at the resort for fools. And she's going to prove it.

The top of her life jacket rubs against the side of her neck above her rash vest. She circles her shoulder to try and move it, but doesn't risk letting go of the camera in case she misses something. She takes a few slow, deep breaths like she used to before getting on her surfboard, envisaging the oxygen flowing through her muscles, easing the burning sensation.

She wishes again that her dad was here. She remembers, a spasm in her gut as she does so, how he had struggled with every single breath towards the end. And he isn't the only one to have suffered from a disease that could have been prevented. Air pollution kills five thousand people a year in Australia, and deaths from mesothelioma are the second highest there in the world.

In her experience, people want to help, but small changes aren't enough. She needs to do something that will make people really sit up and take notice, something that might even nab her a Netflix series. And this is the perfect opportunity.

She watches Zach finish his beer through the zoomed-in camera lens. He throws his empty glass bottle into a plastic trug on the deck. She keeps the video recording, adjusts the focus, and waits. Marc says something, but although she can see his lips move she can't make out what he's saying.

Can you get the bait? Get the beer?

She's normally good at lip-reading, years of practice trying to work out what her dad was saying when they were surfing, his words often whipped away by the wind or the waves. She sees Zach hesitate, then pick up one of the green refuse bags from the deck and pass it to Marc before disappearing inside the cabin.

Her heart thuds in her chest.

She continues to video as Marc hesitates, glances towards the cabin, then hoists the bag up with both hands, balances it on the handrail that runs around the edge of the deck then pushes it over the edge into the ocean. He does the same thing again, and again, until three large bags are floating in the water.

Skye watches them bob around on the surface for a minute or two before they sink out of sight. She has to swallow down the urge to start paddling and recover them. She knows what's in them. Rubbish. From Asana Fushi. Marc is supposed to take it to Thilafushi, an island specifically set up to manage waste from all the resorts in the Maldives. But that comes at a cost, a cost that eats into Asana's profits and, more importantly for him, his bonus.

Devi had seen him dumping rubbish before. A dirty secret carried out by several of the resort managers. Most of the staff knew about it, but no one dared to report it, for fear of losing their job. The cleaner she'd spoken to had certainly known. The thought of bags full of plastic and God knows what else sinking down to the ocean floor where their contents will cause untold damage to marine life makes Skye shudder.

But now she's caught him in the act, and from the footage she's captured it looks like Zach knows exactly what Marc has been doing. She balances the camera on her knees and reviews the footage, checks she's got everything she needs.

A pang of guilt rises up from the pit of her stomach. It will destroy Alexa if she goes ahead with this, but there is something bigger at stake than a friendship. She feels sorry for the girl, but she's known her for less than a week.

She puts the camera back in the dry bag and sticks it under her seat before pulling the paddle from the elastic bungee net on the front of the kayak, where she'd put it to hold it fast.

She looks across at Asana Fushi in the distance, rolls her shoulders again, then slides her paddle into the water and glances back at the boat. The sun reflects off Zach's sunglasses, making her squint. She frowns. She can see him without using the binoculars. The boat is much closer than it was a few minutes ago.

And Marc is staring straight at her.

49. 19 hours 30 minutes left

Marc throws his empty beer bottle on top of the dozen others that are lying in the plastic trug on the deck before he turns off the engine and lowers the anchor.

'Here looks good,' he says. 'I'll set up the rods. We should get some decent mahi-mahi and tuna if we're lucky.'

Zach looks out towards the horizon. The boat is sleeker than the dhoni they went on for the diving trip. This is more modern; constructed of fibreglass, with a smooth white surface, a modern indoor cabin housing the controls with glass windows and a chrome guardrail around the deck.

Marc points over the water. 'You can still just about see Asana in the distance over there if you use the binoculars.' He hands Zach a pair and then digs around in the ice cubes in the cool box and pulls out two bottles. 'Fancy another?'

Zach thinks of the way Cara's eyebrows will rise in disapproval if he comes back hammered.

But she's not here now, is she? And after what happened last night, he deserves a few drinks.

'Go on, then,' he replies, glancing back at the cabin as he hangs the binoculars back up. 'What have you done with the rubbish bags?' he asks.

'I've stuck them in one of the storage containers at the back of the boat for now,' Marc says. 'They were starting to stink. We can drop them off in Thilafushi when we're passing, or I'll get the staff to take them over there tomorrow.'

Zach reaches into the pocket of his shorts for his phone to let Cara know he could be here a while, but it's not there. He checks his other pocket. Not there either. *Fuck*.

'You OK?'

Marc hands him a beer.

'Yeah . . . I think I left my phone in the villa. I wanted to let Cara know I might be back a bit later than I thought.'

He knows exactly where it is. He'd hidden it in Alexa's room this morning as he didn't want Cara seeing it at lunch. He'd meant to collect it when they got back from the restaurant, but in the rush to get on the boat, had forgotten. *Idiot*. At least it's locked.

Marc smiles sympathetically.

'Your wife a bit clingy? Mine used to be terrible. Always needed to know where I was, what I was doing.'

Zach hesitates. 'I didn't realize you were married.'

'Separated. Lilia and I weren't really . . . compatible.'

Zach rubs one hand over the stubble on his chin and pats Marc on the shoulder.

'Sorry to hear that.'

He takes off one of his Reef flip-flops, pushes the sole on to the top of the bottle. The metal top gives way with a hiss and he throws it into the plastic trug.

'Neat gadget.' Marc puts his hand up to shade his eyes.

Zach can see the beads of perspiration on Marc's forehead. He'd expected there to be more of a sea breeze out here, but the heat is unrelenting. At least the water is calm. Marc has been downing beers at a rate of knots, talking incessantly.

'It is,' he replies. 'You wouldn't believe how many times it's come in useful.'

Marc points at his flip-flop. 'I bet they're made out of recycled plastic or something, as well, aren't they?'

'Used rubber tyres, apparently.'

Marc shakes his head. 'No wonder you and Skye Elliot get on so well.'

'I don't really know her that –'

'She said you asked to collaborate with her. So has Ryan Miller. Looks like you've got competition.' Marc takes another swig of his beer with a smug smile. 'She was out here earlier in one of the resort kayaks. Taking more photos for her bloody magazine article, no doubt. I'm surprised she didn't come over and say hello.'

Zach cleans his sunglasses on his T-shirt, looks at Marc, then shrugs.

'Maybe she didn't want to disturb us.'

'She's a pain in the arse,' Marc continues. 'All the staff are having to bend over backwards for her. She doesn't seem to realize that the resort has to make a profit. I can't implement every single one of her environmentally friendly ideas.'

'You've got to admire her for trying,' Zach replies.

Marc takes another gulp of beer.

'She's got no idea how tight the margins at Asana are and how much pressure I'm under to deliver. If you were in my position, I bet you wouldn't say that.'

Zach laughs. 'Probably not.'

Marc turns away for a second, looks out over the ocean.

'Would you say you're a good boss?' he asks.

'You'd have to ask the people who work for me. Why?'

'I think we could help each other out.'

Zach stares at him. Desperation is oozing from every pore on Marc's face.

'Could we?' he asks, deciding to play ignorant.

Marc swallows another mouthful of beer, revealing the damp patches on his shirt as he lifts up his arm.

'I could put you in touch with my contacts out here rather than giving the information to Ryan. If you employed me, that is. Islands need to borrow money in order to build desalination plants. That's what ZH Investments does, isn't it? Finance ethical projects?'

Zach looks at him.

'It does. But now isn't the best time for me to be taking on any new staff.'

'I'm not talking about a staff role. More like a silent partner.'

Zach shakes his head.

'I'm not looking for a partner.'

He watches a deep red flush spread across Marc's face. He's beginning to wish he hadn't come on this trip.

'But I have the contacts you need.' Marc's wheedling voice reminds Zach of his mother's miniature dachshund. 'Surely you can see it's a great business opportunity? We're talking seven figures, possibly eight if things go well. It would be like printing money. I know a lot of people out here who can help make a deal run smoothly.' He hesitates. 'And also people who can stop it happening at all.'

Zach swirls his beer around in the bottle, wanting to slow his drinking pace.

Is Marc threatening him?

He reaches for the guardrail to steady himself as he

feels his head spin. *How much have they drunk?* From the number of bottles in the bin, it's definitely more than he should have had.

'I wish I could, but I can't commit to any additional expenditure right now,' Zach says. 'But I'd love to look at something on a commission basis . . .'

'I'm not a salesman.' Marc flinches as he runs his hand over his sunburnt head.

That's exactly what you are, Zach thinks. *And not a very successful one at that.*

'I know,' Zach says. 'I meant a business-development-type role. If you introduce me to your contacts and something progresses into a formal contract, I'd be happy to pay you a fee.'

Marc throws his empty bottle into the trug, leans down to pull another one out of the cool box and pops off the cap.

'I've done a lot of research on you and your business, you know,' he says.

Zach feels a flutter of fear beneath his ribcage. 'Have you?'

Marc nods, waves away a fly that lands on his arm.

'You could easily afford to pay me something up front. I just need enough to pay off my ex-wife and leave Asana. Maybe set up a small Airbnb in Europe. There's a lot at stake here. It's worth you thinking it through. Properly.'

The insinuation hovers between them as the line attached to the fishing rod makes a whirring sound, stretching tight in the water. Zach points at it, relieved by the distraction.

'I think we've caught something,' he says evenly.

'Forget the fucking fish,' Marc slurs. 'I know you, Zach

Hamilton. And I know what you're hiding.' He lurches a couple of steps closer.

Hold your ground. He's hammered. He doesn't know anything.

Zach swallows.

'Look –'

'Don't *look* me,' Marc snaps. 'It's fucking patronizing.'

The boat rocks slightly in a sudden swell and Marc staggers back against the guardrail. Zach glances out at the miles of empty ocean. No other boats nearby. Asana Fushi is a blur of green in the distance.

'Shouldn't we be heading back?' Zach desperately wishes he had his phone.

'We haven't finished our discussion.'

'I don't know what you think you know about me,' he says slowly, 'but my business isn't going through the best time. Things are quite tight at the moment.' *If only that was true.* Tight *isn't the half of it.* 'I'd love to be able to employ you,' he continues, 'but there's some stuff I need to sort out first. If we do it my way to start with, it doesn't mean things can't change in the future. If any jobs come up, I'll put you at the top of the list.'

Zach watches Marc's chest rise each time he takes a breath, sweat now dripping from his forehead on to his pale blue shirt.

Is he ill? Christ, what if he collapses out here?

'You're lying,' Marc says. 'You saw the desalination plant. Other islands are crying out for that kind of thing. And I've seen your accounts.' He hesitates, takes another swig of beer. 'You're just trying to get me on the cheap.'

Zach glances at the empty bottle in Marc's hand and takes a step backwards.

'Let me look into it a bit more when we get back to the resort,' he says, keeping his voice level. 'I'm sure we can work something out.'

Zach edges towards the fishing rods that are leaning out over the back of the boat and begins to wind in one of the reels.

Keep calm. Tell him what he wants to hear.

'How about we talk about this later over a drink?' he asks. 'Cara and I have got a table booked for dinner and I probably need to be –'

'We're the same, you and I.' Marc is slurring heavily now, his words almost indecipherable.

Zach frowns. 'What are you talking about?'

'You think you're so much better than me, but you're not. I saw you. On that app.'

'What app?'

Marc throws the empty bottle of beer in the bin and pulls out his phone.

'This one.'

Marc staggers towards him and grabs hold of Zach's shoulder, waves his phone in front of Zach's face. Zach turns his head away, trying to avoid the smell of stale beer on Marc's breath.

'You're all the same, you people,' Marc says. 'You pretend to be one thing when you're actually another.'

Zach tries to pull away from his grip.

'I've no idea what –'

'That's you, isn't it?'

Zach squints at the screen, the sun making it difficult to see anything. He can just about make out that he's looking at a photo of himself. He takes the phone out of Marc's hand and studies it more closely. It is him. His name and his photo. On Grindr. A gay dating app. Except, of course, it isn't him. He didn't set this profile up. He's never seen it before.

'I told you we're the same,' Marc says, putting his other hand on Zach's shoulder and gripping his shirt. 'I can see you're unhappy with Cara. I was miserable with my wife too, but I wouldn't have made the leap if she hadn't searched my internet history. Realized what I'd been watching.'

Zach looks at him in confusion.

'But this isn't me,' he says, pointing at the screen. 'It's someone pretending to be me.'

Marc brings his face closer to Zach's, his eyes wide. 'It's OK. You can trust me not to say anything,' he says.

'Get your hands off me.' Zach tries to pull away and Marc lets go, raises his hand in the air and curls it into a fist.

He's going to punch me.

The realization hits Zach a fraction too late. He puts one foot against the side of the boat and shoves his entire body weight forward at the same time. Marc staggers backwards, knocking into the cool box, which overturns, sending empty beer bottles, ice cubes and water skimming across the deck. Zach watches him lose his footing, his arms flailing frantically. Marc falls back, hits his head on the side of the boat and lands in a heap on the deck.

For a few seconds Zach is too shocked to move. He waits for Marc to get up, poised for another verbal onslaught, wonders if he should try and lock himself in the cabin.

But Marc stays motionless and the boat continues to sway in the water.

Zach edges towards him, pokes his arm with his flip-flop,

but Marc doesn't respond. He kneels down, puts his hand on his shoulder and shakes him, but realizes with a jolt of horror that the shadow he can see by Marc's head isn't a shadow at all – it's a pool of blood that is gradually expanding across the white deck.

50. 17 hours 40 minutes left

Alexa wakes up with a numb arm. She shakes it, but it feels as if it doesn't belong to her; it's like a piece of meat attached to her body. She braces herself as the inevitable prickling sensation of pins and needles starts to spread down the limb, bringing it back to life.

She's buried in one of the colossal blue beanbag cushions in the resort library with a pounding headache, an unread paperback discarded next to her where it's slipped off her lap, a line of dried saliva down one cheek making her skin feel tight. She can see the high ceiling above her, and the white wooden shelves lining the walls with a selection of books artistically arranged on them, small cards detailing recommendations by the staff and previous guests. She sits up, leaving a damp imprint of herself on the thick cotton, and checks her phone, her skin sticky in the evening heat.

It's 7.20 p.m. The faint smell of petrol from the bottle in the bottom of her bag lingers on her fingers, mixing with the musky aroma of the reed diffusers sitting on the bookshelves. She has five increasingly anxious texts from her mum and there's an unpleasant gnawing feeling in her stomach from having drunk too much alcohol.

Beyond the tall glass windows of the library the sun hovers just above the horizon, a ball of orange and pink that looks as if it will set the water on fire when it descends.

Normally, she'd be taking photos and posting them on Insta, but not this evening. Within a matter of minutes, the sun will have disappeared completely, and then it will be time for the first fire show. The anger she feels towards Devi is still there, a throbbing in her chest, as constant and regular as her heartbeat.

A WhatsApp message from Skye flashes up.

Hope you're coming to watch the fire show tonight?

Alexa reads it but doesn't reply. *How fucking dare she.* A minute later there's another one.

Devi's roped me in to help – he's doing something special to raise money for his daughter's hospital treatment and had me practising at the crack of dawn this morning in a pair of ridiculous heels. I've no idea how the dancers manage to wear them all night – they're agony! Do come and watch. I know he's not your favourite person at the moment, but I honestly think you didn't see what you thought you did, and I'd love you to be there. I owe you a drink for doing that video for me.

Alexa feels acid bubble up, burning the back of her throat.

Oh God. Has she got this all wrong?

She had no idea Devi had a daughter. She stumbles as she gets up, her hair knotted and damp from where she's been lying on it. The wine bottle is still half full of petrol, heavier than ever in the bottom of her bag as she pulls at the door to get out.

She needs to get the gloves.

She runs along the path that leads from the library to the restaurant, scrapes her hair back off her face into a bun, adrenaline flooding her body with each step. Strings of white fairy lights have been draped across the branches of the trees and in the vegetation either side of the path to illuminate the route, and small flying insects attracted by them keep trying to land on her. She has an acute longing for hard pavements and something other than this humid heat that presses itself up against her face, suffocating her.

The area around the restaurant is buzzing with guests. She glances quickly across the tables but can't see her mum or dad. Maybe they're not here yet. She walks around the side of the restaurant to the small storage room, but it's locked. She knocks on the door, her hand shaking, but no one answers.

Where is Devi?

The semicircular stage has been set up on the beach. Most of the thirty or so seats that have been put out on the sand are already occupied by guests so she stands at the back, looks around desperately for him.

The music starts, the familiar lyrics of Sia's 'Unstoppable' blasting out from tall speakers at either side of the stage as dancers dressed in black holding dozens of LED glowsticks perform a carefully choreographed routine. The audience begins to clap along to the pulsing beat and Alexa holds her breath as Devi appears on the stage.

The spectators cheer, some of them already up on their feet to get a better view. Alexa stands up too.

He's not wearing the gloves. Thank fuck.

Her legs buckle in relief and she collapses on to one of the empty seats in the back row. Dressed all in black to match the dancers, Devi begins to whirl the chains attached to flaming poi around in circles, then changes direction so they form dozens of different shapes. For a few minutes, Alexa forgets where she is, what she has done, entranced by his skills, the way his body moves. And then, when there is a pause in the music, she remembers and it feels as if her throat is closing up. She doesn't even have enough saliva to swallow.

A second track starts playing, and this time Devi picks up two fire fans. Each one has five lit wicks, and he spins them both around in time with the music. Everyone watching is on their feet now, whistling their appreciation.

He bows as this part of his routine finishes and hands the lit apparatus to the dancers, who take it off stage. He picks up a microphone and says, 'You want to see some more?'

Alexa sees his dimples crease as he smiles. The audience cheers its approval.

'I'm going to ask for a volunteer to come up on stage and join me.'

The spotlights are turned on to the crowd and Alexa's insides shrink. She wants to slide off her chair and hide underneath it, but that will only highlight her presence. She sits very still and hopes he won't notice her, the lights too bright to see anything.

'You!' Devi points. 'Come and join me.'

Alexa blinks, her vision still dazzled.

Is he pointing at her?

Her stomach rolls with another wave of fear and she grips the edges of the seat so hard it makes her hands hurt.

'Yes, that's it,' Devi says. 'Be careful coming up the steps.'

The spotlights swivel back to illuminate the stage and Alexa watches as a woman wearing a white dress and high heels heads up the stairs towards him. The woman walks across the stage, turns to face the audience and smiles.

Skye.

Everyone whistles and stamps their feet.

'I'm going to let you into a secret, ladies and gentlemen,' Devi says. 'This lovely volunteer is Skye Elliot. I'm sure many of you have heard of her already, due to the amazing work she does promoting environmental issues. She and I have been practising something very special for a good cause, so if you enjoy this part of the show, feel free to leave a tip in one of the buckets on the stage. Do remember not to try this at home – this is real fire, and you will get burned.'

Devi walks to the back of the stage and returns carrying a black tunic and a pair of gloves. Skye pulls the tunic over her head, twists her blonde hair up into a bun and holds out her arms. Devi slides the gloves over her wrists, pulling them up so they reach almost to her elbows.

Fuck. Oh fuck.

Alexa freezes. The music starts up again, 'Titanium' this time, and the audience starts to clap along to the beat. Devi and Skye perform a choreographed dance routine and the clapping rises to a crescendo. She knows she should say something, but it's as if she's stuck to her chair, prickles of fear crawling up her arms and across her body like dozens of tiny insects eating her alive.

She didn't mean this to happen.

A dancer appears holding two burning chains.

'These are called orions,' Devi says into the microphone. 'They're twenty centimetres long, ten centimetres wide and made of Kevlar, which has a high heat resistance. We're going to show you a couple of moves you can do with them.'

Say something.

He takes the chains from the dancer and hands one to Skye. The audience begins to clap as the music starts again. The flames engulf the Kevlar material and begin to lick up the chain towards Skye's hands.

For fuck's sake, say something.

Alexa opens her mouth, but only a whisper comes out. 'Please stop.'

Her words are swallowed up by the music and the noise of the crowd. She looks around at the people beside her, all smiling, and wishes more than anything that she could turn back the clock.

Skye begins to swing her chain in a circle and Devi copies her so their actions are synchronized. The circles change shape to fiery hearts, and everyone watching gasps. For a few seconds, everything is fine and the horror that Alexa feels squeezing her lungs starts to recede.

They can't be the same gloves.

But the flames stretch and swell just as she allows herself to hope. They crawl off the Kevlar and streak up the chain towards the glove on Skye's left hand, which erupts in a ball of fire. The audience cheers loudly, believing it's all part of the act.

It's only Alexa who sees the look of terror on Devi's face as he lets his poi fall on to the stage, grabs Skye, throws her on to the ground and covers her arm with his body.

The audience falls silent as the track plays on in the darkness, pierced at intermittent intervals by the sound of Skye screaming.

51. 17 hours 15 minutes left

Skye lies on her back and stares at the thousands of stars sprinkled across the night sky above her. If she focuses hard enough on one of the pinpricks of light, she can pretend this isn't happening. Just like she'd done with her dad when they sat on the garden steps in his final weeks. 'Look at them, Skye,' he'd rasped. 'Most of them ceased to exist a long time ago, but they're still part of our lives.' Maybe he'd meant his words to be comforting, but she'd taken them to mean that the biggest stars shine the brightest.

The lyrics of 'Titanium' cut out from the speakers and Devi's face swims into view.

'Stay calm and don't move,' he says. 'Someone's getting the first-aid kit.'

She feels his hand on her cheek, then he's gone.

She's not sure why he's telling her to be calm. She is calm. It's everyone around her who seems to be panicking. She can hear someone barking instructions to the audience over the microphone, then the whine of feedback.

A part of her wonders if anyone filmed what happened; her followers will go nuts for that kind of footage. But she doesn't want them to see her like this, not the messed-up real-life version of herself with her face contorted in pain. She has no desire to share her vulnerability, to admit to a reality that hasn't been filtered, cropped and sanitized.

Ladies and gentlemen, we are taking a short break from the show to ensure the safety of our performers. Please leave your seats in an orderly fashion and make your way to the restaurant, where there will be a complimentary beverage waiting for you.

Something cold and wet is pressed on to Skye's hand. At least she thinks it's cold and wet. The pain is so severe that the sensation seems to blur into something that is beyond anything she has felt before, something that bites down with razor-sharp teeth, trying to cut her into pieces and swallow her whole.

Devi's face reappears above her. She wants to tell him to get out of the way. He's blocking her view.

'We're going to take you to the medical centre,' he says. 'Someone's trying to get hold of Marc.'

A verbal response would take too much effort, so she blinks at him instead. Once for yes. Twice for no. Wishes he could read her mind.

'Do you think you can get up?' he asks.

Twice for no this time.

'Skye.' He waves his hand in front of her face. 'I've taken your shoes off and we need to try and get you up. I promise we'll go slowly.'

She feels multiple hands slide beneath her shoulders.

Don't fucking touch me.

She shouts the words, but they carry on regardless. Why can't they hear her? The stars whirl together in an arc as they sit her up. *The words are only in your head, Skye.* Her dad's voice. *Is he here too? Of course he isn't. He's dead.*

The hands are under her right armpit now, and others are around her waist, pulling her upright. No one seems to want to go near her left side. There is a charred patch on the wooden boards on the stage in front of her, but at least that thick, sweet, foul smell – *burnt flesh* – seems less pungent. Or maybe she's just become accustomed to it.

'Can you walk?' one of the dancers asks her.

Yes, she can walk. Stupid question. There's nothing wrong with her legs.

The huddle of bodies, with hers at the centre, moves as one across the stage, down the two steps at the side and slowly across the beach. She can see the light from an iPhone pointing at her. Someone from the audience is filming, but it hurts so much she doesn't care. The medical centre isn't far from the restaurant, but she needs to just stop and sit down.

Not much further. Focus on keeping your balance.

Her dad again? Or Devi this time? She doesn't know. She just wants to get to wherever they're going. Wants something to block out the pain that has begun to chew through her tendons, devouring sinew in its eagerness to reach her bones.

A door. Someone holds it open. People peel away from the huddle so she can fit through the gap. White walls. Bright lights. Hard metal chairs. Hands guide her to where she can sit down, and she shuts her eyes while voices murmur around her. She can feel her teeth chattering, something she can't seem to stop. She doesn't even understand why it's happening. She's not cold. Something soft is placed over her legs. Tucked in underneath her thighs.

Skye, it's almost time. She can see her dad's face. He's smiling.

She opens her eyes again and looks at the clock: 7.57 p.m. He's right. She hadn't realized.

'The doctor is on his way.' Devi pats the blanket. 'One

of the dancers has gone to the staff quarters to get him.'
He squeezes her shoulder. 'I'm so sorry. I don't know what
happened. Nothing like that has ever . . . there's no reason
it should have gone up like that.'

Skye looks down. The glove is still covering her left arm.
Or part of it is. The other part seems to have melted into
her skin. Pink and black merged together into a charred
stickiness. The bottom part of the tentacles on her octopus have disappeared into the horror.

'I thought I could smell petrol,' she whispers. 'When I
put it on. I thought it was something you used in the show.'

She can tell Devi doesn't believe her. Thinks she's in shock.

The hand on the clock moves forward another notch:
7.58 p.m.

Skye runs her tongue over the roof of her mouth, trying
to gather together enough saliva to swallow.

'I got what I needed,' she says. 'He was there, just like
you said.'

Devi glances at the receptionist behind the counter
in the medical centre, but she is staring at the screen in
front of her, trying to avoid looking at the mess that is
Skye's hand.

He nods. 'And you won't tell anyone about my passport?'

''Course not. You've worked here for this long; I doubt
anyone is going to check it now. Who cares if you're originally from Bangladesh, or anywhere else for that matter?
The important thing is that you get the job done. The
photo really looks like you, anyway. Most people wouldn't
even notice.'

They both look at the clock. The hand moves around
another notch.

'It's all set to go at eight,' she says. 'I wanted to see it go live.'

'I know.' Devi bites his lip. 'I'm sorry.'

Neither of them says anything as they watch the second hand on the clock complete another full circle: 8 p.m. Too late to change anything now.

Devi's knuckles turn white as he grips the chair more tightly, as if he is bracing himself for the impact of what she knows is to come. Skye thinks of her dad, of how proud he'd be. How this is going to change her life. A chance to burn brighter than ever before.

And then, despite the pain, she thinks of Marc and Zach Hamilton. Of how much they deserve this. And how they have no idea what is about to hit them.

52. 17 hours left

Where the fuck are Zach and Alexa?

Her husband was supposed to be back ages ago. Their table was booked for seven thirty. Cara sits on their sofa and looks through the glass panel at the turquoise water illuminated by the lights fixed beneath their overwater villa.

The blacktip reef shark is back.

Two of them this time. Sleek grey bodies that glide smoothly in and out of view, their tails and fins angled to sharp points. She remembers being told they have to keep moving. That if they ever stop, they'll die. It had sounded like a form of torture, reminded her of the fairy tale her mother used to read to her about the woman in red shoes who couldn't stop dancing. Do they not get tired? She feels shattered, and she's barely moved at all today. But maybe that's not surprising. Unexpected emotional bombshells will do that to you.

She's put Zach's phone back under Alexa's mattress. For now. She needs to make a plan. Decide what she's going to say so he can't wriggle out of it. Her husband is good at doing that. Slippery. She looks through the glass panel at the sharks again. This time, she's not going to let him.

She hears footsteps outside the villa and braces herself, expecting him to walk in, but the door doesn't open. She takes a deep breath and lets it out slowly, focuses on keeping calm. Zach hates confrontation; he wants an easy life.

Having seen the message on his phone, the irony of that isn't lost on her.

Does Alexa already know? The thought makes her shiver.

Is that why she hasn't been in touch today?

Numerous possibilities run through Cara's mind, each worse than the last. Alexa cannot find out what her father has done. It will destroy her. And Cara refuses to let that happen.

That noise again. It sounds as if someone is running up and down the wooden boards of the jetty. She opens the villa door and looks outside. In the dim glow of the lanterns she sees a man sprinting towards the end of the jetty then head up the path on to the island and disappear amongst the bushes. Cindy follows behind him but stops and turns around when she hears Cara and jogs back towards her.

'There was an accident in the fire show,' she says, breathing heavily.

Cara lets go of the front door, and it swings back, hitting her foot and scraping off a layer of skin. Images of Alexa lying with a broken arm, blood oozing down her leg, lying motionless on the sand, flick through her head.

'What do you mean, an accident?' Her voice comes out more high-pitched than usual.

Cindy smooths down the front of her silk dress where it's rucked up.

'Someone in the show got set on fire.' She hesitates. 'Can you believe it?'

'Oh my god,' Cara says. 'That's awful.'

'It was horrific, apparently.' Cindy sounds almost excited.

Cara catches a glance of her waffle towelling robe, realizes she has forgotten to change into the dress she was going to put on to go out to dinner. She pulls the cord a bit tighter around her waist.

'I didn't actually see it,' Cindy says. 'I was in a yoga class.' She sounds disappointed. 'But I got talking to someone after it all happened and she said a young woman got picked out of the audience to go up on stage and, as she was whirling the chain around, the flames caught on her glove and set her hand alight.'

Cara shuts her eyes briefly. *Please God, don't let it be Alexa.* Someone from the resort would have come and told her, wouldn't they? A trickle of fear runs through her stomach. Or have they already told Zach? Is that where he is? Has he gone to help?

'I ran back here to get Ryan,' Cindy continues. 'He's gone to see if there's anything he can do. He's had all the latest first-aid training at work. I know we learned it, but it was a long time ago now, wasn't it? I don't know if I'd trust myself to know what to do any more.'

Cara swallows, doesn't give a shit about what Ryan can or can't do.

'Were they badly hurt?'

Cindy shrugs. 'I don't know.' She lowers her voice even though there's no one around to hear. 'But you'd think they'd have procedures in place so that kind of thing couldn't happen, wouldn't you?'

Cara notices the way Cindy runs her tongue over her bright red lipstick. She's shared her titbit of gossip and is now looking for an ally to pore over every inch of the details with. She nods, wanting to avoid a discussion.

'You really don't remember me, do you?' Cindy says. 'You don't remember us flying together?'

'I –' Cara starts to answer, but Cindy cuts her off.

'It doesn't surprise me. I had dark brown hair back then. Was at least seventy pounds heavier. You never liked me. You thought I wasn't up to the job. That you were better than everyone else.'

Cara frowns at her.

'No, I didn't.' Cara thinks back, flicks through her memories, doesn't recognize this description of herself at all.

'Yes, you did. And then, just when we were starting to get more friendly, you left.'

'I barely knew you.' The words come out of Cara's mouth sharply, but there is something in Cindy's description that leaves an unpleasant taste in her mouth. Perhaps that was how she was. She'd fought to get herself into a good position and expected others to do the same, hadn't been particularly tolerant of those who had struggled with the pressures of the job.

'Maybe that's how you remember it,' Cindy says. 'But I looked up to you, and you ignored me. Especially after you got together with Zach. It was always Zach this, Zach that. The perfect couple. You didn't even bother to say goodbye to me when you left.'

Cara tries to think back, remembers having a leaving party but doesn't remember Cindy being there.

'My mother used to say that you should always be nice to people on the way up; you never know who you'll meet on the way down,' Cindy continues. 'Karma's a bitch, but she catches up with everyone in the end. Ryan told me Zach's business is having problems. Looks like it's one thing after another for you guys at the moment. What with that and your diving accident. No lasting effects, I hope?'

Her eyes glitter.

Cara swallows. 'No. Luckily I'm fine.' She studies the woman standing in her white patent high heels in front of her, her chin tilted in defiance. 'Why do you ask? Did you have something to do with it?'

Cindy hesitates, a fraction too long, then shakes her head, her eyes wide and innocent.

'Of course not.'

Cara remembers the panic she felt when she couldn't breathe. She can't tell if Cindy is lying, but she wants to get as far away from this woman as possible. She points at her towelling robe. 'I need to get dressed.'

'Sure,' Cindy says. 'Your husband seems to think he's too important to discuss business with mine, but Ryan doesn't like being treated like an idiot. You can tell Zach from me that he's in for a nasty shock. Zach might just be surprised to see where he turns up.'

Cara shuts her villa door without saying goodbye. Where Zach's concerned, Cindy might have a point. She tries calling Alexa, but her phone goes straight to voicemail. She types a text in capital letters.

CALL OR TEXT ME NOW PLEASE!!! URGENT.

She waits, her phone ready, *please ring*, but it stays silent.

She can't just sit here and do nothing. She has to be proactive. She'll go to the medical centre. *It can't be Alexa.* Then she'll go to reception. Find Marc. Or one of the staff who knows how to contact him. And when she gets hold of him, she can find out where the hell Zach is.

She goes into her bedroom, pulls off her dressing gown and throws on a jumpsuit. Something she can walk in easily. She's just tying up the laces of her Veja trainers, her hands shaking, when she hears the front door open and then click shut.

Please God let it be her.

Alexa is standing with her back pressed against the door, holding her phone, a tote bag on the floor by her feet. Tears are rolling down her face.

Cara runs over and embraces her in a tight hug.

'Christ, Alexa. Where have you been? Are you OK? Someone said there had been an accident at the fire show, and I thought . . . it doesn't matter what I thought. Are you hurt? Did you see what happened?'

She goes to pull away, but Alexa holds on to her. Buries her face in Cara's shoulder. Cara can feel her daughter trembling and has a flashback to her lying on the ground beside the car, her face contorted in pain as blood gushed from her leg on to the gravel.

She cups her hands around Alexa's face as she takes a step backwards.

'Tell me. Are you hurt?'

Alexa shakes her head.

Thank God.

Cara hugs her again.

'It's OK.' She strokes her daughter's hair. 'It must have been awful, but I'm sure the girl who got hurt will be all right. They've taken her to the medical centre, I heard. I saw Cindy and she said Ryan has gone to see if he can help, and there's a doctor here, so she'll be looked after.'

Alexa continues to sob. Cara can't remember the last

224

time she saw her this upset. Even after the break-in she had barely cried.

'Do you want me to find out how she is? I can call Devi to go –'

Alexa shakes her head.

Cara holds on to Alexa's hand.

'Dad isn't back yet, and he left his phone here, so I need to go to reception and try and find out where he is. Do you want to come with me?'

Alexa shakes her head again.

'Go and wash your face, then. I'll get you some water.'

Alexa nods and stumbles towards her bedroom. Cara finishes tying her shoelaces and then picks Alexa's bag up off the floor. The wine bottle rolls out, clear liquid sloshing around inside the glass. No wonder she's in such a state. Alexa shouldn't be drinking at all, but Cara is fully aware that Alexa often consumes more alcohol at the weekends than she does. Vodka shots and cans of cider seem to be the current preferences, but *wine*? Alexa hates the stuff.

She unscrews the cap and the smell hits her straight away.

What the fuck?

She hears the toilet flush and a tap turn on in her daughter's bathroom. Cindy's words echo in her head. *The flames caught on her glove and set her hand alight.* She tries to swallow down her panic as she thinks of the girl lying in the medical centre and screws the cap back on to the bottle. They need to get rid of this. Right now.

53. 16 hours 45 minutes left

Alexa pulls one of the white fluffy towels off the rack in the bathroom to dry her face.

She studies herself in the mirror. Her eyes are bloodshot, ringed by hollow, dark circles. Her hair has separated into lank sections and when she runs her hands through it she can feel grains of sand in her scalp. She covers her ears, trying to block out the sound of Skye's screams, which have followed her across the beach and over the wooden boards of the jetty. She can't make them stop.

What has she done?

The weight of guilt sits like a heavy block in her chest, pressing against her ribs and diaphragm, stopping her from breathing.

Why the fuck didn't she say something?

She watches herself chew the corner of her lip in the mirror. Because they would have found out she was responsible. So long as she stays silent, no one will know it was her. They'll think it was an accident. This kind of thing must happen all the time when people are juggling with fire. And perhaps it looked worse than it actually was. Hopefully they can just bandage up Skye's hand and she'll be fine in a few days.

Her reflection stares back at her accusingly.

'Course she won't be fucking fine.

Alexa glances down at the scar on her leg. It's healing,

but the pink line is still clearly visible. If that can happen after being scraped by the underside of a car, imagine the damage a naked flame can do. She shivers. She remembers getting sunburnt when they went to the south of France last summer. She'd had to sit with a wet towel draped over her shoulder and the raw tenderness when just the sleeve of her dress had touched it had been agony. Her skin had peeled away in paper-thin layers afterwards, as if she was shedding.

She presses her hands into her eye sockets, wanting to disappear into the blackness and flashing lights. She wishes she could go back in time. Just a few hours. *It's not much to ask, is it?*

You can't run away from this. There'll be some kind of investigation. Think.

Did anyone see her go into the storage room by the diving centre? What if one of the staff notices the petrol spillage by the paddleboards? Will they tie the two things together? What if there's CCTV?

Why hadn't she thought about any of this before?

Her phone buzzes on the side of the sink. She swipes the screen and sees her mother's earlier text. It has only just come through.

CALL OR TEXT ME NOW PLEASE!!! URGENT.

It's too late for that now.

She runs the tap again and splashes her face and gulps down some water, hopes it will help to ease the acid that is swirling around with the Chablis in her stomach.

Her phone buzzes again and she opens Snapchat. There are a few messages on their group and she reads the last one from Charlie as she works out the time difference. It's 4.15 p.m. in the UK.

Have you seen the video that's been posted on Skye Elliot's YouTube channel? It's all over social media. Alexa, if ur reading this, ur dad is in deep shit.

She doesn't understand what he's talking about. What video?

She lowers herself on to the edge of the bath as she plays the latest video on Skye's channel. Skye is talking to the camera, then the footage cuts to a clip of Marc boarding a boat. She presses the button frantically to turn up the volume, frowns as she hears Skye say the words 'Zach Hamilton' followed by 'utter hypocrisy', 'significant investment in Sheimark', followed by 'waste dumping', and 'environmental disaster'.

The video cuts away to footage of the boat out at sea. The camera zooms in and she recognizes her father passing a green refuse bag to Marc, who then throws it over the side of the boat into the ocean. The footage replays, in slow motion this time, the bag circled in red as it falls into the water, where it bobs on the surface.

Alexa goes back and plays the video again, convinced she must have missed something. Skye continues to talk about Sheimark's appalling record on workers' rights, its use of toxic chemicals and how investment in the company couldn't be less ethical, but Alexa isn't listening. The video has had tens of thousands of views already, and the numbers on the screen are continuing to climb.

'Mum?' She gets up and walks into the living room, still looking at her phone. 'Mum, have you seen this?'

She holds out the screen and watches the colour drain from her mother's face as the video plays again, the sound echoing through the living room.

It's not until Skye has finished speaking that Alexa realizes the bag she'd taken out with her earlier is lying open on the coffee table and standing beside it is the wine bottle, still half full of petrol.

54. 16 hours 30 minutes left

Zach sits beside Marc on the deck, feels the boat tip slightly from side to side in the water. The sea is still calm, *thank God*, but he doesn't know if it will stay that way. He's not sure how long he's been here, his back pressed against the guardrail, his knees pulled up to his chin – an hour? Two? Long enough for the sky to have turned from blue to a dusky black, the sun no longer visible above the horizon. He knows he has to *do* something, he's just not sure what. The feeling is horribly familiar.

Not now, Zach.

Marc's linen shirt lies ripped open, a mark on his chest where Zach pushed down on it to give him mouth-to-mouth resuscitation. He'd had no idea if he was doing it correctly, but something had obviously worked as eventually he'd felt a weak pulse and turned Marc over into the recovery position. Red liquid had continued to leak from his head, gathering in a small pool. Zach had watched it spread out across the deck, but at some point it must have stopped.

Think, Zach. Think.

He was hoping that Marc would regain consciousness and they could go back to the resort. He's been telling himself to give it *just another few minutes* in case he opens his eyes, *please God, just wake up*, or starts moving. But he hasn't. He keeps checking his pulse and thinks Marc's is around forty-five beats per minute. He doesn't know exactly what it's supposed to be, but his is eighty-five, so he's pretty sure this isn't good.

Zach has been going over and over what happened in his head but still doesn't understand it. He hadn't even pushed him that hard.

Was it his fault? If he dies, would it be classed as self-defence? Manslaughter?

Zach doesn't know that either. Part of him still hopes that he's going to wake up in a minute and find this has all been some kind of horrendous nightmare.

A fly lands on Marc's chin and crawls over his lip, heads towards his nostrils. Zach waves it away, but it comes back.

Do something.

He stands up slowly, his legs numb, and winds in the reels on the fishing rods, lifts them off the back of the boat and lies them down in the storage racks. He stumbles across the deck into the cabin, looks at the chrome steering wheel surrounded by levers and dials.

I don't know how to pilot a boat.

He's seen people do it but has never done it himself. There's a radio fitted into the dashboard next to one of the levers, the hand-held device to talk into attached by a black spiral coil of black cable. A set of keys are in the ignition.

He should call someone. Tell them what's happened.

What if they don't believe it was an accident?

Fuck.

Zach opens the cupboard beneath the small sink and finds three rolls of blue paper, the catering version of kitchen roll. He pulls one out and unwinds it until he is holding a sizeable ball. Hopefully enough so he doesn't actually have to touch the blood. The thought of getting the warm, sticky liquid on his fingers makes his stomach turn over. He carries the ball of paper, together with the roll, outside on to the deck.

Maybe Marc will be sitting up complaining of a headache?

Zach shuts his eyes briefly, makes a wish like he used to when he was little, but when he opens them again Marc's body is still lying in exactly the same position as when he'd left him. He swallows.

He holds his breath as he kneels down, can't bear the thought he might inadvertently catch the scent of Marc's aftershave, something that belongs to him. He sticks the wad of blue paper on top of the blood and lets the blood soak into the soft material, pulling more and more off the roll and adding it to the pile until the redness no longer shows through. He tears off another few sheets and uses them to pick up the saturated lump of tissue from the deck, carries it a few feet to the back of the boat, where he throws it overboard, then retches. It begins to sink as soon as it hits the water, disappears out of sight in seconds.

There are a few red smears and splashes of crimson on the deck, and he forces himself to go back, unroll more blue paper and wipe them up, lifting up Marc's head to clean the worst of the blood off the deck.

He throws that stained paper over the side as well, and then leans over the back of the boat and washes his hands in the sea, shakes them to get rid of the water, pretends he can't see them trembling. A few hours ago, he'd thought the messages on his phone were the worst thing he had to deal with.

He kicks out at the side of the boat, then hits the

fibreglass shell with his fists as hard as he can, again and again, until his knuckles are scraped and raw. He'd had a plan to sort everything out, and now this happens.

It's all such a fucking mess.

For a moment he thinks he might cry. There's no one around to see. He could scream as loud as he likes out here and no one would hear.

What good would that do?

He's going to have to take Marc back to the resort. Tell them he slipped on the deck and hit his head when they were fishing. He's cleared most of the blood up, so it's not going to look as bad as it was. If Marc tells people that Zach pushed him, he'll have to lie. Explain the guy has just suffered a head injury, so it's no wonder he's confused.

He takes a deep breath, then bends down and puts his hands under Marc's armpits – *don't think about it* – and drags him inside the cabin. He takes one of the folded orange beach towels that are lying on the seat and places it under Marc's head and spreads out another over his legs. The material falls into the contours of Marc's body.

He can keep an eye on him here.

Zach picks up the beer bottles that haven't rolled off the deck and sticks them in the bin, then leans over the steps at the back of the boat, fills the empty cool box with seawater, throws it over the deck and uses more blue tissue-roll to rub away the last remaining stains.

He thinks he can see the lights from the resort in the distance. *Are they from Asana?* He's not a hundred per cent sure, but he's going to aim for them anyway. Marc had said Asana was in that direction earlier, so he'll just head towards the lights and hope he's going the right way. The bubbling sound of the engines starts up as he turns the key in the ignition. He pushes the throttle forward, moves the boat very slowly towards the anchor so the rope goes slack. Marc had just pressed a button on the dashboard earlier to let it out, so he tries pressing the one with an arrow pointing up to reel it in. There's a grinding sound, and when he looks over the back of the boat he can see, with relief, the rope being wound back into the boat, then a clunking noise as the chain follows. The mechanism stops shortly after the anchor appears out of the water.

First hurdle completed.

He turns the boat so it's pointing in the direction of Asana Fushi and edges the throttle forward.

'I'm taking you back,' he says loudly towards the orange towels. 'We're going to get you to a doctor.'

Has he got enough fuel? The gauge shows it's only just above empty. Marc had said when they set off that they didn't need to fill up, but now Zach wonders if he was just keen to get going. He has no idea what he'll do if the engine cuts out, but for the moment he concentrates on keeping the boat moving through the water.

If he looks straight ahead, he doesn't have to think about Marc lying on the floor beside him. He prays the noise of the engine will wake him up.

Focus on the lights.

Just keep going, and focus on the lights.

An hour and a half later, he approaches the jetty. He knows the boat must be running on fumes as the needle is in the red, and his body is stiff with tension.

Almost there, Zach. Just a few more metres.

He moves the throttle back to slow down as he goes over the reef, concentrates on keeping the boat between the marker poles.

Thank God there is a jetty on this side of the island. All the restaurants and bars are over the other side, so no one tends to come here at night.

He edges the boat in behind the resort dhoni and ties it up to one of the posts. Letting out a deep breath, he repeats the version of events that he's going to tell everyone to himself before crouching down next to where Marc is lying on the floor. He checks no more blood has leaked on to the towel under his head.

'I'm going to get you some help,' he says.

He puts his fingers on Marc's neck but can't feel the now familiar faint beat. Holds his hand over Marc's nose. He's not breathing. Zach's blood rushes into his ears. He tries feeling for a pulse on Marc's wrist . . . nothing.

Oh Christ.

Marc's skin is pale, almost waxy.

He's dead.

He can't be dead.

He was breathing. How can he be dead?

Fuck.

Think, Zach. Think.

Even if he says it was an accident, the press will be all over it, dragging his reputation through the mud. Skye will probably put it on her bloody YouTube channel. He can't afford for that to happen. He doesn't need any more problems. There's nothing else for it. He's going to have to get rid of Marc's body.

The thought occurs to him that if Marc had died a

couple of hours ago he could have dumped his body in the sea, but now he can't even do that. For a start, Marc is taller and heavier than him and he doesn't think he has the strength to be able to lift him over the side of the boat, but even if he could, the lagoon here is far too shallow. His body would float, or be spotted immediately in five feet of clear blue water. And everyone would know Zach was the last person to see him, not to mention the fact that his clothes will be covered in Marc's DNA. And he can't risk taking the boat back out again as it's almost out of fuel. He's going to have to think of something else. He presses his fingers into his temples.

There's no going back now.

He breathes through his mouth as he pulls the stack of towels off one of the cabin shelves and shakes them out before putting them over Marc's body. He focuses on thinking about clear mountain spring water and doesn't allow himself to reflect on the fact that he's covering up a corpse. Taking the keys out of the engine, he locks the cabin door, hopes that if anyone does peer through the window, all they'll see is a pile of orange towels, that they won't notice the slightly sweet, stale odour he swears he can smell already.

He needs to hurry, prays Cara hasn't already raised the alarm and told anyone he's missing.

He wipes his sunglasses on his T-shirt as he notices the tiny red stain near the hem. Smaller than his fingernail, but still there. The thought of what it is makes him want to tear his top off and scrub it clean, but the only place to wash it is in the sea, and then he'll be stuck wearing a T-shirt that is wet as well as stained. He needs to be calm. To think.

Breathe.

He remembers the gardeners in the resort pushing around their wheelbarrows full of dead leaves, knows they are stored nearby overnight. He swallows.

He's going to have to do this. He doesn't have a choice.

55. 15 hours left

Devi sits on the hammock swing, the stiff strands of rope digging uncomfortably into his buttocks, and prays Skye will be OK. A bunch of wilted yellow-and-white frangipani flowers lies on the sand beside him; he's supposed to be taking it to Ryan and Cindy Miller's villa to replace the jasmine he'd put in there earlier. She's allergic to that too, apparently. As well as the colour orange and the numerous other things on her list. If he was the resort manager at Asana, he'd take flowers out of the rooms altogether. They only last a day before the petals start dropping and the pollen stains the linen.

Where's Cara? She should be here by now.

After what happened to Skye, he's not sure she'll turn up at all. The hum of panic amongst the guests at the bar was palpable, even in the face of a free drink – which could sometimes soothe the trickiest of customers. The doctor had told him to leave the medical centre, that there was nothing else he could do. He'd changed in his room and then come straight over here, but even though he's replayed what happened in his head over and over again, he still can't understand what went wrong. He's done that trick hundreds of times before.

Skye's words linger in his brain.

I thought I could smell petrol when I put it on.

Had she just imagined it?

He doesn't keep petrol anywhere near his uniform, for obvious reasons. And none of the staff except him use that storage room.

Sometimes accidents just happen.

He undoes the top button on his collar and rolls up his sleeves. The heat sticks to his skin, even this late at night.

He's tempted to lie down, but that would feel too much like giving up. He's already adjusted his position from standing to sitting, pushing into the sand with his feet to swing the hammock gently backwards and forwards on the beach.

She's not coming.

She'll be here.

One thought to carry him forwards, the other while he swings back.

He checks his phone again. No new messages.

No news is good news. Isn't that one of the phrases the tourists use?

He's not sure. Cara isn't here, and she should be.

Has he missed her? Got the wrong meeting place?

He can't have. He'd got here almost fifteen minutes earlier than they'd arranged to meet, and he's been sitting here for over an hour. He would have seen her if she had turned up. He's a hundred per cent certain there's only one hammock swing in the resort, and this part of the island is deserted at this time of night. Everyone else is in the bar or at one of the restaurants. He checks his WhatsApp again, but there's nothing new, and no response to the message he sent her fifteen minutes ago when his patience had begun to wear thin.

She'll be here. She's got too much to lose.

He'd told Asma that Cara had offered to give them some money. He knew he'd have to explain that kind of amount appearing in his bank account and he doesn't like lying to his wife. A memory of him running his hand over Cara's red swimming costume, her breath warm in his ear, flashes into his head. *Unless it's absolutely necessary.*

His earlier certainty begins to trickle away.

He looks over towards the jetty, where two waiters, Ryan Miller and the resort doctor are helping Skye into a speedboat. A crêpe bandage covers most of her left arm. At least it wasn't her face. His mother had accidentally splashed burning oil on herself when she was cooking, years ago, and the patch of skin on her cheek is still hard and knotted, an artificial bubble-gum-pink colour that no one fails to notice. She'd been the one who had told him to get out of their country, start a new life somewhere else. Somewhere he could work hard and achieve something. She'd spent her savings getting him a fake Maldivian passport, using his brother's photo to ensure he could get a work visa after his own passport had been confiscated by the traffickers he had paid to get him a job here in the first place.

One of the waiters gets into the boat with her. Devi hopes the doctors can fix the damage, wonders if she'll need a skin graft. She'll be taken to Malé, the closest island with facilities to treat serious burns. He'd offered to go – he knows the hospital better than most people – but the doctor had said it would be better if he stayed here to answer any questions. Devi had felt a sense of dread at the thought of an investigation but hadn't wanted to miss this meeting with Cara.

The speedboat pulls away, the lights on it bobbing up and down in the water. The other men walk away, back to the other side of the island, towards the restaurants and bars. Devi digs his heels into the sand to stop the motion of the hammock, stays very still so as not to draw attention to himself. He can see the game-fishing boat moored up behind the dhoni against the stone wall of the jetty.

Marc must be back. Devi's stomach clenches and he wonders if he's seen Skye's video yet. If Marc is forced to resign, Devi wants to be the one who is asked to step up. He's been here longer than Marc; he could run this place with his eyes shut. And the pay rise would mean he didn't have to worry about Imani. But right now, he needs to explore every possible avenue to ensure he gets the money Imani needs.

Come on, Cara. Where are you?

If she doesn't turn up, is he actually going to tell Zach what happened with his wife? He can't imagine having that conversation. What would be the point? It's the money he wants; he doesn't have any desire to ruin the Hamiltons' marriage. Maybe he'll just have to focus on getting a decent tip off Zach instead. A mention of how generous Mr Miller has been might do the trick. These businessmen always like to beat the competition.

A movement on the jetty catches his eye and he stares into the darkness. Someone is walking around by the fishing boat. It doesn't look like Marc. This man is shorter, slimmer. Devi frowns. He's pushing something. Devi narrows his eyes to try and see better. A wheelbarrow? What's Azeem doing, gardening this late?

Devi watches the man struggle to roll the barrow slowly along the stone jetty and then off on to the sand towards the back of the beach. The man disappears into the shadows cast by the bushes, then reappears a minute later without the barrow, carrying what looks like a spade. Devi blinks. He looks familiar. The hair. The glasses.

Zach Hamilton.

What is he doing out here?

Devi continues to watch as Zach walks to the back of the beach, sticks the shovel into the sand, puts his foot on the blade and begins to dig.

56. 14 hours 45 minutes left

How the hell has he got himself into this mess?

Zach lets go of the spade for a second and rubs his face with the back of his hand, feeling grains of sand scrape against one of his numerous mosquito bites.

No time for that. Just dig. And get a fucking move on.

His hand trembles as he pushes the spade into the sand. His heart is pounding so hard he's scared it might burst.

Stop fucking panicking.

Focus.

And pray no one walks this way.

He's deliberately picked this isolated spot close to the jetty, and at this time of night all the guests should be in the main bar or one of the restaurants. The small strip of sand that rises up out of the sea here is only about ten feet wide, then it is swallowed up by dense vegetation; bright green bushes that stretch all the way across the back of the beach and are now a black silhouette in the dark. Even if someone does walk past, he could crawl in amongst the leaves and branches and no one would see him.

It won't come to that.

He whispers the words like a mantra, both to reassure himself and to stop his teeth chattering, a clicking that echoes in the darkness.

Does Asana Fushi have security guards?

God, he hopes not. The last thing he needs right now is

to explain himself to a man with a gun. Marc would have been able to tell him, but Marc is currently lying in the wheelbarrow that Zach has pushed as far as he can into the bushes behind him, his body covered in two orange towels.

He's killed someone.

He's a murderer.

The thought makes his foot slip off the spade.

Breathe.

He focuses on the sound of the waves breaking on the shore, wills himself not to fall apart.

Not here. Not now. Pull yourself to-fucking-gether.

The wheelbarrow creaks, making him jump.

Thank God for the gardeners.

Without the wheelbarrow, he has no idea how he'd have got Marc's body off the boat. As it was, he'd had to tip the barrow over on to its side in the small cabin, then fight to roll Marc's body into it before trundling it across the fold-out aluminium gangway on to the jetty.

Who knew a dead body could be so heavy?

He squeezes his eyes shut, trying to block out the horror of his hands touching dead flesh. Of Marc's hair falling in lank strands over his puce forehead.

Had he cleaned the deck of the boat thoroughly enough?

He thinks so. But he can't be certain. He wipes his forehead with his arm to get rid of the perspiration. Grains of sand have edged their way underneath the straps of his flip-flops and grind painfully against his skin every time he pushes the spade into the ground.

He'd thought sand was soft, easy to dig through, easy to move. For the first quarter of an hour or so, it had been.

Like scooping up caster sugar. But then it had got wetter, the grains sticking together in clumps, and now it takes all his effort – *don't cry* – to push the shovel into the tightly packed denseness. His shoulders ache and he can feel the muscles in his back going into spasm.

How long does it take to make a hole big enough for a body?

He wishes he was still wearing his watch; then he'd know how long he's been here instead of having to guess. Before he started digging, he'd thought perhaps an hour, but it already feels like at least two. And it's still not finished. He remembers reading somewhere that graves are supposed to be six feet deep, but he's six foot and there's no way he's going to get down that far. Four, if he's lucky. Maybe only three. The hole is up to his stomach now when he stands in it. *Is that deep enough?* He's made it a couple of feet wide and he's aiming for around four feet long – he hopes he can bend Marc's body to fit him in, but the thought of having to touch him again makes his head swim.

What if rigor mortis has set in?

He retches.

The deeper he gets, the harder it is to lift the sand out and dump it by the side of the hole. He's already had to climb out a few times and push the piles he's created away from the edge to stop them falling back in on top of him. His hair is full of the stuff, grains that get under his finger-nails whenever he wipes his face or scratches his scalp.

Something flicks against his cheek and he swats away another mosquito.

Cara is going to go mental at him for being so late. No wonder he hasn't been able to tell her about the problems he's been having with the company. He should have talked to his mother. Nothing fazes her. She'd have told him what to do. But he couldn't face admitting how bad things are. Not yet.

He might not have a choice if ZH Investments continues to haemorrhage money. Or if Victoria decides to make a fuss.

There's water in the bottom of the hole. He can hear a squelching sound when he moves, feels it covering his flip-flops. He's not far enough down, *nowhere near*, but he's going to have to stop.

A noise cuts through the waves breaking on the shore. Leaves rustling. Zach scans the silhouettes of the bushes and the flat sandy beach. Nothing. Or nothing he can see. He shivers, bile rising in his throat at the thought that someone is watching him.

Don't be paranoid.

He waits, tries to pinpoint where it's coming from. *The bushes?* He can't see anything move along the dark line that stretches across the back of the beach. Zach stands very still. Waits. More rustling. Closer this time.

Christ, is someone there?

He adjusts his hands on the shaft of the spade as a large fruit bat emerges out of one of the trees, swoops down over his head and flies off into the night. Blinking frantically, he fights the urge to scream.

Just get this over with. Bury him.

He pulls the wheelbarrow out of the bushes, pushes it to the edge of the hole and tries to lift up the handles. It's a struggle. Marc demonstrates a stubborn unwillingness to move.

Come on, you fucker.

Zach grunts as he lifts his arms higher and, just as he thinks he's going to have to try something else, Marc's body slides out into the hole. Zach lets the wheelbarrow fall back on to the sand. The dead man lies crumpled in the small space, the orange towels twisted around his torso. Rigor mortis clearly takes longer than a few hours to kick in.

Zach takes the bundle of keys from the boat out of his pocket, throws them in on top of Marc's body, together with Marc's mobile, which he's turned off, and then fills the hole back up with the sand he's just spent hours digging out.

He'll tell Cara the boat had engine issues. That it stalled at sea and had taken them ages to fix; that the radio wasn't working and neither of them had a mobile. If anyone asks, he'll say Marc headed back to the staff quarters when they got back to the jetty and he hasn't seen him since.

Can he lie convincingly enough to make it look like the truth?

He swallows. Of course he can. He's done it before and got away with it. He pushes away the image of Victoria that pops into his head, shoves the spade into the empty wheelbarrow and kicks the sand around over the hole, stamping and flattening it out until it blends in with the rest of the beach.

As he trundles the wheelbarrow back towards the garden storage area, covering up the tracks as he goes, he looks back. In the moonlight, one patch of sand still looks slightly darker than the rest. It should dry out by the morning. He really hopes it does, or he's totally fucked.

57. 14 hours 30 minutes left

The call comes through at 6.30 p.m. He slides his phone out of his pocket where he's got it on vibrate so as not to annoy Marie.

'Have you seen it?'

He doesn't answer Vincent straight away, needs a few seconds to try and gather his thoughts, which are still being dragged away from the game he's been playing with Jamie. He gets up off the sofa and makes his way out of the living room, shuts the door quietly, leaving his son rolling his toy-truck over the obstacle course of cardboard boxes they have set out on the floor.

'Have I seen what?' he asks.

'The video. It's everywhere. Just type his name into Google and you'll see exactly what I'm talking about.'

He rubs his eyes, types it into the search bar and clicks on the link, watches the video with the sound turned up enough so he can hear. It ends, and there's a pause before the caller speaks again.

'You know what to do.'

He doesn't answer. Doesn't want to think about having to leave Marie and Jamie again when he's only just come back from a trip. And this time it will be for even longer.

'Hello?'

'I'm still here. I'm just trying to think.'

'There's nothing to think about it. Get out there as soon as you can. There's a flight in a few hours, which you should make if you move your arse, and when you get there, do exactly what we agreed.'

The phone goes dead. He rubs his forehead, wishes he'd never answered it, then goes to the cupboard in the hall, pulls out a small suitcase which has everything he needs in it, already packed.

58. 14 hours left

Cara runs her fingertips over her eyebrows, smoothing them down as she waits for Alexa to come back. Following a long confrontation with Alexa, during which she had locked herself in her room for over an hour and refused to say what she was doing with a bottle of petrol in her bag, Cara had told her they needed to deal with the situation. She'd persuaded her to take the bottle somewhere away from the villa and get rid of it. But her daughter has been gone for ages and Cara is beginning to worry something might have happened to her.

What if someone's seen her? Asked her what she's doing?

There's a click as the door opens. A streak of night sky lit up by tiny pinpricks of light flashes into view and the knot in Cara's stomach loosens, but it's Zach who steps over the threshold into the living room.

'Where have you been?' she asks.

Cara keeps her voice deliberately neutral. Her husband takes a step backwards as he sees her sitting on the sofa, her legs curled up underneath her. A plethora of emotions flickers across his face. Surprise, anger, embarrassment, followed by something that looks like fear.

Does he suspect that she's found out what he's been hiding?

They've been together so long, been through so much over the past nineteen years, and until earlier this evening she'd have sworn she could read her husband like a book.

She might not always have wanted to see what was on the pages, but they always lay open. Now she's no longer sure of anything. It's as if someone has peeled away a layer of cellophane packaging and, for the first time, she's able to clearly see what lies underneath.

At least Alexa isn't here.

The thought flashes through her head, followed by the question of how long she's got until her daughter gets back. She had considered pouring the petrol away down the bathroom sink but was worried it could somehow be traced back to them – are the plumbing pipes linked to other villas? Could the fumes set light to something? Better to pour it away in the sea and then chuck the bottle into one of the various litter bins dotted around the island. Cara feels as if there is something heavy inside her, weighing her down whenever she thinks about what her daughter has done.

It was an accident. That's what Alexa had whispered when she'd seen the wine bottle on the table, and Cara hadn't asked any more questions, had just nodded, wanting more than anything to believe her. An accident was a perfectly plausible explanation. They happen all the time. And juggling with fire isn't exactly safe.

Was it though?

She can't think about that right now.

'You know where I've been.'

Cara sees his Adam's apple bob up and down as he swallows and glances at Alexa's bag, which is lying on the coffee table. 'Out fishing with Marc.'

He flashes her a brief smile, and she wonders how many times he's lied to her in the past, how often she's simply swallowed his deception as she's stared at his perfectly white veneers.

She's only ever seen what he wanted her to see. She had trusted him not to do anything stupid, had moulded their lives around him to make everything as easy as possible. But now she realizes she has no idea who she's looking at. She wonders when the lies started, how long their marriage has been a sham. Was it something gradual that had happened over many years, or was there one defining moment that she had somehow missed?

'You said you'd be back hours ago,' she says. 'Our table was booked for seven thirty.'

He doesn't answer.

'And you're filthy,' she adds.

Zach looks down at his T-shirt, runs his hand through his hair.

'I know, sorry. There was a problem with the boat. The engine cut out and wouldn't start again. I had to help Marc fix it and it took a lot longer than we thought it would.'

Cara points at his top. 'What are those marks?'

Does he flinch, or is she imagining it?

'Just engine oil,' he says. 'I need to get in the shower. We didn't even catch much. Only a couple of red bass.'

The door clicks shut behind him.

'Have you and Alexa already eaten?'

He pulls off his flip-flops and stamps his feet, grains of sand falling on to the mat.

Cara swallows. 'I know, Zach.'

'You know what?'

'I know what you've done.'

She says the words calmly, her tone undermining the

252

enormity of the bomb she has just thrown into the room. The sentence that signals the end of her marriage deserves to be yelled. Screamed, even. But the most important things often die quietly, leaving something bigger than themselves behind. And if she allows herself to shout, the rage that is bubbling away just beneath the surface of her skin will break through and she isn't sure what will happen then.

'What are you talking about?' Zach frowns, but even in the dim glow of the living-room lamps she can see the flush on his cheeks. 'I haven't *done* anything, Cara. I'm sorry I'm late, but it wasn't my fault the engine died, for Christ's sake.'

'I'm not talking about the b—' Cara starts to reply, but before she can finish Alexa walks back into the villa. She looks at Zach, then at Cara, who shakes her head a fraction, just enough for Alexa to understand.

No, she hasn't said anything to Zach about the bottle.

'You've been gone ages, Dad,' Alexa says as Zach starts to walk towards the main bedroom.

'I've just had this conversation with your mother,' he replies. 'We had issues with the boat. She can explain. I need a shower.'

Cara sees small lines form between Alexa's eyebrows at his gruff tone.

'Has Mum shown you?' Alexa asks.

'Shown me what?'

'The video.'

'What video?' Zach asks, stopping in his tracks.

'The one Skye posted on her YouTube channel. It's pretty much gone viral already. Is what she said true? What the hell were you doing, Dad?'

Cara watches Zach's hand tremble as he rubs the stubble on his chin.

'What are you talking about?' His face drains of colour as he pushes his glasses up on his nose. Alexa walks over to him, swipes her phone screen to find the video, and holds it up in front of him.

'This,' Alexa says. 'I'm talking about this.'

He glances at his wife while Skye delivers a scathing verdict on his behaviour as if he's hoping Cara can somehow help. Cara looks away as Skye starts talking about Sheimark and their spectacular fall from grace. She studies the glow coming from the glass panel in the floor and tucks her legs further up underneath her.

'I wasn't dumping rubbish,' Zach says as the video cuts out. 'Marc asked me to pass him one of those bags. He said he wanted to put it in one of the containers at the back of the boat because it was making the deck stink. I had no idea he was doing that.'

Neither Cara nor Alexa says anything.

'I'm telling the truth!' He raises his voice as Cara glares at him.

'And what about the investment in Sheimark, Zach?'

He doesn't bother to deny it.

'Whether you dumped rubbish or not,' she says eventually, 'doesn't actually matter. God knows how many people have seen that video, and they won't believe you. Skye has proof that you invested in Sheimark and, as you're the owner of a company whose brand is all about being environmentally friendly, no one is going to believe anything you say.'

Zach runs his hand through his hair and Cara hears the

sound of dozens of grains of sand scattering across the wooden floorboards.

'I'll get someone in the office to issue a press release,' he says.

Alexa rolls her eyes.

'It's a bit late for that, Dad. Even my friends at home have seen it.'

Cara sees Zach bite his lip as he looks at her.

'Is this what you meant when you said you knew what I'd done?' he asks.

Cara nods briefly. She's not going to bring up the message she saw on his phone. Not now, not in front of Alexa. Her daughter has no idea what her father is capable of and, after everything she's gone through, Cara needs to protect her.

'I tried calling you to tell you,' Cara says. 'But you didn't answer.'

Relief flickers across Zach's face.

'I didn't have my mobile with me,' he says. 'I must have left it here. Have you seen it?'

Cara shakes her head. The tiny seed of hope that maybe he hasn't done what she thinks he has floats away with his words. All he's done since the moment he walked through the door is lie. Is there anything he wouldn't say or do to cover his back?

Think, Cara.

ZH Investments is finished. She can see that, even if Zach can't. He'll be more toxic than Ratner was after denigrating his product so publicly. And if the company goes under, they will have no income. Any attempt to deny what the video appears to show will just draw more attention to it. Zach is the person who made the company so attractive to investors in the first place, and with his reputation in tatters no one will want to be associated with it. She can hear their friends discussing it now in scandalized whispers.

Marc might confirm Zach's version of what happened with the rubbish – but he's in just as much trouble himself. He's the one who has been captured on film dumping it into the ocean. No doubt someone will have told him about the video – she can imagine how fast gossip spreads around the staff quarters. She's surprised he isn't banging down their villa door, trying to get his story straight with Zach. Maybe he has. More missed calls and messages to add to the one she has already seen on the phone under Alexa's mattress.

She considers her options, follows them through to their inevitable conclusion. *What should she do?* The swift stab of revenge she'd get from confronting Zach now, however sweet, would be short-lived. She needs to take her time, wait for the half-formed plan sitting in her head to fully crystallize.

If Zach decides to ruin his life, that's his problem. But if he thinks he can ruin Alexa's life too and leave Cara to walk away from their marriage with nothing to show for it, he has severely underestimated her.

59. 12 hours 30 minutes left

Alexa stands with her head under the rain shower and liberally pumps Aesop Citrus Melange body wash out of the dispenser attached to the stone wall. She rubs her hands together for the third time until a foam waterfall cascades down her body and into the drain surrounded by tropical greenery. It doesn't matter how many times she does it, she can still smell petrol. Maybe it's suffused into her skin. Maybe it will never go away. Like the nauseous feeling in her stomach – as if she's woken up after downing too many vodkas.

She should have said something. Called out. Stopped it.

She turns up the temperature and feels the water prick her skin like hot needles. It hurts, but she won't let herself move, thinks about Skye going through so much worse. All because of her. She'd watched a reality TV programme with her mum last year following some woman who'd had reconstructive surgery after getting burnt in a house fire. She pushes the valve round further, increasing the heat until the scar on her leg begins to shriek in pain, begging her to stop. She makes herself count to ten before she allows herself to step out, pulls one of the white fluffy towels off the rack and wraps herself in it, walks back inside the bathroom, her reflection a deep crimson in the mirror.

She puts her hand up to her cheek, imagines it blistered,

her skin peeling off. The tips of her fingers charred lumps of flesh.

Could she live with that?

Alexa looks at her reflection in the mirror. She's fucked up, big time. And her dad has no idea. What if her mum says something? *She won't.* Her mum knows she saw her with Devi on the deck of their villa. She plays the scene in her head all over again. The angle of their bodies, the way Devi bent over her mother.

Skye hadn't slept with him.

She knows that now, can't believe she jumped to the wrong conclusion. Maybe if she tries hard enough, she can wipe this afternoon out of her memory. She's going home in a few days, and then she'll never have to think about it again.

It's so much easier to pretend it never happened.

Her brain flashes back to getting rid of the wine bottle. It had taken her much longer than she thought it would to find somewhere suitable. Eventually, she'd waded into the shallow sea in the dark, poured out the petrol, washed the outside of the glass in the water and then walked back up the beach, stuck it in one of the litter bins at the side of the path. She'd pushed it right down in amongst the empty crisp packets and ice-cream wrappers that were already in there, hoped it would be swallowed up, any link to her and what she's done completely erased.

She walks out of the bathroom and stops short when she sees her dad crouched down by the side of her bed, pulls her towel more tightly around her, self-conscious.

'Dad! It's after midnight. What are you doing?'

He stands up quickly and drops his phone, which skitters across the floor, coming to a halt in front of her feet.

'Sorry,' he says. 'I should have knocked. I just came in to borrow your charger.'

'Haven't you got one in your room?'

'Your mother's using it.'

Alexa bends down to pick up his phone and, as she hands it to him, she catches a glimpse of the message that pops up on the screen.

'Why is Charlie's dad texting you?' she asks.

Zach shoves the phone into the pocket of his towelling robe, his face flushed.

'He's seen the video.'

'This is going to be bad for your company, isn't it?'

Zach hesitates then shakes his head.

'Nothing I can't handle.'

Alexa stares at him, her damp arms feeling the chill of the air-conditioning. She wants him to leave so she can get into bed, but he hovers awkwardly, as if he's waiting to ask her something.

Please don't let Mum have said anything about the fire show.

'What?' she says.

Zach runs his hand through his hair.

'Nothing. Doesn't matter.' He turns to walk out.

'Aren't you going to take the charger?'

Alexa pulls it out of the plug socket and hands it to him. He smiles briefly before shutting the door behind him. Alexa listens to his footsteps as he walks across the living room then kneels down on the floor and looks under her bed, not really knowing what she's expecting to see. The wooden floorboards are bare, their surface polished until it shines, but she can't shake the feeling that he hadn't come in to borrow her charger at all.

As she pulls on a T-shirt and climbs into bed, she clicks on Skye's YouTube channel and looks at the comment she's posted.

Asana Fushi is one of the most beautiful places in the world. Dumping rubbish threatens to destroy the ecosystem — and this is happening around the world. People need to take notice and change their behaviour before it's too late. #Environmentaldamage #SaveOurSeas #ClimateChange #ZachHamilton

She plays the video again without sound, can't bear to hear about her dad's mistakes all over again. She focuses on the footage of Zach handing Marc the bag, and then Marc dropping it over the side of the boat. She spots the obvious cut in the footage and knows her dad was telling the truth. He hadn't dumped any rubbish overboard. Skye has edited the film to capitalize on his profile to raise her viewing figures. Some of the guilt that has been weighing her down lifts slightly, giving her room to breathe.

Skye isn't as truthful as Alexa thought she was. And if she's lied about this, what else has she lied about?

60. 9 hours 30 minutes left

Zach reaches out across the gap in the crisp, white cotton sheets on their four-poster bed and nudges his wife.

'Wake up,' he mutters. The fan hums as it spins above him, giving off a high-pitched whine that has been drilling into his head for the past few hours.

'What is it?' she mumbles, her voice thick.

'I need to talk to you about what we're going to do.'

She rolls over so she's facing him, and yawns.

'It's the middle of the night, Zach. What d'you mean, what we're going to do?'

'About the company. I've been up most of the night going through the cashflow, trying to sort things out, but it's not looking good, Cara.'

He doesn't want to panic her, but *not good* is a massive understatement. Things weren't looking great for the company before they came away, but now it's a complete shitshow. He can't believe how fast something can spread on social media. Every time he looks at that bloody video, the views have gone up by hundreds of thousands. He's had to turn on his *out of office* on his emails, something he hasn't done since starting the business, just to try and stem the flow of messages. Investors demanding that he issue a response, threatening to pull out left, right and centre.

And he hasn't been able to get hold of Victoria. The

illuminated numbers on the clock on his bedside table tells him it's 3.30 a.m. here, so 11.30 p.m. in the UK – she usually responds no matter what time he messages, but she hasn't answered any of his texts. He'd promised her he'd talk to Cara on this holiday, explain the situation and break the news to his wife that he's leaving her. He has no intention of doing that, of course, but if Victoria has seen the footage she'll know how much trouble the business is in, and Zach realizes he might now be a significantly less attractive prospect than he was a week ago. *What if she goes straight to Cara?* Then he's completely screwed.

His mother has tried phoning him, but he's let the calls go straight to voicemail. Until he's got another plan in place, having just buried the person he needed for his last one to succeed, he doesn't want to make things worse than they already are. If that's possible.

He rubs his eyes. They itch, and his skin feels as if it is being sloughed off by the grains of sand that continue to fall on to his pillow, despite his shower earlier. The stuff gets bloody everywhere.

'How bad is it?' Cara asks.

'Bad.'

There's a silence. Zach wishes his wife would reach out to comfort him, or edge a bit closer so he doesn't feel as if they are on opposite sides of the king-size mattress, but she stays exactly where she is.

'What are your options?' Cara asks.

He notices she doesn't say 'our options', or even 'the options'. 'Your' puts the ball firmly in his court.

'I don't know yet.'

She mumbles something and turns over again, pulling

the sheet with her so he feels the breeze from the fan against his exposed skin.

'What did you say?' he asks.

'I said I'm sure you'll come up with something.' She hesitates. 'It's your forte, Zach.' She buries her head further into the pillow. 'You always find a way to make the bad stuff disappear.'

That's no fucking help.

His wife can't even be bothered to stay awake to talk to him. *Bloody typical.* Why is he always the one who has to deal with everything? He's trying his best, but he needs someone to discuss this with. Cara always expects him to fix all their problems, as if he's some kind of fucking magician.

He swallows as the image of Marc's body, his limbs unnaturally contorted below a splash of orange, flashes into his head.

Don't think about it.

He tries to pretend those last few hours of his life never happened, pretend he hadn't rolled a body into a wheelbarrow and then tipped it into a hole in the sand. Lying in bed next to his wife, he can almost convince himself it's true. The visceral horror has started to blur around the edges. The more time that passes, the easier it will get. He visualizes waving goodbye to Marc after docking the boat at the jetty. If he does it enough times, at some point he might actually believe it.

He practises the look of surprise he's going to have on his face when he's told Marc is missing. A raise of the eyebrows, not too high, a slight widening of his eyes. The skin on his palms is chafed from where the handle of the spade has rubbed it raw, and he has two blisters which feel ready to burst, the liquid inside them hard when he presses them. He offers up a prayer that no one will find the body, or at least not until after he's left Asana Fushi.

What the fuck is he going to do about the company?

If ZH Investments goes under, they'll have no income. His salary will disappear and his shares will be worth nothing. They'll have the house, but it's heavily mortgaged and will have to be sold if they can't make the repayments. And they still have Alexa's school fees to pay. He can't imagine having to scale back his lifestyle. Doesn't want to have to explain to his friends why he's driving around in a Ford Focus and moving to a terraced house in a less salubrious neighbourhood. He doesn't deserve it after all the work he's put into making the business a success.

Could he ask his mother for a loan?

He's not subjecting himself to that kind of humiliation. And even if he did, at this point, he doubts whatever she could afford would be enough.

He looks at Cara lying motionless on the other side of the bed and shuts his eyes.

Think.

Ideas flicker through his brain in that place between being awake and asleep, the fan still whining, until something clicks and he opens his eyes in the darkness. It's not what he was hoping for. *A last resort, but maybe a possibility.*

Cara's right. He can make things disappear. After all, how difficult can it be when he's done it before?

61. 8 hours 30 minutes left

Her husband is a liar. Not only a liar, but a liability as well.

Cara lies very still in bed with her eyes closed, conscious of Zach less than three feet away, the sheet covering her body stretched taut. She focuses on breathing slowly in and out, pretends she's asleep. But sleep is the furthest thing from her mind. She's wide awake, thoughts fizzing in her brain like a series of tiny electric shocks. She's been analysing the last few years of their marriage with the benefit of hindsight, revisiting things they've done, snapshots of key events that stand out in full colour rather than the black-and-white monotony that constitutes everyday life. When did it all start? How long has he been lying to her?

Since Zach set up the business, he's always been busy. The time they spend together has become squeezed into ever smaller pockets, but they used to still *have* time. Somewhere along the line, she and her husband have slipped away from each other. They have been living mostly separate lives – still the perfect couple at any public event, but she can't remember the last time they sat down and talked about anything more important than what they were having for dinner. And that's if he comes home to eat at all.

Does she even want him in her life?

It's the question she's been asking herself over and over, for months, and she keeps coming up with the same answer.

Needs, maybe, but not *wants*. She no longer wants him. She doesn't think she has for some time, if she's honest with herself. *Needs* is something completely different.

Zach's income is what keeps them afloat. Allows them to have the kind of lifestyle she's become accustomed to. Even if she went back to work, she wouldn't earn a tenth of what he does.

Her husband has faults – she's not naïve – and she'd come out here with the intention of issuing an ultimatum. Her or me. A clear choice. One which she'd hoped it would be easy for him to make. He'd either see how much of an asset she was, or choose to walk away, and then she'd take him to the cleaners in a divorce.

But now Skye had leaked that video Zach's reputation isn't just shaky, it's been ripped into a million pieces.

And she has Alexa to consider.

She can't get the message she saw on his phone out of her head. It's burned on to the inside of her eyelids and reappears every single time she shuts them.

How could he do that? To his daughter? And his wife?

She knows there's no point in asking him. He'll just lie again. Like he's lying about whatever he was up to with Marc. They were probably getting hammered, or God knows what else that he clearly thought she'd disapprove of. He'd come back to the villa looking as if he'd been dragged through a bush backwards – to quote one of his mother's favourite phrases. She doesn't even care what he was doing; she's just thankful he wasn't here when Alexa came back. That he doesn't know what his daughter has done.

If she had been paying attention, maybe she would have

realized what was going on earlier. She's considered telling him she knows. Allowing it to spill out in a torrent of boiling rage, letting Alexa discover what kind of a man he really is. Something that would destroy the very heart of him. But he'd find a way to wriggle out of it. Come up with some excuse, tell her she's overreacting, that she's imagining things, dismiss it as yet another symptom of the menopause.

She needs to be clever. Her half-formed plan has crystallized into something more solid, but can she bring herself to go through with it?

Zach's snoring starts up again, irregular sounds that go silent for a few seconds; just enough time to lull her into a false sense of security and make her think they've stopped. She closes her eyes briefly, thinks again about the message on his phone, imagines how detached he must have felt to do that, how insignificant she and Alexa must be to him.

Her skin prickles. She slides herself slowly out of bed and turns around to study him – his eyes are still shut and his mouth is half open, strangulated sounds coming from his throat. She looks at her pillow lying next to his and for a second wonders what it would feel like to place it over his face and hold it there.

She turns away and pads silently across the floorboards into the bathroom, switches on the small light by the sink and rummages in her washbag to find what she's looking for, moving things about carefully so as not to make a noise, still listening out for his snores from the bedroom.

She rubs a couple of drops of lavender oil on her temples, turns off the light after smoothing her hair down in the mirror and stands for a minute in the darkness, half remembering a line from a long-forgotten play she'd studied at school. *Macbeth*. Something about being unfinished . . . but the words are just out of reach.

She rubs the goosebumps that have risen on her arms as she walks slowly across the floorboards before sliding back into bed. Her last thought before she falls into oblivion are the words she was trying to remember in the bathroom a few minutes earlier.

What's done cannot be undone.

62. 7 hours left

Alexa pulls the blanket over her feet. She's sitting in the hammock on the deck, letting it swing from side to side, staring out over the vast expanse of water. The sunrise is lighting up the horizon in a pink-and-orange glow. She can't sleep. It was cooler out here and she'd hoped she could drift off listening to the sound of the waves, but that hasn't happened. Her mind is buzzing and won't settle, despite her mindless scrolling.

Fuck.

Everything is such a mess. She can't stop thinking about finding her dad crouched down on the floor in her bedroom. He'd seemed embarrassed, as if she'd caught him doing something he shouldn't. She's sure he had just invented the crappy excuse that he needed to borrow a charger. She knows full well he already has one in his room, and her mother has her own – she's seen them both plugged in.

Why would he lie?

A thought slips into her mind like a gush of cold water. Had he seen her on the beach rinsing out the wine bottle? He can't have. He would have said something, wouldn't he? He's not the kind of person to hold back. Since the break-in, they've got closer than they used to be. She knows he feels guilty he wasn't there. Maybe he had seen her and was checking to see if she'd hidden something under her bed?

She prays the rubbish bins are emptied regularly and the staff don't look through them too closely.

She runs over their conversation again in her head. Maybe he'd been about to ask her about it and then the message from Charlie's dad had distracted him. She'd met Vincent once, briefly, at Charlie's. He had said a quick hello before disappearing into his study. Charlie said he travelled a lot for work, and she'd got the impression they weren't that close. Everyone at school knows he has a dodgy reputation; there are rumours he makes his money from something to do with drugs and his online travel agency is just a front. Alexa hadn't wanted to believe them, but she knows Charlie is the go-to person when her friends want to score. Ket, loud, molly – he can get his hands on pretty much anything.

Charlie's mum had been cool, though; she'd offered Alexa a vodka and Coke and given them bowls of popcorn to eat while they binged something on Netflix.

She checks her phone again. A new WhatsApp message pops up from Skye. She reads it, a sour taste filling her mouth.

I guess you've seen the video. I'm sorry I used a bit of artistic licence. I know your dad didn't actually dump the trash bags in the water, but he was on the boat and he must have known what Marc was doing. Did you know that 100,000 marine animals and 1 million seabirds are killed by marine plastic pollution every year? And I didn't lie about his investment in Sheimark. I think anyone who is such a hypocrite deserves to be called out, no matter what it takes, don't you? People won't change unless they're forced to take notice. I knew your dad's name would get everyone's attention, and I was right. It's had over a million views on my YouTube channel already.

I'm OK, by the way. Thanks for asking. Second-degree burns, and I might need a skin graft. Not sure if the octopus is going to look quite the same afterwards. The good news is I should be allowed out soon, so we can catch up for a chat and you can tell me why you did it. I'd really love to know. Because it was you, Alexa, wasn't it? I saw you running away at the end of the fire show. And one of the waiters, Farid, who came with me on the boat to the hospital, told me he saw you going into the storage room earlier in the afternoon. Carrying a bottle.

And I bet I could tell you what was in it, couldn't I, Alexa? After all, petrol does have a pretty distinctive smell.

63. 6 hours left

Zach holds out his plate as the chef standing behind the display counter slides on a freshly cooked heart-shaped waffle, showers it in cinnamon sugar and drizzles on melted chocolate. Normally he'd avoid anything like this – an overload of carbs in the morning means he loses the ability to concentrate, but he's knackered from too little sleep and knows he'll need every ounce of energy to get through today.

The breakfast buffet is set up each morning in the largest restaurant in the resort. The dark wooden building has a thatched roof, but the sides are open, overlooking the beach, where the tables are set up for guests. Every possible breakfast option Zach can think of is on offer at one of the counters: fresh fruit, yoghurt, honey dripping from honeycombs, sushi, cold meats, cheeses, sausages, bacon, muffins, pastries – the list is endless.

Ryan is behind him, his plate piled high with waffles and blueberry compote.

'The food is incredible, isn't it?'

Zach nods, not wanting to start a conversation.

'We should have a chat at some point, if you've got time.'

'Yes, that would be great. I'm a bit busy this morning,' Zach says. 'Cara and I are heading out for a private-island picnic, but maybe we can catch up later in the bar?'

Ryan looks at him. 'I've seen the video.'

Zach swallows. 'Well, as I'm sure you know, Ryan, things aren't necessarily always what they seem. My lawyers are already on the case.'

Ryan nods. 'Good luck with that. Reputation is everything in this industry.'

Zach starts to walk away, but Ryan carries on speaking.

'I wanted to give you a heads-up.'

Zach turns around.

'What about?'

'I had a chat with Victoria, your FD. Several chats, actually. She was particularly helpful when it came to providing information about that Sheimark investment. Not sure your lawyers are going to be able to dispute that one. Turns out she doesn't feel valued in her current position, so she's going to come and work for me instead. Help set up a branch of the business in the UK.' He slaps Zach on the shoulder. 'What was it you said at that conference? *Defeat your enemies with success.* I took a leaf out of your book. No hard feelings, though. Business is business, right?'

He walks away, leaving Zach to stumble back to where Cara is sitting at the edge of the beach, an attempt to stay as unobtrusive as possible. He prays none of the other guests have watched the video. Or if they have, that they don't recognize him.

He needs to speak to his solicitor. Tori had signed an NDA, the bitch. He'll sue the shit out of her. If she expects him to support her with the baby after this, she's got another think coming.

The waiter carries over the glass of freshly squeezed orange juice Cara has ordered, along with Zach's latte. He's crying out for a hit of caffeine after that news.

'*Shukuriyyaa*,' Cara says.

The waiter nods.

'Busier than usual in here this morning,' Zach says, peering at the man's name badge. 'Isn't it, Farid?'

Farid nods again as he lowers the tall glass and long silver spoon on to the table in front of Zach.

'We opened a little later than usual,' he says. 'Mr Geddes is off, as he's unwell.'

Cara frowns. 'Nothing serious, I hope?'

Farid smiles. 'I am sure he will be fine, Mrs Hamilton.'

'He seemed OK when we got off the boat last night. We were both just knackered,' Zach says, taking a sip of his drink, wincing at the bitter taste. No matter how many times he's asked, they still can't make a decent cup of coffee. *Smile. Act normal.*

'You were out with him yesterday?' Farid asks, wiping up the ring of water Cara's glass has left on the table with his napkin.

Zach nods. 'Game fishing. We didn't catch much.'

He watches the desire to ask more questions flicker across Farid's face as the waiter delays his exit by continuing to wipe the already dry table.

'We're going over to the deserted island for a picnic today,' Cara says. 'I was hoping to speak to Marc before we went. Will he be around later?'

Zach looks at her. *Shut up, Cara.* Too much chat about Marc and it'll start to look suspicious. He needs to change the subject, but Farid has already started to answer.

'I'm not sure, Mrs Hamilton. I guess we'll have to wait and see how he's feeling.'

Now change the subject.

Zach leans over the table and puts his hand over Cara's, a gesture so out of the ordinary that he feels her instinctively start to pull away before acquiescing. She looks across at the surface of the lagoon, which is barely moving, as if it's already too hot to make the effort.

'At least it's calm,' she says. 'It shouldn't take us that long to kayak. How far do you reckon it is?'

Zach shrugs. The island they are aiming for is currently a green dot in the distance. He wonders if the staff have taken the boat out already to set up the picnic, whether they noticed any smears of blood that he'd failed to clean off the deck.

He can feel the sun on his bare arms already. One of the blisters on his hands popped this morning and his palms feel sore when he presses them against his thighs, despite the plasters he's covered them with. The pain brings back flashes of last night: his back spasming, the sand rubbing against the strap of his flip-flops, the twisted monstrosity half hidden under the orange towels at the bottom of the hole. He shivers as he wonders how high the tide comes up the beach, whether it ever reaches as far as the bushes. *Christ, he hopes not.*

He just needs Marc's body not to be found straight away. Preferably never. At least until he's back home and the seawater coming into the hole has destroyed any DNA evidence.

'Done?' he asks Cara.

She swallows her last piece of French toast and nods as she wipes her mouth.

'Are we taking anything back for Alexa?' says Zach.

Cara shakes her head. 'She said she didn't want anything.'

He leans forward over the table and tucks a strand of loose hair behind her ear.

She grabs his hand, frowns as she sees the plasters.

'What happened?' she asks.

He pulls away.

'It's nothing. Just a couple of blisters from holding the fishing rods yesterday. Listen, I did a lot of thinking last night, Cara.' He hesitates before continuing. 'The business is in real trouble. We had a few financial issues before that video came out, which I should have told you about, but now . . .' He rubs the stubble on his chin as he lowers his voice. 'Now, I think some of our investors might pull out, and things are going to get very difficult.'

Cara doesn't say anything.

'I've been through all the options,' Zach says. 'Trust me, I barely slept last night.'

'What exactly are you saying?' Her green eyes study him.

He clears his throat.

'I don't know. I guess . . . I guess if you've got any ideas, now is the time to tell me.'

She doesn't answer as she folds her napkin into a neat square and pushes her chair out from under the table.

'I'll have a think,' she says. 'Can't Victoria help? I thought a good finance director would be able to come up with some options?'

He swallows. Pretends to straighten his mat on the table as he shakes his head.

'I think this is a bit beyond her capabilities.'

Cara doesn't break eye contact. 'Shame,' she says. 'You made it sound like she could work miracles. I didn't think there was anything she couldn't do.'

She starts to walk away from the table across the beach.

'I'll call into the diving centre and pick up the kayaks,' he shouts after her. 'Just make sure you and Alexa have packed everything and are ready to go.'

Can he really do this?

It's one thing having dark thoughts in the middle of the night, quite another carrying them out. Especially when they involve your wife.

What kind of a man is he? What is he capable of?

He already knows the answer to that. He wonders if the question he should be asking himself is what *isn't* he capable of.

64. 5 hours left

Cara walks back to the villa alone. She needs to remember to take suncream; there's already a hot line along the skin on her arm where it slipped beyond the shade of the umbrella during breakfast. She makes a list in her head of the other items to pack in her rucksack. A hat, a bottle of water, a sarong, a long-sleeved T-shirt and her phone.

Isn't there something else?

Whatever it is prods at her brain, trying to make her aware of its presence, but she's too preoccupied thinking about the plan she came up with last night. She'd hoped that having a good breakfast would settle her nerves but, in retrospect, fresh orange juice might have been a mistake. Acid poured on top of acid. Eating away at her insides.

She reaches the bleached wooden boards of the jetty, the villa only a hundred or so feet away, when she sees Devi walking towards her, carrying two laundry bags crammed full of dirty linen.

Shit. Shit. Shit.

She'd completely forgotten she was supposed to meet him last night. There's no way she can avoid him unless she turns around and walks off in the opposite direction. She fixes a smile on her face.

'Devi!'

'Mrs Hamilton.'

'Cara, please. It's nice to see you.'

He lowers the laundry bags so they are resting on the jetty. Her heart sinks. She needs this interaction to be quick so she can get back to the villa.

'I think we must have missed each other last night,' he says. 'I waited for you on the beach by the hammock, but you didn't turn up.'

She keeps her smile firmly in place.

'I'm so sorry. Alexa wasn't feeling well, Zach was out and I didn't want to leave her on her own.'

His forehead creases. 'You should have sent me a message to let me know.'

The silence between them stretches into something awkward, and she looks down at her feet, wiggles her toes against one another, feels the grains of damp sand that have stuck to her skin dig into her as she tries to think of something she can say to finish this conversation.

She points at one of the laundry bags. 'I hope Marc isn't giving you too much to do?'

'I haven't seen him today,' Devi says.

Cara raises her eyebrows. 'The waiter at breakfast said he wasn't well.'

A ringtone buzzes from the pocket of Devi's trousers.

'Aren't you going to get that?' Cara asks.

'It can wait.' He smiles. 'Have you been out for a swim yet? Such a lovely day for it.'

'No . . .' Cara trails off, hesitates. 'Zach and I are going to kayak over to the island for a picnic. Alexa still isn't feeling great, so I don't think she'll come. Maybe she and Marc have picked up the same bug.' She lets out a tight laugh.

Devi nods, lets go of the strap on one of the bags.

'Maybe. I spoke to Imani, Mrs Hamilton. She's very excited that you have agreed to help us.'

Cara feels her cheeks flush. She tucks a loose strand of hair behind her ear.

'That's good. I'm just in the process of sorting out the donation.'

Can he tell she's lying?

'Of course,' Devi says. 'I know it takes a bit of time. I could always speak to your husband, try and hurry things up a bit?'

Cara swallows. 'I don't think that will be necessary. I'll WhatsApp you later.' She looks at him, standing very still, as usual, rubbing his thumb and forefinger together in small circles. 'I heard about what happened at the fire show,' she adds. 'So awful. Is there going to be any kind of investigation?'

Devi looks down at the jetty, avoiding her gaze.

'I'm not sure yet.'

'Perhaps Marc will try and figure out what went wrong once he feels better. Have you heard how Skye is?'

'The hospital is deciding whether she needs a skin graft.'

Cara feels the acid bubble up from her stomach and burn the inside of her throat.

'The oddest thing happened last night, Mrs Hamilton.'

Cara tilts her head slightly to one side, her smile still glued on her face.

'Oh yes?'

'When I was waiting for you by the hammock, I thought I saw someone on the beach,' Devi says. 'Digging.'

Cara stands very still, suppresses the shiver that travels down the length of her spine.

Fuck. Had Alexa buried the wine bottle? Why hadn't she just thrown it away like she'd told her to?

'Did you?' she asks.

He doesn't reply.

Is he blackmailing her for more money? Christ, has he dug it up? Will it have Alexa's fingerprints on it?

She sees he has curled one of his hands into a fist and that his smile has disappeared. She bites the dry skin on her lip, tastes salt mixed with the tang of metal. Devi's phone buzzes again, the noise breaking his train of thought, and she seizes the opportunity.

'I'll leave you to get that. It was good to see you, Devi. I'll be in touch when I've sorted things out.'

Her arm briefly touches his as she squeezes past, and she flinches. Any feelings of desire have shrivelled away into something hard and unpleasant. Zach will be back any minute. She quickens her pace, forces herself not to run as a trickle of sweat slides down her back.

The front door of the villa clicks shut as she steps inside, her eyes taking a few seconds to adjust to the dim light. Alexa's empty bag is still on the dark wooden table and her throat tightens when she sees it. She shivers under the chill from the air-conditioning, kicks off her shoes and walks over to her daughter's bedroom.

Alexa is sitting on her bed, a can of diet Coke on her bedside table, a discarded banana skin and bare grape stalks lying on the sheet in front of her.

'Everything OK?' Cara knows it's a stupid question as soon as the words are out of her mouth.

'Did anyone say anything about Skye at breakfast?' Alexa asks.

Cara shakes her head. She'd heard several of the guests talking about the accident as they'd carried their plates piled high with pastries and exotic fruits around the buffet, commenting how dreadful it was that something like that could happen, but she isn't going to tell Alexa that. Give it a few days and the gossip will fade. It always does. Especially if people have something else to talk about.

'Have you said anything to Dad?' Alexa asks.

Cara perches on the side of the bed.

'No, of course I haven't.' She hesitates. 'He's got a lot on his mind, and I think it's best if we keep what happened between us. He's gone to collect the kayaks and then we're going to paddle over to the private island for our picnic.' She puts her hand on Alexa's arm. 'Do you still want to come? You don't have to if you don't want to, you know. You look shattered.'

'Do I?' Alexa takes a swig of Coke as her phone buzzes. She switches it to mute. 'I was hoping the caffeine would have kicked in by now.'

She tips her head forward and rolls it around in a circle as she rubs her shoulders. Cara waits, the tips of her fingers itching.

'I think I'll be OK to go with you,' Alexa says slowly.

'Are you sure?' Cara pulls her eyebrows together, as much as her Botox allows. 'You could sit out on the deck in the hammock if you stay here, catch up on some sleep.'

She can see her daughter weigh up the options as if she's walking along a tightrope, not knowing which way to fall.

If you push her, she'll do exactly the opposite of what you want.

'As long as you're happy to face the staff when they come and pick us up later,' Cara adds, 'then that's fine.'

She knows she's hit the right note when she sees Alexa's eyes widen a fraction.

'Maybe I'll stay here.' Alexa leans back against the pillows. 'I'll have a sleep, and I might go for a swim.'

Cara squeezes her daughter's hand as she hears the door to the villa open.

'Whatever you think best. I'll let Dad know.'

She holds on to Alexa's hand a little longer, then reluctantly forces herself to pull away. She has a flashback to them clinging to each other while one of the intruders pulled the cable ties tight around Alexa's wrists and ankles. Physical contact between them has been minimal since then; they're both scared of dredging up feelings they have tried hard to forget. Cara couldn't protect her then, but she will now.

'Thanks, Mum.'

Cara smiles as she shuts Alexa's bedroom door behind her. Zach is already in their bathroom, fishing about in his washbag to find his travel-sickness tablets.

'You ready?' he asks. 'I've tied the kayaks to one of the posts under our deck.'

Cara nods as she squeezes out a dollop of factor-fifty suncream and rubs it over her face and arms.

'Almost. Alexa's not coming. She doesn't feel great, and I think the last thing she needs is to be out in full sun for five hours straight. She's going to stay here and have a sleep.'

'Right.' Zach tweezers a couple of stray eyebrow hairs from his glabella, oblivious to her watching him in the mirror.

'I'll just grab a couple of things to put in my rucksack,' she says.

As she goes to walk out of the bathroom, Zach moves across to stand in the doorway, blocking her path. He reaches out and holds her face in his hands, kisses her briefly on the lips.

'I've had an idea,' he says. 'I'll explain it properly when we have our picnic, but I need you to listen to me without freaking out, OK?'

Cara hesitates, then nods.

She'll listen, but she has already decided what she's going to do. The thought makes her stomach squirm, as if it's full of snakes slithering over one another.

It's one thing if her husband destroys his own life by fucking up; she could even cope with him ruining hers. But hurting Alexa is something else. Protecting her daughter has always been, and always will be, her biggest priority.

Zach has no idea the lengths she'll go to in order to keep Alexa safe.

65. 4 hours 30 minutes left

The three yellow kayaks float in the crystal-clear water like oversized bananas. Zach climbs down the steps attached to the deck and lowers himself into the sea as Cara watches. The water in the lagoon only comes up to his waist – there are still a few hours to go until high tide. Thank God Alexa decided not to come – he wasn't sure how he was going to persuade her not to join them, but luckily she's saved him the trouble. He can't work out whether it's the incident at the fire show that's affected her or if she's still having issues with Charlie. Either way, as long as she stays in her room for the next few hours, he doesn't care. He unties one of the kayaks and pushes it up against the steps, holds out his hand to help his wife.

She hesitates, adjusts the straps on her rucksack before she climbs in and picks up her paddle.

'We don't need all three of them,' she says. 'Now Alexa's not coming.'

'Yes, we do.'

Zach unties the towline on one of the two kayaks still attached to the pole and knots it around the metal ring on the back of the other so they are fastened together.

'I'll explain in a bit,' he says. 'Can you hold this against the steps with your paddle so I can get in?'

Cara nods and Zach clambers awkwardly into the seat.

'You can stick your rucksack down by your feet if you want,' he says.

Cara shakes her head. 'It's fine. It's not heavy.'

Zach shrugs. 'Suit yourself. Let's paddle out. You can see the island over there.' He points in the direction of a small green blob surrounded by white sand. 'The guys in the diving centre said it would take about an hour to reach it, maybe less, depending on the current. The staff have already been over this morning to set up the picnic and they've left snorkelling gear out for us as well. Apparently there's an octopus that lives on the reef, and they said to be careful of the triggerfish. They're not usually aggressive, but it's their breeding season, so it's best to avoid them.'

'I'm not an idiot, Zach.'

He recognizes his wife's tone and knows she's rolling her eyes behind her VB mirrored aviators. She'd bought them in Duty Free, and he doesn't like them. Not brand friendly. *But who is he to talk?* She lifts up her paddle then lowers it into the water and follows him.

He paddles out to sea, keeping an eye on the island ahead, trying to ensure he doesn't drift away from the route he's aiming for. After ten minutes, he's sweating, drops of perspiration running down his forehead into his eyes. His breakfast starts to curdle in his stomach despite the tablets, and he wonders if they should have left earlier. The sun is gaining height in a cloudless blue sky, and the heat is relentless. No sign yet of the rain that has been forecast for later. He doesn't believe it will actually materialize – the weather has been perfect since they got here. The skin on his arms is already uncomfortably hot and the blister plasters on his palms are starting to peel. He stops paddling and waits for Cara to catch up.

'OK?'

She nods, takes a swig of water from the bottle in her rucksack.

'So why did you bring the other kayak?'

He looks at her.

'I need you to trust me. OK?'

She hesitates as she rests her paddle on the front of her kayak, then, 'OK,' she says.

He wishes he could see her eyes behind her sunglasses. *Does she really trust him?* He wouldn't blame her if she doesn't; she probably shouldn't. He wants to tell her that the last few months have been one disaster after another, that he'd never meant to hurt anyone, that everything has just got horribly out of hand. And he's been digging ever deeper holes, sometimes literally, in order to try and fix things, but nothing has worked and he's run out of options.

He swallows.

'I think we should disappear.'

For a few seconds, there is silence, apart from the sound of the water lapping against the fibreglass hulls of their kayaks.

'What do you mean, disappear?' Cara asks.

'Just that.' He tries to paddle to bring himself alongside her, but she moves backwards, away from him.

She doesn't trust him.

'Look, we've got the perfect opportunity,' he says. 'We'll leave some of our stuff on the island and capsize two of the kayaks offshore. People will think we've drowned.'

Cara continues to stare at him.

'And where will we actually be, Zach?'

'We can both fit in the other kayak. We'll paddle it back to

287

the resort, dump it somewhere close enough to be able to swim to the villa, and collect Alexa. They'll assume one of us tried to come back to get help but didn't make it.' He holds up his wrist to show he's wearing his Apple Watch with the smashed screen. 'We'll leave this in the water so they can trace it.'

'And when we get back to Asana Fushi, then what?'

'We leave. We'll catch the boat that goes on one of the day trips to Malé, then fly back to the UK.'

'The authorities will know we got on a plane, Zach. They'll be able to trace our names on the flight list.'

'Don't worry about that for now,' he says. 'You just need to trust me.'

'And then what?' Cara asks. 'What happens when we get back to England? What are we supposed to do then?'

'I can take some money out of the business before everything goes to shit and we can start again. Somewhere else.' He knows it doesn't sound convincing when he says it out loud, but at least she hasn't rejected the idea outright.

She cocks her head, lets go of her paddle briefly and runs one finger across her eyebrow, slumping forward a little.

'And how are you going to get cash out of a failing business? Ask Victoria to sort it out for you?'

He glances over the side of the kayak, pretends he's seen something in the water. He doesn't want to think about Tori right now. She'd texted him this morning saying she'd discovered she wasn't pregnant after all. *Thank Christ.* That this latest public exposé had been the final straw and she'd decided to take up a position with another company. Ryan Miller had been telling the truth.

'No,' he says. 'I'm perfectly capable of managing that myself.'

'You just expect Alexa and me to go along with this idea?' Cara asks.

'If you have any better suggestions, Cara, then I'm all ears.'

'Why didn't you talk to me about it earlier? Tell me what you'd done? We're supposed to be a partnership.'

'I'm talking to you now. And I'm telling you: we don't have another option. If we don't do this, we are going to end up with nothing. You've seen the reaction. The company is going to go under.'

'I thought Victoria was handling things while you're away,' Cara says, her tone icy.

'She's not responding to my emails,' Zach says. 'I can't get in touch with her. At least if we do this, we can salvage something from the business. I can get hold of enough cash for us to start again. A new life.'

He pushes his sunglasses on to his head and winces at the brightness, which is making his head hurt. The water is much deeper now they are out beyond the reef, in the channel between the two islands. The aqua colour of the lagoon has deepened into a midnight blue which stretches away for what feels like miles beneath him. He imagines the creatures that are lurking in the depths, remembers one of the waiters saying they'd had to stop the guests feeding the fish at dusk as it was attracting tiger sharks.

Nothing is going to attack a kayak. It's fine.

'I know it's a lot to take in,' he says, 'but I think this is our best chance of coming out of this godawful situation with something.' He turns his kayak around so he's facing the island. 'Have a think about it, yes?'

Cara nods slowly, takes another swig of water, then puts the bottle into her rucksack and paddles off ahead of him.

Zach watches her, his mouth dry. He considers stopping again to get his bottle out of his bag, but he can't get the image of Marc's face out of his head. He tells himself he'll have a drink when they reach the island. Just another thirty minutes of brisk paddling.

He's surprised Cara reacted so calmly to his suggestion. But then he hasn't told her the whole truth. If she knew he has no intention of hanging around as soon as they get back to England, she might not be so amiable.

66. 3 hours left

Cara's arms ache as she steps out of the kayak and pulls it up on to the soft white sand. She'd thought the beach on Asana Fushi was stunning, but this is even more beautiful. It's just the kind of desert island she'd seen in picture books when she was little. A few palm trees dotted around in the centre, surrounded by a sprinkling of vegetation, small enough that you could walk around the circumference in under five minutes. Tiny pale pink shells, smaller than her little fingernail, cover the shoreline. And just below the surface of the shallow water she can see reds, purples, yellows and blues – a vast carpet of live coral.

Four wooden poles have been stuck into the sand, a piece of white cloth suspended between them for shelter and three beanbag-style linen cushions arranged around a low table covered in different-sized boxes. It's a shame they aren't going to be here long enough for her to appreciate it.

Shade. It's what she needs right now. Anything to get out of this blistering sun, which beats down on her head despite her baseball cap. She walks across the beach, not waiting for Zach, who is struggling to pull the two kayaks out of the water. As she gets closer, she can see the boxes on the table are wicker hampers and a couple of cool bags. A bottle of champagne floats in a silver bucket amid a half-melted pool of ice cubes.

She sits down on one of the cushions and gulps a few mouthfuls of water from her flask, watches Zach stagger up the beach towards her and slump down on another cushion.

'Bloody hell, it's hot,' he says.

She nods, holds out her water bottle towards him as she unclips her life jacket.

'Want some?'

He shakes his head, fishes around in his rucksack. 'I've got some. That sun has given me a cracking headache.'

He lies back on the cushion and massages his temples.

'You really want to go through with this?' Cara asks.

'I don't see what else we can do.' He stifles a yawn and stretches out his arms, rolls them around in circles to relieve the muscle strain from paddling. Cara copies him. 'Do you?' he asks.

She notices the plasters on his hands have come off, and the skin is red raw around his blisters.

So many secrets.

'I agree we need a plan,' Cara says. 'If the company is going to go under. But people quickly lose interest in stuff on social media. You can issue a statement denying you knew anything about the dumping of the rubbish, say your investment in Sheimark was an attempt to improve working practices and sustainability from a position of power as a significant investor.'

She watches the muscles in his jaw tighten before he replies.

'If it weren't for the fact that the company was already in trouble, that would be a good idea. But we were already haemorrhaging cash on other projects. The investors aren't happy. Reputation is everything in this business. If they pull out, we wouldn't survive that kind of loss.'

He sits up, drinks some more water.

'If you want me to go along with what you're suggesting,' Cara says, 'we need to be completely honest with each other. Is there anything else you're not telling me?'

She notices the fraction of hesitation before he shakes his head.

''Course not.'

She's spent so many years seeing her husband as others do: as an innovator, a leader, someone who can command control of a room. And now she's not sure if he was ever any of those things. Whether his wealth and family privilege acted as a kind of disguise, and now that it's been ripped away she can see what's really underneath. Someone who, when it comes down to it, will always care most about himself.

'Promise?' she asks. Her world spins on its axis as she throws him a lifeline, one last chance.

He nods, and she expects to feel a return of the hot rage that had surged through her when she first saw that message, but she doesn't.

Right now, she feels absolutely nothing.

He gestures towards the ice bucket and wicker hampers. 'Do you want anything?' he asks.

She shakes her head. She's not hungry after that huge breakfast and she needs to keep a clear head.

'Shame to let such a lovely lunch go to waste, but if this plan is going to work, we need to get going,' he says. 'Give ourselves as much time as we can before anyone misses us.'

He takes a T-shirt out of his rucksack and lays it on the

sand before handing her the bag. 'Can you take this in your kayak so it doesn't get wet? Give me something of yours.'

Cara gets off the cushion and puts her sarong on top of Zach's T-shirt as he picks up the snorkelling gear.

'We'll take this with us. Dump it with the kayaks.' He winces as he steps on a patch of sand that isn't in the shade and he has to hold on to her shoulder as he scrabbles to get his feet back into his flip-flops. She stands very still, refuses to give in to the urge to shrug him off.

He smiles at her, and kisses the back of her neck.

Don't flinch.

She shuts her eyes, imagines him doing the same thing to Victoria, wonders how nineteen years of marriage have come to this.

'Shall we go, then?'

Cara puts her lifejacket back on, tightens it so hard into her skin she can no longer feel where he kissed her, follows him across the beach and climbs into her kayak. He pushes her into the water, manoeuvring his own boat together with the one tied behind it with his paddle so they are both floating in the shallow lagoon over the reef.

'Should have taken the glass-bottomed ones,' he says. 'Could have had a good look at everything underneath us. The coral must only be a couple of feet away here.'

She nods, trying to ignore the slithering she can feel in her stomach. Random thoughts float through her head – attempts by her subconscious to divorce herself from reality as she paddles over the multicoloured underwater garden towards where the edge of the reef drops away sharply.

She watches Zach's arms as he pulls each stroke: right,

then left; right, then left. *Is he getting slower, or is she imagining it?* She paddles past him, feels her heart pump with the exertion. Fifteen minutes later and they are back out in the dark blue channel, the ocean floor now impossible to see and the deserted picnic island a small circle of green surrounded by white sand in the distance.

She can see Asana Fushi in the opposite direction, the overwater villas tiny brown dots off to one side of the jetty. They are too far away to see anyone lying on Asana's beach.

Which means no one can see them either.

Zach unties the tow rope from his kayak, pulls the empty boat alongside him and tries to flip it over in the water, but it keeps slipping out of his grasp.

'Fuucck.'

His voice is slurred.

'Can you help me with this?'

She paddles over and reaches for the carry handle at the back of the kayak, helps him flip the boat over, watches it slowly float away. He breathes heavily as he picks up the masks and fins from where they lie by his feet and throws them into the sea too. They sink into the blue, deeper and deeper, until finally they disappear altogether.

How many metres is it to the bottom? Twenty? Thirty? More?

The snakes she felt earlier in her stomach are wriggling around so much now that she has to shift position. She grips her paddle a bit harder. He undoes the strap of his Apple watch and throws that into the water too.

'I'll swim to you, and then we can . . . Cara?' He holds up his hand to shade his eyes against the sun. He's staring directly at her, but it's as if he can't see her. She waves, and he frowns. 'Thought I'd lost you there for a minute.'

'No,' she says calmly, 'I'm still here. You can't get rid of me that easily.'

He starts to stand up, wobbles and is forced to slump down again.

'I'm going to swim over to you.' He runs his hand through his hair a couple of times as he repeats what he's just said. 'Do you feel OK?' he asks. 'I'm absolutely shattered.'

'Paddling is hard work,' she replies.

He raises himself out of his seat and half jumps, half falls into the water. Cara watches him try to swim towards her, more labouring doggy-paddle than the stylish front crawl she's used to seeing him do length after length in their pool at home. His kayak starts to float away, caught by the current.

She pulls her paddle through the water, left, then right, pushing her kayak backwards, away from him. He stops swimming, treads water as he looks around for her, his forehead creased in confusion.

'Cara! For fuck's sake, come towards me.'

She leans over the side of her kayak and shouts to him.

'*Have you told her yet, Zach? Tick, tock. She's going to find out sooner or later.*'

He spits out a mouthful of water as a wave splashes him in the face, rubs his eyes. She sees him frantically kick his legs to stay above the surface.

'What are you talking about?' he says after a pause. 'You need to bring your kayak closer; I can't reach you.'

Cara doesn't move.

'Do those words sound familiar to you at all?'

Zach frowns.

'I don't remember. Jesus, Cara. Do we really have to do this right now?'

She moves her kayak back a few more feet. 'Too tricky? I'll give you a clue, shall I?' she adds. 'Someone messaged them to you on your phone.'

Zach tries to swim towards her but gives up after a few strokes as he sees her back away even further.

'OK! OK, I'm sorry. Look, it was just a fling. It's over. It didn't mean anything.'

'Are you talking about Victoria?' Cara asks.

'Yes!' he shouts. 'I'm sorry. Just come and get me, please.'

Cara keeps her kayak exactly where it is.

'The thing is, Zach, the message I read wasn't from Victoria. I know you two have been texting, but I don't actually give a shit about that,' she says. 'I've known about your seedy little fling for months. All those late nights in the office. It doesn't take a genius to work it out. Victoria isn't the problem here. The problem is what you did to Alexa and me. Do you want to know what else that message said? *Get me my money, or I'll be back for another visit. Only a coward leaves his family to face the music.* Now do you remember who sent it?'

Cara hesitates, watches Zach's face as her words sink in.

'Yes,' she says. 'That's right. Vincent Pearce. I saw the message from him on your phone,' she continues. 'You knew he'd broken into our house, and you did nothing. You abandoned us. You left your wife and daughter with those *animals*, Zach. How could you? I guess you thought if you didn't bother showing up at all, they might give up and go home. But they didn't, did they? They only left because that delivery driver spooked them.'

Zach treads water, trying to see what's below him.

'I'm sorry, Cara. I had no idea he would actually do something like that.'

'So you did know? That he was in our house? With two of his *friends*?'

Zach disappears below the surface and reappears a couple of seconds later, struggling to catch his breath.

'I'll explain properly if you let me get in the kayak.'

'No, you can explain now.'

'Cara . . . please . . .'

'Now, Zach.'

'He'd lent me some money, OK? A lot of money. A loan to tide things over until the company was out of trouble. He didn't want to lose his investment, but the loan wasn't official. Vincent is involved in some shady stuff – I didn't ask for details. I had nowhere else to go – no bank was going to lend me what we needed, so I took what he was offering. But when I couldn't meet the interest repayments, he said he wanted all of it back. I didn't have it. He chased me for weeks, and I kept ignoring him. And then he called me and said he was at our house and that I needed to bring the money. I thought you'd hit one of the panic alarms . . .'

He trails off as he disappears underwater again for a few seconds in the swell.

'. . . and the police would come.'

'We didn't have a chance to get to any of the alarms,' Cara says. 'Your daughter and I were too busy having cable ties zipped round our wrists and ankles.'

'I didn't know what else to do!' he shouts. 'I panicked. I'm sorry, OK? I'm really sorry.'

'You could have called the police, Zach. Like any other normal human being would have done.'

'Vincent told me he'd kill you if I did.'

Cara raises her eyebrows.

'Right. And I don't suppose your failure to act had anything to do with the fact that if the police had found out they'd know you were involved with organized crime – yes, I've heard the rumours too – you know gossip spreads like wildfire amongst our friends – you would have been arrested and it would have been the end of the business?'

'I'm sorry. Honestly, Cara, I'll do anything to –'

'It's too late to be sorry,' she says. 'It's one thing leaving me with a bunch of psychopaths, but it's quite another to leave your daughter with them.'

'Just let me get into the kayak and we can talk about it.' He shuts his eyes briefly before opening them again.

'Your disappearing act would never have worked,' Cara says. 'I imagine you thought I'd play the doting wife, the sucker, as always. Then when we'd get home you'd launch the second half of your performance and vanish with Victoria.'

'I wouldn't –'

'I'm not as stupid as you think I am, Zach.'

'Cara . . . honestly, Victoria and I are finished. It was one night, and I –'

She can't bear to listen to his lies any more. She takes his rucksack and throws it towards him in the water.

'I'm giving you a chance, Zach,' she says. 'You might be able to catch up with your kayak if you start swimming now. You can use it as a float, and there's shade and a nice picnic waiting for you on the island if you can make it back a mile. You swim further than that at home. You just don't tend to do it after you've taken a double dose of sedatives.'

Zach swallows another mouthful of water, splutters loudly, and she wonders for a minute whether he's choking.

'You remember taking your travel-sickness tablets, don't you?' she says. 'It's easy to mistake one white tablet for another if they're in the wrong packet.'

She turns her kayak around so she's facing away from him and back towards the green dot of Asana Fushi in the distance.

Can she really do this?

She feels a twinge in her chest, but nothing significant enough to move the stone that has embedded itself where her heart should be. He started this. The enormity of what he's done cancels out any possibility of forgiveness. He left Alexa; now she's abandoning him. There's something satisfying in the circularity of it.

She puts her oar in the water and starts to paddle, ignores the frantic splashing and shouts coming from behind her.

Left, then right. Left, then right. The same strokes in a steady rhythm, over and over as the surface of the ocean speeds past beside her. Eventually she allows herself to pause. She stops the kayak and looks back over her shoulder. Blue water stretches out all around her, the small ripples on the surface sparkling in the sunlight. A yellow shape in the distance which must be one of the kayaks. But no sign of her husband.

Zach has completely disappeared.

67. 2 hours 45 minutes left

Alexa sits on the lounger. The cushion smells faintly of her mother's Gardénia perfume. She experiences a sharp prick of nostalgia, a sense of suddenly being alone. She glances at her phone, scrolls through her latest messages on Snapchat. It's the hottest day of their holiday so far and the deck scorches her feet when she steps on it without flip-flops. The lagoon sparkles in front of her, too bright to look at even through her sunglasses.

Only five days to go and she'll be out of here.

Even that thought doesn't ease the tightness she can feel across her neck and shoulders. It's as if someone has tied her muscles in a knot.

Maybe she should have gone on the picnic. She hasn't been able to sleep, the wi-fi keeps cutting out and she's uncomfortably hot, even in the shade. At least there would have been a breeze out in the ocean. She'd dangled her feet in the water but has been too scared to lower herself in entirely in case she gets too close to the coral again, and she's worried about sitting on the beach or by the main pool in case the staff ask her about Skye.

She adjusts her bikini top, covers up the red line under her bust where she'd missed a bit when she put the sun-cream on and gazes across the blue water to the deserted island in the distance. It's too far away to see properly, but she feels a lump of envy in her throat as she imagines her parents sitting on the powder-white sand, drinking champagne and eating prawns the size of lobsters off a skewer.

She needs to rehearse her story so that, when Skye is allowed out of hospital and comes back to Asana, it's word perfect. Tell her the waiter must have been mistaken. Be able to say it without a flush of colour rising up her cheeks.

What if more than one person had seen her?

Maybe she should say she was drunk, which would explain why she was carrying a wine bottle, then she could claim she'd gone into the storage room to try and find Devi. Say that Cara had been looking for him to fix a lamp that wasn't working in their villa. Her mother will cover for her if it comes to it, she knows she will.

What if there's an investigation? Could they trace what was on the gloves?

Dozens of questions she doesn't know the answers to whirl around in her head, but she can't risk googling anything in case it can be traced on her phone.

Alexa hears the sound of an engine and shades her eyes with her hand as she looks out over the water. It's the resort boat that collects guests from Malé if they choose not to take the seaplane. She watches it negotiate the marked channel, staying clear of the coral reef as it makes its way to the landing jetty on the other side of the island.

She bets most of the guests are from the UK. They all have that washed-out, anaemic look – a combination of hours of long-haul travel and months without sunshine.

All of them except two.

She pushes herself further back into the cushion on the lounger as if it will somehow hide her from view. Two policemen are sitting at the back of the boat wearing the

Maldivian uniform of sky-blue shirts with navy epaulettes. Alexa feels the liquid in her stomach freeze solid as she watches the boat disappear out of sight around the curve of the island.

They're coming to speak to her about the fire. Then they'll arrest her and she's never going to be able to go home.

68. 2 hours left

Cara's legs tremble as she grabs hold of the carry-handle on the back of the kayak and pulls it up on to the beach by the diving centre. There are a few others lying next to one another on the sand, black life jackets flung across their bright yellow shapes, reminding her of a swarm of wasps. She should check in with the staff, tell them she's brought the boat back, but they'll ask about Zach and she can't face any questions right now.

She leaves her kayak next to the others and heads back to the villa, walks the long way around on the beach to give herself time to think about what she's going to say to Alexa, and to avoid bumping into Marc, who will definitely ask her about Zach. Hopefully he's still feeling like shit and has decided to stay in his room.

The straps of her rucksack dig into her shoulders with each step, and her flip-flops sink into the white sand. She wonders if Zach's life-vest is still keeping him afloat, whether he made it back to his kayak. The waiter's comment about tiger sharks runs through her head; she wonders how many of them live in the depths, how often they come up to feed.

'Alexa?'

Cara calls out her daughter's name as she opens their villa door, but there's no answer. She slides her rucksack off her back and leaves it on the floor along with her baseball cap, wincing at how stiff her shoulders are.

'Alexa?'

Still nothing. The villa is silent, apart from the low hum of the air-conditioning unit. The polished floorboards and furniture that seemed so luxurious when they first arrived now feel rather unwelcoming. She slips off her flip-flops and walks past the coffee table, avoids looking down through the glass panel into the water, struck by the horrific thought that at any second Zach's face might float into view.

That's impossible. He's at least a couple of miles away.

'Alexa?'

She knocks on her daughter's bedroom door, opens it when she doesn't get a reply. The room is empty, but the sliding glass doors out to the deck aren't fully closed. There is a small gap on one side and she can see someone sitting on one of the loungers outside.

She steps out on to the deck, sees the small white buds sticking out of Alexa's ears and realizes she has her AirPods in. Alexa jumps as she taps her on the shoulder, lets out a shriek as she turns around on the lounger.

'Fucking hell, Mum!'

Her face is white, and Cara can see she's been crying. She holds up her hands.

'Sorry, sweetheart. I didn't mean to scare you.'

'You could have called out or something. I didn't know it was you.'

'I did knock, and call,' Cara says.

'Not loud enough.'

Cara bites her lip. *Alexa's right.* She doesn't like being taken by surprise now either. Most of the time Cara thinks she's over it, but when she feels an unexpected hand on her arm, or hears people shouting, it all comes rushing back.

Zach deserves whatever happens to him.

'I'm sorry. Are you OK?'

Alexa hesitates, then shakes her head.

'The police are here,' she whispers. 'I just saw them arriving on the boat from Malé.' Alexa wrinkles her nose as her eyes fill with tears. 'Skye knows it was me, Mum. She sent me a WhatsApp and said one of the waiters saw me going into the storage room before the show carrying a bottle.'

Cara hesitates. 'That doesn't prove anything.'

She sits down on the lounger next to Alexa, and her daughter throws her arms around Cara's neck and buries her face in her shoulder.

'I don't want to talk to the police, Mum. I can't. I know I shouldn't have done it. I didn't mean for Skye to get hurt – it was meant to be Devi. I thought he'd done something, but I think I got it all wrong and . . .'

Cara rubs her daughter's back, unused to this display of emotion.

'We'll sort it, don't worry.'

'How are we going to sort it, Mum? The police will arrest me. What if they've worked out there was petrol on those gloves? What if someone saw me getting rid of the bottle?'

The conversation Cara had with Devi flashes into her head and she feels her heart flutter. The police will ask the staff if they saw anything, and Devi made it quite clear that he had. She can't tell Alexa. Now is not the time. She disentangles herself from her daughter's embrace.

'If the police are here, then we need to leave,' she says. 'Now. Before they have a chance to ask you anything. I don't imagine they'll pursue you once we've gone. It won't be worth their while unless they have solid proof, and if they do, we can get a solicitor involved.'

She rubs the palm of her hand where it's chafed from the kayak paddle.

Zach didn't protect Alexa. But she will.

'We'll get on the boat that goes back to Malé – the one the police came in on goes back again in about an hour, and I can move our flights online.'

She stands up, squeezes Alexa's shoulder. 'Come on. Get up. You need to pack, but anything you don't really need, leave here. The less we have to carry, the better.'

Alexa doesn't move from the lounger.

'Where's Dad?' she asks.

Cara swallows. 'Isn't he here?'

Alexa shakes her head. 'Didn't he come back with you? I've been trying to call him, but his phone goes straight to voicemail.'

Cara looks out over the water, the brightness making her eyes hurt. Her forehead feels tender where the brim of her baseball cap didn't quite shade it.

How long could someone survive in the sea out here?

'Dad and I had a row when we got to the island,' she says slowly. 'He stormed off with one of the kayaks and said he was coming back to the villa. I thought he'd get here before I did. Why were you trying to call him?'

Alexa fiddles with the corner of her towel, picking at the threads until they come loose.

'I was going to tell him the police were here. I wanted

to ask him what to do.' She glances at her phone on the lounger beside her and Cara feels her stomach squeeze.

'What were you arguing about?' Alexa asks.

Cara grits her teeth. She doesn't want to do this, but she has no choice. She needs to do whatever it takes to get Alexa to leave.

'I saw a message on Dad's phone. From Vincent Pearce. He was one of the men who broke into our house that night.'

Alexa frowns.

'Charlie's dad?'

Cara shuts her eyes briefly.

'Yes,' she continues, 'and Dad knew about it. At the time, I mean. He knew Charlie's dad was in our house, threatening us, and he didn't do anything to stop him.'

'There's no way he'd do that.' Alexa moves to stand up, but Cara holds on to her wrist.

'I only just found out,' Cara says. 'I had no idea, and I didn't want to have to tell you. Vincent loaned Dad some money. Dad couldn't pay him – the business is in trouble – and Vincent has been chasing him ever since.'

Tears well up in Alexa's eyes.

'I can't believe he'd do that to us. Why didn't he just call the police?'

'Apparently the loan wasn't legal. If the police had found out about it, Dad would have been arrested too.'

'So he prioritized not being arrested over our safety?'

Cara doesn't answer. 'I don't know,' she says finally, 'but none of that changes the fact that you are my priority. You always have been and always will be. And we need to go home. Now.'

'Without Dad?'

Cara nods.

'I'm leaving him, Alexa. I can't stay with him now. I need you to pack quickly so we can get out of here before the police come looking for you.'

And before Devi knocks on the door.

It won't be long before he realizes the police are here. Then he'll tell them what he saw on the beach and give them a master key to get into the villa.

There's no way she's going to let that happen.

69. 1 hour left

Cara sits next to Alexa on the boat, her back pressed up against the seat as droplets of spray splash against her face. Her black wheelie case is squashed between her legs, the hot plastic sticking to her skin. Asana Fushi recedes into the distance behind them. There are only two other guests on board apart from themselves – a couple who must have just got engaged. The woman can't stop staring at the diamond ring on her finger. Two carats at least. She had smiled at Cara, briefly, but Cara had looked away, unable to bring herself to smile back.

She recognizes the men at the controls. The one steering the boat also works in the diving centre, but he is busy chatting to his friend, and apart from giving the standard safety briefing and offering them a bottle of water, neither of them has paid much attention to her or Alexa.

She had felt as if she couldn't breathe as she'd walked out of the villa and along the jetty to the other side of the island. She'd expected the police to appear at any second, and could see that Alexa felt the same way. As they had made their way up the sandy path, she'd had to tell Alexa not to let the tears welling up in her eyes spill over when her case with its stupidly small wheels got stuck on a tree root. She can still feel the damp patches under her arms, the tight knot in her stomach that is only now starting to loosen the further the boat gets away from the resort, bouncing as it cuts through the swell.

She glances at her daughter, leans over and squeezes her hand.

'All right?' Cara asks.

Alexa nods, but one hand fiddles with her helix piercing.

'It's going to be OK,' Cara says, keeping her voice low enough so the honeymoon couple can't hear, although, over the noise of the engine, she thinks that would be impossible. 'I've changed our flights, and we'll be there in plenty of time to check in.' She gets out her mobile and forwards Alexa's boarding pass to her phone, watches her add it to her wallet. Alexa Mireille Hamilton. Zach had insisted on Mireille. After his mother. Cara has no idea how she's going to manage *that* situation when they get back.

One thing at a time.

'We're flying British Airways to Heathrow. BA568. Departs in four hours, so 5 p.m. Malé time, as they're an hour ahead of Asana,' she says.

'Are we sitting next to each other?' Alexa asks.

Cara nods.

She squeezes Alexa's hand again before turning away and looking out over the blue water. She can see the picnic island off to one side in the distance – the powder-white-sand beach, the palm trees in the middle and the sailcloth held up by four poles. No sign of any kayaks. Or Zach. She adjusts her grip on the guardrail, her knuckles bleached white.

A series of worst-case scenarios plays out in her head. She imagines the police will be waiting for them when the boat docks in Malé, that she'll watch while Alexa is handcuffed, separated from her, taken into custody and locked away somewhere. Or a security guard at the airport will take one look at her daughter's passport before asking her to step aside and telling her they need to have a chat.

She takes a deep breath and lets it out slowly, trying to stay calm, but knows she won't be able to relax until the plane is in the air on the way back to the UK.

She thinks of her Zach, of all his things still in the villa: his clothes hanging in the wardrobe, a pair of his swimming trunks drying outside on the deck. And then she thinks of Vincent's face a couple of inches away from hers, so close she could feel his breath on her skin, his eyes staring at her through the slits in his balaclava. He knew who Alexa was. It had been a game to him, waiting to see if the penny would drop. She shivers.

How could Zach have done that to them?

She takes her hand off the guardrail and frowns as she realizes the tips of her fingers are covered in something black. They feel tacky when she rubs them together. She fishes in the pocket of her dress for a tissue, puts it over the neck of her bottle of water and tips it upside down before rubbing the tissue over her fingers. The staff obviously haven't cleaned the boat properly. *What is it? Oil? Tar?* She rubs a bit harder to get rid of it and her stomach somersaults as she looks at the damp tissue. It's turned a dark red colour. *Jesus. Is it blood?* She swallows, trying not to gag as she drops the tissue on the floor and kicks it under the seat in front of her to get it as far away as possible.

'I thought Dad wanted to spend more time together because he was worried about me,' Alexa says quietly. 'I thought he wanted to talk about what happened to see if we could tell the police something that would help catch those men. But he didn't care about me at all. He only cared about being found out.'

Cara looks at her but doesn't reply. What is she supposed to say? That despite all his faults, Zach still loved her? That he'd done what he thought was for the best? That he cared more about himself than either of them? There's an element of truth in all these thoughts, but before she can decide what to say Alexa continues speaking.

'As far as I'm concerned, Mum, when we get back home, I never want to see him again.'

70. 5 minutes left

He hadn't wanted this job. But at the end of the day, money is money, and when Vincent had offered to double his fee when he said no, he hadn't felt he could turn down the offer. After all, he has a reputation to maintain.

For this kind of task, a certain level of detachment is required. The less he knows, the better. He's not usually interested in the whys and wherefores, the reasons that have led up to this point. Emotional involvement clouds judgement and leads to mistakes. It distinguishes the professionals from the amateurs in his field. As a rule, he only needs to see a photo, to be told the when, where and how.

But on this occasion, it's slightly more complicated. He's never seen the man in the photo Vincent showed him before, but he knows who he is, has even been in his house. Twice. The first time, he'd tied up his wife and daughter. It seems Zach Hamilton would rather sacrifice his family than pay Vincent what he owed. That's real desperation for you. He feels that unfamiliar tug in his gut again as he thinks about what he's going to have to do.

Malé airport is already crowded. People congregate in groups beneath departure boards, staring up at them, trying to work out where to go. Lines of tourists pushing trolleys full of suitcases join queues that shuffle slowly forward towards the banks of check-in desks.

He stands very still and looks again at the information he's been sent on his phone. The constant low-level hum that surrounds him, punctuated by loud shrieks of laughter, is distracting.

He prefers to work when it's quiet. It helps him to concentrate.

That last job had been a shitshow. Vincent's planning has become sloppy. Just because he'd never been caught before, it didn't mean it couldn't happen. Things aren't run how they used to be, and he knows he's the one who will have to serve time without complaining if something goes wrong.

That's why they'd decided he needed to come out here. They could have waited until Zach Hamilton got home, but an accident on holiday is easier to cover up than it is on home turf. And thanks to that influencer's video, they knew exactly where he was. Now he just needs to get to Asana Fushi, and he's booked on the next seaplane transfer to take him there.

He glances at his watch. Probably just enough time to get a coffee. The screens above the British Airways check-in desks flicker as the number of the next flight flashes up. BA568 to London Heathrow. Departing at 5 p.m., currently no delays. The queue is already starting to build up. He's got a few days to get this done, and then he'll be catching that flight home again.

Vincent has told him to get the job done cleanly. Drowning is his method of choice. Easily dismissed as an accident if there's no obvious bruising. But he's been instructed to do whatever is necessary to ensure that Zach Hamilton realizes that when it comes to Vincent Pearce, failure to repay a debt is not an option. They need to set an example or the business will collapse, like a pile of Jenga blocks.

The thought that had occurred to him yesterday when he was driving home down the motorway niggles in his brain. What if he ignored Vincent's orders? From what he's heard about Zach Hamilton, he's certain he'd be willing to pay to stay alive. And between the two of them, he's sure they could come up with a way to make Vincent think he'd done as he was asked. He wouldn't need his boss after that kind of pay-off and, if Zach disappeared, Vincent would never have to know he was still alive. He knows the people who could make it happen. Early retirement would become a possibility. Vincent knows it's on the cards in the next few years anyway. He could come back out here for a holiday with the family. Jamie and Marie would love it. A step up from making sandcastles on Branksome beach.

Don't be ridiculous.

Vincent would kill him if he found out. That tug in his gut again as the image of a man lying in a car boot pops into his head. But if he was careful, Vincent wouldn't find out, would he? He blinks, shakes the thought away.

Focus.

He heads towards one of the small cafés he can see ahead of him, the smell of coffee cutting through the stuffiness and stale perspiration. A teenage girl knocks into his arm, her eyes fixed on her phone. She stumbles slightly, one of her AirPods falling out of her ear.

'Sorry,' she says.

'No problem.'

He bends down to retrieve the white earpiece and notices the scar on her shin as he hands it back to her.

'Thanks.'

He takes in her long brown hair and gold nose ring, registers her familiarity and smiles, a reflex reaction to cover his shock.

It's her.

She glances across the departure lounge, and he can see her staring at her mother. Neither of them is supposed to be here. And if they're here, where the hell is Zach?

She smiles back at him, but he breaks eye contact as he assesses the situation, wishes she'd chosen some other place to be today, that she'd arrived five minutes earlier, or later.

He should really call Vincent. But he knows what Vincent will say. They have a set of rules for this situation. If he can't find Zach, his family is the next best option.

71. Zero minutes left

Cara watches the man with his black rucksack tightly strapped over both his shoulders study her daughter. She'd experienced a feeling she can't articulate when he'd bent down and picked up Alexa's AirPod. An internal warning system that has been honed to perfection over many years. One that Alexa has only just started to develop. One that warns her to step away, to move to the other side of the road, to cover her drink. It was sharp, almost painful, like an electric shock that has morphed into a kind of hypersensitivity to the noises around her.

She starts to walk towards Alexa, oblivious to the dozens of tourists who are milling aimlessly around her in the departures hall. Her daughter has stopped moving. Her limbs are unnaturally frozen, her hand gripping the handle of her carry-on case as if it's stuck to her. Alexa gazes at her wordlessly as Cara breaks into a jog in a desperate effort to cover the fifty or so feet between them as fast as possible. She realizes with a growing sense of horror that the man standing next to her daughter is whispering something to her. Alexa's eyes grow wider as his lips move.

Even worse, she realizes he has his hand around her daughter's wrist and is squeezing it tightly, like a vice.

She tries to scream, but no sound comes out.

There is a loud humming in her head as she squints in the brightness of the strip lighting above her. Her legs are

317

heavy weights, each foot glued to the shiny stone floor as she assimilates his features. His shaved head. Dark eyes. Understanding floods through her body; it's like being plunged into ice-cold water.

It's him.

It can't be.

It's definitely him.

The face she'd glimpsed briefly through a bathroom window. The man she'd seen while she was scuba diving. The person who haunts her dreams.

Why is he here? What does he want?

She knows the answer to that question before her brain has finished asking it.

Zach. This man is here to collect what Vincent is owed. Cara realizes with a jolt of horror that it's the first time she's felt any regret at leaving Zach floundering in the sea. If he was here now, she'd hand him over without a moment's hesitation if it meant this man would leave Alexa alone.

She can't breathe. Twenty feet to go, and her legs are lumps of jelly that refuse to obey her instructions to move forward, getting themselves tangled up in the suitcase she'd forgotten she was still dragging behind her.

The man holds up his hand, a sign not to come any closer. He takes a phone out of his pocket and starts to pull Alexa backwards with him across the lounge, leaving her case lying abandoned on the floor. Cara takes another step forward, but Alexa shakes her head, her eyes fixed on her mother. Cara's breath escapes in a sob.

Please God, no. Don't take her away from me.

Has he got a knife? A gun?

Why else would Alexa be shaking her head?

Cara doesn't know what to do. She can't think. Her brain is a blank white canvas, paralysed by indecision. She's terrified anything she does or says will just make everything worse. She looks around desperately for someone – anyone – to help her.

The man moves with Alexa across the floor, his hand still tightly clasped around her wrist, a macabre dance in which their bodies bump together in an unnatural closeness. The entrance to the terminal is less than a hundred feet away, and Cara knows, feels it deep in her bones, that if she lets him leave she won't see Alexa again.

She takes another few steps towards them, but Alexa shakes her head again, and the man frowns.

There's an unexpected crash as someone in the café drops their tray, and Cara watches their cup smash as it hits the ground, pieces of crockery and brown liquid spreading across the terminal floor. The man turns his head to look and Cara seizes the opportunity. She lets go of her case and sprints towards the two policemen who have emerged from beside one of the check-in queues.

'Please,' she gasps. 'You have to help me. That man –' She turns around to point at him, and for a second her vision clouds over as she realizes she can no longer see him. Or Alexa.

Fuck.

He can't have gone, not yet. Not that fast.

She glances frantically at the various groups of people, shapes and colours merging into one until she finally spots him trying to edge around an extended family group who are standing with their luggage trolleys, oblivious to his efforts to get past.

'. . . that man' – she jabs her finger towards him – 'has taken my daughter. Please. You have to help me.'

For a few seconds, the men in blue uniform just stare at her, and Cara wonders if they've understood, whether they think she's a lunatic. The man has almost reached the set of doors that will take the two of them outside.

'Please,' Cara says. 'Please, you have to help me.'

But as she says the words, her eyes still fixed on her daughter, she knows it's too late: they won't be able to reach Alexa in time. She's too far away, and the man has started to jog, his rucksack straps lifting on his shoulders as he pulls Alexa along with him.

Cara's heart thumps, electric shocks pricking the bottom of her stomach. This can't be happening. Not now.

One of the policemen looks where she is pointing, then back at her, and reaches down for the radio attached to his shirt. He mutters something into the mouthpiece in a language she doesn't understand. She starts to run across the floor towards the doors, not caring now whether or not the man has a knife, desperate not to let Alexa out of her sight.

The man reaches the automatic glass doors and they slide open smoothly, and the two of them step through, only to come face to face with another policeman standing on the street outside. Cara stumbles to her knees in relief as she watches the silent altercation through the floor-to-ceiling windows, sees the man let go of Alexa and hold up his hands before he turns and runs away, pushing past the crowd of tourists standing on the pavement.

Cara throws her arms around her daughter when the policeman brings her back inside.

'Thank you,' she tries to say, but her mouth is too dry and her lips get stuck on her teeth. She holds on to Alexa's hand, her face ashen as she glances back outside at the policemen. A few more appear, all shouting instructions to one another as they run down the street, searching amongst the crowd of tourists.

But she knows it's pointless. The man has vanished.

Epilogue

February 2024 – Two months later

'Thank you. Yes, me too. Speak soon.'

Cara sits down on one of the bar stools by the slate-topped island in her kitchen, surrounded by the last few packing boxes. The only things she wants to keep from her life with Zach; she's given away most of them. Time for a fresh start. The dampness of the February afternoon hangs in the air and she pulls her cashmere throw more tightly around her shoulders as she looks out of the bifold doors to where the removal men are packing up the garden furniture.

She can't believe it was only eight weeks ago that they landed in the Maldives. If she shuts her eyes, she can still remember the heat of the sun on her face as she stepped out of the airport terminal in Malé, can still feel Zach's hand on hers when they sat down on the seaplane. Part of her can't believe he's gone; she still expects to hear a knock on their door and for him to walk back in.

She glances at her mobile lying beside her. She's just finished a call with her family liaison officer. They'd had them frequently to start with, after Zach's kayak was found, but as the weeks went on and there wasn't any other news to speak of, the updates have become less and less frequent, and she knows at some point soon they will stop altogether.

Occasionally she catches herself missing him. But not as much as she thought she would. He's slipped out of her life with minimal disruption, one of the advantages of him not having been fully functional within it to start with. The insurance pay-out will give her enough to start again, although the bank demanded the sale of the house following the collapse of the business. Zach hadn't told her he'd remortgaged it.

She glances at the clock. Alexa will be home from school soon. Not the same one she was at eight weeks ago. A new one in the area they are moving to. When they'd first got home, she hadn't wanted to let Alexa out of her sight. She'd driven her to her new school, waiting outside until she'd seen her go in through the gates, had insisted on putting a tracker on her phone and had refused to let her go into town with her friends. But as time went on, she'd found herself slowly relaxing. The house no longer needed to be locked up like Fort Knox, she'd stopped looking over her shoulder every time she went out, and Alexa had started seeing her friends again, promising to call if she was running late. Vincent Pearce hasn't been in touch, and she's under no illusions that he would have been by now if he'd wanted to. Made a personal appearance, or sent someone else. Maybe Zach's absence has satisfied him, or maybe he knows they have nothing left worth taking.

Alexa has reacted surprisingly well to the news that her father is missing, presumed drowned. Amongst a myriad of other emotions, the relief on her daughter's face had been evident when Cara had told her about his rucksack being found in the kayak. As if it had conveniently removed the necessity for her to confront him about the break-in. What he'd known and when. Whether he really had deserted her. Cara knows it's sometimes easier not to have to deal with the whole truth.

Her phone buzzes. She expects it to be her daughter asking for a lift because she can't be bothered to walk home from the train station. The two of them have been edging back towards each other and the way things were before the break-in.

But it's not Alexa.

It's a message from Devi.

Hello, Mrs Hamilton. I hope you are well and are bearing up in the circumstances. I know we haven't been in touch since you left, but I thought you might be interested to know I have been promoted to resort manager at Asana Fushi. I'm contacting you now as I have something I think you might be interested to see.

She grips the phone more tightly, her vein beating a visible pulse under her skin.

Please don't let it be anything to do with Alexa getting rid of that bottle.

She'd seen Skye on TV recently. Presenting a follow-up to her initial exposé on Zach. Her hand appeared to have healed without the need for a skin graft, *thank God*. Alexa told her that Skye had sent her a message asking if she wanted to tell her side of the story – something Cara had vetoed from the start. There had been no mention of Farid and what he thought he'd seen. But then Cara hadn't expected there to be, once she'd contacted him directly as soon as they got home. Following a payment equivalent to two months' salary into his bank account, his memory of what he'd seen that afternoon had become somewhat hazy. Cara's fear that Alexa could be prosecuted had gradually ebbed away, and now, it's something she rarely thinks about.

She clicks play on the video that appears and holds her breath, her stomach contracting at the thought of what she's about to watch.

The video fades in and out of focus, taken on a phone by someone in a crowd of people chanting and holding up banners. She recognizes the location as the quayside in Malé near the airport; she can see the seaplanes lined up in the water behind them. At first, she can't work out what is going on, but after a few seconds she realizes that the people in the crowd are protesters, brandishing various torn-up sheets and cardboard signs with different slogans daubed on them in coloured paint. ALLOW THE MALDIVES TO HAVE A FUTURE. ONE EARTH, ONE CHANCE. RISING SEA LEVELS ARE KILLING US. ECO-FRIENDLY IS THE WAY FORWARD #ASANA. SAVE THE CORAL REEFS.

The camera swings around, the presenter's commentary about rising sea levels only just audible over the loud chanting. She frowns, confused. The crowd cheers again, and as she looks closer she experiences the sensation of the floor being ripped away from beneath her feet. The video pauses. It's been edited so that a circle appears around the figure of a man in the crowd. The video zooms in.

Zach.

Without his glasses, he's harder to recognize, but it's definitely her husband. He has his hand up to his forehead, shading his eyes, and seems to be staring at something. The video zooms out again to reveal another man. He's crossing the road, heading into the airport terminal at Malé. Cara squints, her heart thudding in her chest. It's the man with the shaved head who tried to abduct Alexa. She watches as he stops, looks in Zach's direction and raises his hand. Zach holds up his thumb, and then disappears into the crowd.

Fuck.

The video finishes, and she waits, her body trembling, as another message pings on to her screen.

It was a nice surprise to see your husband again, Mrs Hamilton. After that night when I watched him digging a hole on the beach, and then all that business with his kayak being found, I didn't think it was possible.

Cara frowns. What hole? What is Devi talking about?

This video was taken by one of our guests a couple of days after you left. They sent it to me as one of the slogans mentioned the Asana resort. As you can see, Zach isn't easy to spot, and it was only when I zoomed in that I realized it was him. It seems as if your husband is a man who likes to bury things, Mrs Hamilton. Did you know that the manager here, Marc, hasn't been seen since the evening he took a boat trip with your husband? The official line the staff have been told is that he left without working his notice to spend time with his family, but I don't think that's actually the case, do you?

Something slithers in the bottom of Cara's stomach.

What the fuck did you do, Zach?

I trust that you are comfortable now that you are home, Mrs Hamilton, and that your husband had life insurance? I presume any payment would be immediately cancelled by the insurance company if there was proof he was still alive? Perhaps now that you have seen my side of things, this would be an ideal opportunity for me to take you up on the generous offer you made while you were here. My daughter would really appreciate it.

A name and a set of bank details follow the message. Cara feels a shiver run down her spine. Zach's life insurance was adequate, but not overly generous, and after their new house purchase, she's going to find it difficult to stretch to that kind of payment. Her phone pings again.

Of course, there are very many good causes that need funds nowadays, aren't there, Mrs Hamilton? Nothing is more important than preserving the planet for the next generation. Perhaps you would be kind enough to forward double what we originally agreed? Thanks so much for your kindness – I'll make sure to keep in touch regularly going forward.

Acknowledgements

I would like to thank the entire team at my amazing publisher, Penguin, for all their support over this past year – both with this book and also *The Beach Party*. I feel very lucky to have been able to work again with Harriet Bourton, Vikki Moynes, Lydia Fried, Ellie Hudson, Ellie Smith, Jane Gentle and Gray Eveleigh, and I couldn't ask for a better team. No doubt there are many others behind the scenes, and I am so grateful for all your efforts.

Thank you also to Charlotte Daniels, who has somehow managed to come up with a cover that I adore as much as the one for *The Beach Party*, and to Sarah Day, for her copy-edits, that I feel were possibly some of the most challenging she must have ever encountered, with two timelines in different time zones, along with an hourly countdown (shall we both agree to never do that again?!)'.

I would also like to thank my agent, the wonderful Sophie Lambert at C&W, for all her support, as always, and also Alice Hoskyns – both are incredible women, who are always there if I need something, and who also give such honest and helpful feedback.

Being an author can be a lonely job at times, and I'd like to say a huge thank you to all those other authors who I feel very lucky to count as friends. We support each other when times are tough and laugh so much too. In particular, Lauren, Laura and Zoe, the D20s, the Ladykillers and

Lesley and Lauren, who, over the past year, have been my co-hosts of the podcast *In Suspense*.

To my oldest girlfriends, Anna, Ceril, Els, Lynn and Nanna; I am so lucky to have you all in my life – I just wish we got to see each other all together more often, along with Gill too! And a big thank you to Ceril for kindly reading an early draft of this book for me.

A big thanks also goes to Helen Fields and Anna Williams, who very kindly answered my questions about decomposing bodies. Any inaccuracies are entirely my own.

Please do leave a review, shout about it on social media or recommend it to a friend – it is invaluable to authors when readers spread the word.